ALLIED
★ IN ★
VICTORY

General Charles "Crusty" Carlisle: Surviving his ordeal in the Pacific, he returned to the War Room on Kill Devil Road. There he faced a battle to protect one of his own—from an old family enemy . . .

Sergeant Eddie Donnely: At Bougainville he saw things no man should ever see. In the Philippines he fought behind Japanese lines. But what scared him more than anything was the struggle to be a loyal husband, and a father to his child . . .

Penny Belvale: Back in the States, her husband was a guilt-ridden, traumatized war survivor. She became a warrior, obsessed with getting revenge on the sadistic prisoner of war camp commander who shattered her life forever . . .

Colonel Chad Belvale: He fought well enough with the Free Poles in the battle for Cassino to earn the wrath of General Preston Belvale. Then, when Stephanie Bartlett told him goodbye in London, he turned to another woman—his ex-wife . . .

Lieutenant Sloan Travis: A lone and tortured fighter in the heat of battle, he earned the Medal of Honor—and almost gave up his dreams . . .

Books by Con Sellers

Brothers in Battle
The Gathering Storm
The Flames of War
A World Ablaze
Allied in Victory

Published by POCKET BOOKS

MEN AT ARMS

BOOK 4

ALLIED IN VICTORY

CON SELLERS

POCKET BOOKS

New York   London   Toronto   Sydney   Tokyo   Singapore

An *Original* Publication of POCKET BOOKS

POCKET BOOKS, a division of Simon & Schuster Inc.
1230 Avenue of the Americas, New York, NY 10020

ISBN: 0-671-66768-8

First Pocket Books printing July 1992

10 9 8 7 6 5 4 3 2 1

POCKET and colophon are registered trademarks of
Simon & Schuster Inc.

Printed in the U.S.A.

To my sons, Leonard and Shannon, without whose help this book would not have been finished.

We dedicate this book in memory of our dad.
—Leonard and Shannon Sellers

CHAPTER 1

REUTERS—London, Nov. 20, 1943: This right little, tight little island is readying early for the Christmas season, despite the war. German air attacks have dwindled, thanks to the gallantry of the RAF, but there are few luxuries to be found, and most gifts will be handmade. Of course there will be no lighted displays. The RAF took an early present to Jerry last night. British and Canadian Lancasters, Stirlings and Halifax bombers made the heaviest raid of the war on Berlin—2,300 tons of bombs dropped in 30 minutes. Merry Christmas, Adolf.

Stars & Stripes, Europe—Somewhere in England, Nov. 21, 1943: With the arrival of Division Headquarters and Headquarters Company from the Italian and African theaters of war, the Big Red One is complete again. Increments of the outfit had been strung out from Sicily and Tunisia to Britain. Seasoned veterans of two seaborne landings and the hard-fought Tunisian and Sicilian campaigns, the unit is taking a well-deserved rest. General Eisenhower calls the outfit his Praetorian Guard, referring to the powerful and elite Roman regiments that protected emperors from civilian uprisings and the mutinies of other legions. They were the emperor's most able and trusted troops.

Ask any GI who wears the First Division patch, and

he will say that the United States army consists of the Big Red One and about 500,000 replacements.

Chad Belvale stood for long moments, breathing in damp evening air, settling back into what England is, once more. Stephanie, damn it; England and Scotland meant Lieutenant Stephanie Bartlett, commander of antiaircraft guns. It seemed a century ago when there had been soft warm rains for them and fog not so much chilling as gently shrouding them to keep the harshness of the world away from lovers. Chad winced, remembering the petite woman who had shown him the depths and the laughter of love.

He stood at one edge of the Piccadilly Circus, where he had first met Stephanie in a bomb shelter, and where together they had later rescued a child from a shattered and blazing building. It was there reporters and photographers had exposed the romance between them. That was bad, because Stephanie's husband was fighting the Jap takeover of Singapore, bad because it was common, but not gossiped about, knowledge that many English women, married or not, preferred to share their lonely love with invading Yanks—overpaid, oversexed and over here, the Brits said. The publicity had caused him to be temporarily separated from Stephanie, and the Japs had widened the gap to uncrossable by capturing her.

Thank God and the family high brass for springing her from behind the POW wires. The truth was, if Stephanie hadn't been captured with Penny Belvale during the fall of Singapore, no way would a fortune have been spent to have Malay pirates infiltrate the prison camp and bring the women out. Chad had worried less about Penny, his own daughter-in-law, than he had over Stephanie. But Penny was watched over by the generals—Chad's father, Preston Belvale, and the earthy and hard-nosed head of the related clan, Charles "Crusty" Carlisle—two men with money, rank and power, and a demonstrated willingness to use all three.

He breathed deeply of the busy chill air spiced with the frantic excitement of men and women snatching for whatever happiness they could grab tonight. Nobody promised them tomorrow, and if the bombers came, even the rest of the night was not guaranteed.

Stephanie ought to have been here, but she wasn't. General Belvale had contacted Chad immediately when the women reached Australia, but there was no personal message from Stevie, and the general had sidestepped direct questions. The Belvale-Carlisle treasury had sprung Stephanie and Pretty Penny Belvale from the horrors of a Jap prison camp. The money paid for desperate and dangerous men to care for them and to guide them to freedom across half a world of enemy-held country. But Stephanie wasn't here and she wasn't back home in Scotland; he had checked. Where the hell was she? If somebody was deliberately keeping her from him, that would be somebody's ruby red ass. Who could it be, but Stephanie herself? Why, damn it—*why?*

Maybe Stephanie meant not to contact him again; maybe the guilt she carried about her husband had grown too heavy; maybe the guy was dead—which might ride hard on her stubborn sense of honor. Whatever, she ought to let him know. A top-heavy Limey taxi cruised by, its tiny running lights glowing. Chad gave it time to thread its way through the crowd and then stepped out into the narrow street. He didn't much know where he was headed and cared less. He had an inclination to get drunk, but he didn't know how he would react. Poised a moment on the sidewalk, he thought he might stomp the hell out of the nearest guys and perversely enjoy taking the hard fists and boots in return.

Not good for the image of American troops overseas; if a field grade officer acted that way, what did that say of the ordinary soldier?

Ordinary soldier, hell. There was nothing ordinary about the GIs of the Big Red One. Whoever had said it, the quote about uncommon valor being a common occurrence fit the rugged doggies who were now spread out and fairly well hidden among the civilian buildings of Blandford Forum and outlying villages. They bedded down in evacuated club rooms, schoolhouses, closed factories and the like. Their minor clashes at Oran and Hammam-bou-Hadjar, the not so minor fight at Saint-Cloud, alerted them to what lay ahead in Tunisia and the beating they took at Kasserine Pass blooded and toughened them for all time.

By the time they stormed ashore at Gela Beach in Sicily, they were battle-hardened, cynical veterans that nobody fucked with, in or out of combat. When the division pulled back to Algeria after the rugged Tunisia campaign, troopers found much of Oran marked Off Limits and a special whorehouse set up with choice ladies, for officers only. Enterprising GIs ran a three-quarter up to the locked gates of the Villa Della Rosa, hooked the winch to the iron design, and pulled the thing off its hinges. Since the men were all well armed, mean and usually drunk, MPs became understandably edgy about trying to arrest them. If they did manage to lock up some rowdy celebrant, his CO freed him.

When the provost marshal complained to General Terry Allen about his men raising hell all across town, Terrible Terry told him to kiss off. He said: "We took this goddamned town once, and we can take it again."

4

The assistant CG was still Little Teddy Roosevelt, and he thought the Villa Della Rosa incident was funny as hell.

Chad peered at one blacked-out pub sign and then another, as if it made a difference where he boozed up. The outfit did its drinking in Blandford and its surrounding villages with those ludicrous names—Tolpuddle, Piddletrenthide—and wasn't that a mouthful?—and Milton Abbot, Latin enough to have been carried over from the high tide days of the Romans. Confusing was Piddlehinton and Puddletown, but always good for a laugh. The name of the town of Shambles might have fit more than the civilians wanted, but the Big Red One remained on its good behavior in this part of the world.

Pushing past a blackout blanket hung at the pub's door, Chad waded through drifting blue eddies of cigarette smoke, and beery laughter washed over him. British pubs had the same general odor—beer, smoke and damp woolen uniforms. British sailors at the bar grudgingly made a place for him, and he bought them a round of warm dark ale.

Joking with them once the problem of his exalted rank was solved and they accepted him, Chad felt almost human for a while. But the image of Stephanie came back again and again to nag at him. And the full-color memory films of the ongoing battle in Italy rolled behind his eyes.

Sure, it was important for the outfit to hike out for field problems every day, if only to keep their legs in shape. But keeping troops in condition wasn't Chad's idea of active soldiering. The Corps CG had ordered him back from Italy, and he had gladly complied because there was the chance of meeting Stephanie again in her home country. He didn't often use the family clout, but he considered it now. His battalion could mark time under his executive officer, Major Lucien Langlois, the ornery Cajun. And Chad could go back to the line.

Since there was no word on Stephanie, he would rather be back with the fiercely dedicated Polish Brigade in Italy and its boss, the swashbuckling Colonel Jerzy Prasniewski. The historic abbey atop Monte Cassino would soon be taken, had to be taken, to deprive the Kraut artillery observers of pinpointing fat targets in the valley below. High above the village and its rocky fields, the OP looked down on practically every Allied position and called in too damned accurate 88mm fire. Chad wanted to be there when the Krauts were kicked out.

When he returned to official observer status and word came of the upcoming invasion of France, he could be quickly flown out to rejoin the regiment. Terry Allen might not like Chad going out of channels, but he would understand; Allen was not only a fine field commander but a combat soldier as well.

"Gentlemen," Chad said, lifting his glass, "here's to me being there when we crack the Gothic Line. That's what Jerry calls his defense positions in the mountains of sunny Italy."

One soldier put down his glass. "Bugger all. You'd change this cozy warm pub to slog through freezing mud in effing Italy?"

"Right," Chad said.

They looked at him as if he was crazy. Maybe he was.

INTERNATIONAL NEWS SERVICE—Gilbert Islands, Nov. 22, 1943: This has been another day of furious fighting on Tarawa atoll. Aircraft, naval guns and artillery hammer Japanese pillboxes, and they fall one after the other, but not until all the men inside are dead. Many die by holding hand grenades against their chests and blowing themselves up, rather than surrender. Surrender? The word does not exist in the Japanese army, and propaganda tells them how they will be tortured if they are taken.

Platoon Sergeant Eddie Donnely lay quiet and unmoving against the jungle floor. His nostrils filled with the odor of rotting vegetation, and he could taste its primeval filth. His cheek was pressed against the smooth stock of his M-1, and both hands caressed a grenade. He stifled the urge to scratch where he itched, which was almost everywhere on his body. Heat rash caused that, and jungle rot, and skin problems brought on by contact with strange plants whose juices were malevolent to back up sharp thorns. Add the constant stings and bites of insects and the fungus probing deeper into ear channels, and you totaled up one miserable son of a bitch.

It didn't make him feel any better to know that the Japs were suffering, too; let them. They were more at home in the jungle because they were more animal than human. And what was an army brat—animal, vegetable or mineral? Eddie only knew that he had little in common with civilian kids born away from army posts.

Eddie's old man had died in his second war, and died fighting. That was the unwritten regulation: tough it out and take some of the bastards with you.

(Barracks talk: In the old-old army, the legal offspring of soldiers were called brown-spit babies, because they were tough as mule's ass and weaned on PX chewing tobacco.)

That was a saying of his father's time, "brown spit." Most barracks talk changed with the times between wars; some lasted forever. A small centipede walked twisty and slowly across Eddie's face, and he fought the urge to smash the damned thing. Its bite wasn't fatal, but the swelling and pain hung on for a long time and could make a man wish he was dead.

The night squirmed alive, cheeping and clicking. He could sort out the jungle noises now, but he listened more for the little pools of quiet. That was when the insects fell silent for yards around an intruding footstep. If you listened hard enough, you could follow a Jap's passage by the silences and the chittering that sprang up behind him.

Eddie was taking his turn on OP, a one-man observation-and-listening post pushed out ahead of the lines. His job was to warn the platoon of an attack or infiltrators trying to sneak into the perimeter. He wasn't far away from the nearest foxholes, but it was lonely out here.

The centipede furry-footed off his face, and Eddie let his breath out noiselessly. Directly to his front, a spot of blackness went quiet. He eased the pin from his grenade and held the handle down. The puddle of silence drew closer, maybe too close.

Letting the spoon pop loose, Eddie counted— one, two, three—and threw the grenade, arching it up and over.

BLAM!

The jungle flowered red and orange. Some fragments whizzed back over Eddie, clacking into brush and shaking leaves down. The Jap screamed twice, the first time a shriek of shock and agony, the second one weak and trailing off. The light printed bright scars against Eddie's eyelids, and faded to leave greenish circles. He blinked them clear in a hurry.

Infiltrator. More might be coming, one by one, to try to slide into a foxhole with a bone-tired GI or simply toss a grenade into that pre-dug grave. They had cute tricks like whispering in English to find the positions: "Hey, Joe, where are you?" "Watch it, Mac, I'm coming in." The man who answered called his own death. Shrewd they were, learning just enough English. How many doggies spoke a word of Japanese? Only the regimental interpreters, Nisei from Hawaii or California.

Those from California had been handed the shitty end of the stick; in the panic that swept the country after Pearl Harbor, their families were locked away in desert concentration camps. Still the second-generation Japanese-Americans volunteered; the first outfit that was practically all Nisei had been the 100th Infantry Battalion. But so many Japanese-Americans signed up for the army that it became the 144th Regimental Combat Team. Their motto was a Hawaiian beach-boy saying: "Go for broke"—shoot the works, bet all you have, make it or break it.

Stateside Nisei called the island group *ka-tunks*, meaning the sound made by a coconut when it's thumped. The mainland Nisei were known as Buddha Heads. Whatever, they were a significant force in Italy. Word was that the RCT was man for man the most decorated outfit in the ETO, if not in the whole army. They had more to prove, and they were doing it.

The night settled its black skirts again; here and there the insects cranked up their songs or their territorial challenges. Eddie unhooked another grenade from his belt and crooked a sweaty forefinger through its ring.

Gloria's wedding ring; she had shopped with him, choosing a simple and inexpensive band of gold. Solid girl, thoughtful woman; she knew he wanted to take care of all expenses himself. The Carlisle-Belvale money didn't mean a damned thing to him, and he intended to keep it that way. It was bad enough, marrying into a gold braid family that was overrun with rank, from lieutenant generals down to lowly shavetails.

General or not, old Crusty Carlisle was a hell of

a soldier, and Eddie had enjoyed driving for him in Hawaii a long time ago. He hadn't intended to become the old man's kin. Gloria had come to him by way of a GI hospital and more or less by accident, or a meeting designed by fate. She had been married before, to an officer, of course, but a slob that an act of Congress couldn't make a gentleman. He'd had to resign his commission and beat it beyond range of Crusty's vengeance.

Gloria—she was more woman than he had ever known, and that was saying a lot. She was honest clear through, with honest appetites. Eyes closed, snuggling his face to the smoothness of his rifle stock, he saw Gloria painted vividly on his mind. He watched that wondrously patterned and finely tuned body as it moved across the bedroom to stretch languorously upon the bed.

Watch it, Donnely, he warned himself. You're thinking too much about your wife. That's why men who are already married to the army shouldn't become bigamists and take another wife. It dulls your wits; in time it could kill you and men you are responsible for.

(Barracks talk: If the army wanted you to have a wife, it would have issued you one.)

Gently to his left front came the string of small silences. "Come on," he whispered against his rifle. "Just a little closer, you bowlegged little shit." He threw the grenade; it ripped open the blackness when it exploded. Against the dazzling flare, crouched figures came running, long bayonets reaching ahead.

"Attack!" Eddie yelled. "They're coming!"

"Banzai!" squealed the Japs. "Banzai, banzai!"

ASSOCIATED PRESS—Egypt, Nov. 23, 1943: President Franklin Roosevelt, Prime Minister Winston Churchill and President Chiang Kai-shek continued their Cairo conference today to plan Allied operations in Asia.

No statements were issued.

Major General Charles "Crusty" Carlisle soaked blissfully in steaming water, a Bull Durham roll-your-own drifting smoke around his head. His arthritic shoulders enjoyed the wet heat. He figured it might take a week or so of steaming baths to boil the salt out of his wrinkled hide, the skin so blackened by the tropic sun. And he knew damned well he couldn't waste that much time. At least he had gotten a chance to join the shooting war for a while. Too old, hell. The marines he had island-hopped with would say different. A fine bunch of boys, those jarheads. They fought hard and died hard. Was there any easy way to die? Some forms had to be better than others.

If he was given a choice, Crusty would choose to go suddenly and sharply, buying the farm in combat as opposed to wasting away in a hospital, the pain growing night by drawn-out night until the morphine didn't do much good. But it wasn't Crusty's time yet. Torpedoed troopship, hungry sharks and Jap-held islands—he had out-toughed them all. Now he warmed body and soul in this hot tub, courtesy of the Aussie army in Darwin.

Hey, Lord, thanks for giving me a hand.

Don't thank Me; you just lucked out.

"Whatever works," Crusty said. "I'll keep a line plugged in, anyway."

"Sir?" The Australian batman—counterpart of the dog-robber in the American army—stood by with a large, fluffy towel.

"Nothing to do with you, lad. Just carrying on a little chat with God."

The man flinched. Now his eyes matched the towel. "Oh—yes, sir."

11

"Leave the towel," Crusty said, "and get out of here. I prefer to dry my own ass."

Dropping the towel to a chair, the orderly fled, forgetting to pop his heels and say sir.

Sighing, Crusty luxuriated awhile longer in the bath. The official notice had gone out on his return, lifting his name from the Missing in Action list. And after an hour of frustration with telephone priorities and screwed-up equipment, he'd finally spoken to Preston Belvale.

"You ought to know damned well," he had said, "that only a silver bullet can kill me, and then only when I'm out howling at the moon."

"Kee-rist," Belvale had said. "No more playing gung-ho at your age. Your orders for the ZI are being cut right now. So come on home and stop screwing up the personnel files. Oh . . . and Gloria sends her love."

Zone of Interior, hell; if Crusty wasn't ground down to a nub, he would tell Preston to kiss his money-maker and use the stack of mimeographed orders to blow his nose, or any needful orifice. But the truth was, he was tired and just about out of gas. It was time to rest and get pumped up again.

Gloria sent her love. What a girl—what a woman; he hoped Sergeant Donnely appreciated her. He must; even though Eddie had seen more ass than a toilet seat, the cocksman of the islands discovered what Crusty already knew about this very special girl and latched on to her. Pinching out his cigarette, Crusty rolled the butt into a ball and flipped it expertly into the toilet. So Donnely was perceptive; that didn't mean the tiger could change his stripes. Right now there were no women where Donnely was soldiering, so fidelity was automatic. Anywhere near a combat zone, soldiers tended to grab for what might be their last piece of ass. Once Donnely got back to savor the temptations of Australian fleshpots, how far would that cleaving only to each other go?

Sighing, Crusty climbed out of the tub, admitting that he envied Donnely, envied any tough young soldier capable of raising hell on the knife edge of destruction. He wouldn't blame any man for giving in to the powerful primal urge for the survival of the race. It was always so in wartime, nature's need to replace the sons gone forth to die. Nature did not realize that uncountable billions of those males-to-be would perish, already entombed in latex.

"Too damned serious," he grunted, and toweled himself roughly. He had already been damned serious. He had put in for two Distinguished Service Crosses and Silver Stars all around for the marines who had fought their way through Jap-held islands and left a swath of destruction behind them. The gunny gave him name, rank and serial number of the living and those buried shallow on jungle atolls and deep in the sea. Hell, it was hard enough just nursing that leaky old boat across so many miles of the enemy sea, a sea crisscrossed by Nip planes and submarines. The piloting was by guess, by the stars and by God. Rarely did they have to fight, and when they did, they put up a hell of a battle. The GI who died from internal injuries—the kid Woodall—Crusty still carried his dog tags. Woodall had been put in for a medal, too, if only for helping to kill that big damned shark that tried to sink their seagoing raft.

"It wasn't all luck," he said. "Some of it was good soldiering. And don't tell me that You didn't have a hand in it."

Could be.

CHAPTER 2

Allied Headquarters, South Pacific—Nov. 24, 1943:
The major Japanese defensive positions in the Gilbert
Islands, Tarawa and Makin atolls, finally fell to hard-
driving American forces today. Enemy ammunition
was exhausted and only a few shell-shocked Japs
were left alive for U.S. Marines to clean out.

American casualties on Makin are 64 dead and
154 wounded; Japs: 450 dead and 15 prisoners.

Tarawa losses were much greater: 3,500 killed or
wounded against about 5,000 dead Japs, 17
wounded POWs and 129 Korean laborers captured.

Blood, bright or dark, swift or slow—it all came
down to the blood, sweat and tears promised by
Winston Churchill and war leaders before him.
Every little pimple island in the Pacific called forth
American casualties in excess of normal strategic
value. Preston Belvale sighed.

MacArthur was getting a new approach under
way, island-hopping and bypassing defended garrisons, leaving them to starve out as the Imperial
fleet got herded toward home. These carefully emplaced and fortified islands would have cost many
casualties, tackled head on. Skipped over, they
would wither, cut off by the U.S. Navy so that no

food, clothing and sometimes no fresh water reached the troops. How long to cannibalism?

And to madness beyond that instilled in them by their aristocracy.

Raw airstrips appeared where only primeval jungle had flourished, inching blue markers across the map, growing ever nearer to the red marks of Japanese holdings. They were the reason ground troops had to dig out Japs and hack out jungles, to extend the protective cover of fighter planes over navy forces and to move forward the striking range of heavy bombers so the Jap home islands could be thoroughly and properly gutted.

This new concept of air power overshadowed traditional naval tactics and weighed heavily upon foot soldier maneuvering. Shades of Billy Mitchell, that farsighted, too vocal advocate of army aviation. Helped by the press, he gave a convincing demonstration of sinking an obsolete battleship from the air. He had been far ahead of his time. Proving himself so damned right that the hide-bound admirals and generals of the day were embarrassed to be shown wrong. They court-martialed him so they could go back to sleep unchallenged. Air strikes had already changed conventional warfare and would no doubt recast the face of the world.

But so far the basic rule of war—if rules there were—still called for the infantry to plant its scarred and muddy boots on enemy land before true victory could be claimed.

Lieutenant General Preston Belvale handed the yellow TWX—teletypewriter exchange—message to Gloria Carlisle Donnely for filing. Piling up paperwork was standard operating procedure for the army, tons and tons of it warehoused for little reason, except that one day some bemedaled postwar general, looking back in worry, would raid the files to cover up some of the obvious blunders.

He gently massaged a good cigar, clipped the end and lipped it, but didn't light it. At times the dry flavor was more soothing without smoke. He rubbed his bum knee and wondered why gloom insisted upon hanging just off his flank. Crusty Carlisle had made it through torpedo attacks and troopship sinkings and pitched battles against what should have been overwhelming odds. The ornery old bastard took on the Jap navy, outpost garrisons and the trackless sea, and then sailed into Darwin on a captured ship. Reports said the craft was one of those rickety pearlers that used to eke out a trader's living coasting from island to island. It was a shock to the Aussie navy to meet it come-helling into their sea-lanes, running before the wind, its tattered sails flying.

Right now Penny Belvale was probably flying home from Australia with the English servicewoman, Stephanie Bartlett. They were another gamble that had paid off, in a long, tenuous reach across land and sea to pull them out of the Jap POW camp. On the radiophone, Penny had sounded tremulous but determined; she was family, and Stephanie—if Belvale read the signs right—might soon become a relative in name as well as in spirit, if Chad Belvale could persuade her to marry him; the last that Belvale had heard—and that was from the pre-Jap camp days—she wouldn't abandon her POW husband.

Belvale applauded her for that. She must be one hell of a woman for Chad to be so intense about her. And that meant she would fit the family mold. Still, Belvale wondered why there had been no personal message from her to Chad, nothing beyond a tight-lipped thank-you-very-much. He would learn more when their long flight touched down. Still, he could not help thinking of Kirstin, Chad's first wife and mother to Owen and Farley.

This was no time for mourning the death of Kir-

stin's second husband, but must be a call for celebration in the big hall at Kill Devil Hill, where
polished armor and honored banners looked down
in triumph. Yet the nagging depression remained.
The blood, the thought; it was always the blood;
for these centuries past, the family roots were both
nourished and drained by it.

He lighted the cigar with a worn Zippo and sat
at his desk. The family would fade away without
a commitment to its destiny. Preston Belvale was
not the one to avoid clan duty set so deep into the
bone. There were the toilers born, and the poets,
the kings and the charlatans, the shallow and
changeable directions of other tribes, those who
did not even resist the blurring of once-proud
names. And there were the Belvales, the Carlisles,
so early given the duty to advance the cause; there
were the lances and shields and war hammers; the
clash of arms that came ringing through the hot
race of heartblood. . . .

. . . Unhorsed, Sir Arundel of Belvale braced his
back against the stone wall. Mailed fists gripping
hard upon the hilt of his broadsword, only light
chain mail circling his head and shoulders as he
awaited the charge of the heathen. They slunk like
hyenas just out of his reach, their black rags flap-
ping in drafts of searing desert wind.

Were they awaiting the arrival of their archers
with those short horn bows? Broadhead arrows
weren't needed to pierce the light armor he wore.
Yet they hesitated to close with him, waving their
crooked swords and yapping. No crusader could
discern the workings of the heathen's tangled
mind.

At times they fought like foaming-mouthed dogs,
refusing to give a pace of ground. Other times they
fled ignominiously at the first sounding of steel.
These desert vermin feinting and taunting before

him could be cowards or martyrs. The difference meant little at the nonce. Arundel was brought to bay, the stag dragged down by curs.

Flexing his arms, he thought, No, not a great windblown stag, but a wounded bear. Let them come, for England and Saint George. His fine war-horse lay dead just past the crumbled mounds of this nameless village, this heap of dung abandoned the past fortnight. Fatigued from a battle two days before, Arundel had grown careless returning from a spy patrol ordered by the king. The heathen had hidden their light-bodied horses and set a trap, and he had ridden willy-nilly into it.

A thin, squat man darted suddenly at Arundel, coming low and swift as a ranging hound. Arundel took his arm off at the shoulder and backhanded the blade to catch another man behind the knees and upend him squalling like the hamstrung swine he was.

His comrades dragged him mewling beyond sword range. They danced in fury and braved themselves by shouting. Arundel did not deign to count them, for they were like barnyard weasels or a pack of dungeon rats, swarming and chittering until they fancied themselves strong enough to attack. Pulling in deep breaths of baked air, Arundel vowed to dispatch some of them to their barbarian hell.

Richly dressed, a gold spire glinting atop his wrapped leather and metal helmet, another fool stepped proudly forward. The scimitar whistled at Arundel's head, a dazzling crescent of blue steel, unbelievably sharp.

A mighty downward blow from Arundel's broad-sword threw bright sparks into the hot air, and the scimitar spun glittering away in the sun. The chief heathen leaped back shaking numbed fist.

"Again!" Arundel called. "Come to me again, savages!"

This time they lunged forward in a shrieking wave, darkening the sand and blurring the sky with their swirling robes, spearheads stabbing at him, curved swords slashing up and down and around. He cleared a space immediately before him, but a sharp edge sliced deep into his right arm. Kicking one man in the belly, Arundel wheeled to present his stronger left side to his attackers.

"For Saint George and England!" he roared. "For God and country!"

The flat of a blade slapped his temples and drove him to one knee. His sword point found a soft body and pierced it. Then his weapon was knocked from his hand. His outstretched hands found a thin throat, and he tried to tear it free of the squirming body.

"A Carlisle—a Carlisle!" The great shout leaped down from heaven itself.

"A Carlisle!"

"A Belvale! To me, Carlisle!"

And thence came the thundering hooves of the mighty warhorse in full armor, the bone-crushing swings of mace, and the heathens scuttled for safety, yelping like camp dogs. The hamstrung man cried for pity, but the ball of spikes at chain's end of the mace opened his skull. One Moor leaped aback of a mount and loosed the others to gallop snorting away, the blood scent swelling and snorting their nostrils.

Lord Osric Carlisle, fully suited in battle armor, lifted his visor.

"Long have you been gone from camp, cousin."

Steadying himself, Arundel put a hand upon a stirrup. "May God's eye be ever upon you. My mount is downed, and I would fain cling to you as we return. Did our monarch send you to seek after me?"

"No."

"I thought not."

Recovered sword shoved through his link belt, and only a bit uncertain in the knees, Arundel held to the stirrup and glanced back to find the heathens fled from sight. They would return to gather trappings from the dead horse and butcher the horse itself for meat. A fearless battle mount deserved a more honorable end. If horses had souls, then eternity might be tempered by the heathen grooms dispatched to follow him.

Carlisle said, "There was a time when the most victorious knights were celebrated—aye, even lifted higher in the nobility, given baronies and lands."

Sweating, keeping pace with the horse's walk, despite the blood dripping down his arm, Arundel said, "And now, cousin?"

"Now our monarch mistrusts any name that is spoken louder than his own."

"He has naught to fear from me. And I must hold true to my oath as well as my name."

Carlisle nudged the horse. "Was there ever a king whose crown rode easily upon his brow?"

"Yet each must depend upon the strong arm of the faithful."

"Mayhap it will be ever so."

Belvale controlled a coming-back-to now flinch when Gloria touched his shoulder. She said, "Another TWX from Hawaii; Nancy reports that her favorite patients are well on the road to recovery."

Thumbing his mustache, Belvale hid his eyes behind a screen of cigar smoke. The family was bred to wars, but he wondered if its fabric had ever been this strained. Divorced from Major Keenan Carlisle, the Jap's nemesis in Asia, Captain Nancy Carlisle had been an NP nurse at Tripler General Hospital on Oahu when her ex-husband was flown in as a near-dead survivor of Wingate's Raiders.

As if one lightning bolt wasn't enough, Lieutenant Farley Belvale arrived in terrible shape from combat fatigue. Nancy fought the establishment for better treatment for him and the other mentally wounded. Time and modern transportation had shrunk the world, and regulars could depend upon meeting friends and enemies again and again in different outposts. But a onetime husband and a nephew coming together in one place with Nancy seemed less a miracle than a minor curse.

Since the divorce, Nancy had become her own woman, independent of the restraints and throttling traditions of Kill Devil Hill. How, Belvale wondered, could two people who had once been in love remain friendly? Perhaps Farley was a mutual focus for them, a need to whom they could give freely.

Gloria said, "Nancy says that Farley will soon be transferred to Letterman General in San Francisco. The psychiatrists think he's coming along nicely, but advise against him seeing any more combat."

"Yes," Belvale said. "There are other posts; look at us."

She looked away. "And too many outposts. No letter from Eddie for weeks, and all those bloody island landings. . . ."

Belvale waited a moment, then said, "See if you can raise Chad for me in England. The War Department wants more close-in reports on that Polish Brigade in Italy."

Which meant that the invasion of France was on the back burner and that the winter campaign in Italy was going painfully slow.

British Broadcasting Company—London, Nov. 24, 1943: A late report from the Gilbert Islands states that a Japanese submarine torpedoed and sank the

American escort carrier *Liscome Bay* off Makin atoll. The 700 dead must be added to the price for the capture of Tarawa and Makin.

Helene's flat was in the Prince Albert Consort Courts, not far from the shipyard where the *Queen Mary* had been launched. Those sheds and docks were pocked with fragments from near-miss bombs, but the crib of the great *Queen* was whole, waiting another round trip of the world's biggest troopship. Sometimes she coasted in here, pampered and nosed by busy tugs; as often she anchored off Scotland to unload cargoes of GIs. Owen Belvale would never forget the five-day unescorted dash from New York, one of 17,000 men and their equipment in her steel belly, hurrying so that Operation Torch, the invasion of North Africa, could begin. U.S. destroyers and planes followed her a short way from Pier 29 in New York, then dropped off because they couldn't match her speed. The French liner *Normandie* would have made for a great sister act, but saboteurs had fired her at the dock and she settled in the mud.

The *Queen* was met close to her home by escorts of the English navy and cruising Spitfires. What a prize she would be for German U-boats, but again, good security and her speed kept the *Queen Mary* at her wartime job.

The sea—almost anywhere in Southampton, you could lift your head and taste the gray sea. Once it had been exciting to Owen, a call to adventure. Now it was the promise of a threat. How many more seas to cross before time and luck ran out?

He used the key she had given him, and eased into the small flat. Owen often moved quietly around her, afraid to break the spell and send the faerie queen to flight. She was still at work in the ammunition plant and should be back by twilight. If he hadn't known that, his senses would have told him she wasn't home.

Even when she wasn't in it, the flat throbbed with her, swaths of bright scarlet, lingering exotic scents and sensuous shadows lurking. Owen Belvale heeled the door shut behind him, arms full of bagged goodies, some bought on the civilian black market and some traded from GI mess halls. Early on, his troopers had learned to save oranges and even lemons, delicacies long vanished from the open market, and as for the tooth-grinding D ration bar—it was still chocolate enough to draw hungrily admiring girls.

He remembered H Company's Corporal Russamano pocketing fruit at the mess line. "Better than money," he said. "Go stand on a corner and juggle a couple of oranges and here come the Piccadilly commandos, ready to wheel and deal."

"Damnedest thing," Sergeant Pelkey added, "is walking along Piccadilly past the guys hawking newspapers—'*Sunday Post! Sunday Post!* Hitler in hiding'—and dropping their voices to say, 'Rubber goods, rubber goods.' Curbside condoms ain't a bad idea. It's better than the girls standing up to screw, believing they can't get pregnant, especially if you're short like me an' she's a giraffe."

"Yeah," Russamano laughed. "Nose to nose and your toes are in it; toe to toe and your nose is in it."

Now, few men went into London on pass, except those who had scored during their first tour in England and had steady shack mates. Local British servicewomen were usually as lonely as the GIs. Homegrown lasses from AA sites and healthy Land Army girls came looking. The civilian country girls were young, below draft age, and more apt to be thinking of marriage.

And what was Captain Belvale thinking?

Standing for a long moment, he felt the echo of her, the vibrancy of her, the aura that radiated from Helene Lyons. He moved to the tiny kitchen and put away the presents. He had arranged three days' leave for himself—hours and sunrises, hours and moonsets with Helene, and maybe forever.

If he made it through the invasion of France with his heavy weapons company and whatever followed. The landing would be only the beginning— if it wasn't stopped bloody on the beach and thrown back into the sea. Then the war might stretch into infinity.

The thought of the future or a non-future was something he had not dwelt upon before. The risk went with the job, although any soldier who claimed he wasn't afraid was raving mad or a rotating liar—a liar any way you looked at him. The trick was to do your job despite fear, knowing that nobody promised you a tomorrow.

And now? Owen frowned and took down a gin bottle from the top shelf. Helene was now, and it bothered him to think beyond her; he couldn't imagine a world without her at its center. One sniper's bullet, one sizzling mortar fragment, a potato-masher grenade landing close, and there would be no more Helene for him. There, in whatever dark drill field awaited soldiers, he would be alone in eternity.

He had never chased after women, keeping sex in perspective, holding to duty and country and family traditions. Sex was good, and often a relief, and he thought he knew all about it, barring the sickening stuff. He had been wrong. Owen dropped into a chair and poured a stiff shot of gin. Helene was sex in its many facets, cutting edges and drowsy comfort, and there was only one Helene. She not only raced in his blood, but clawed into the bone and laced through flesh turned fragile for her.

He downed the gin without flinching; he was becoming used to it, maybe a little too much. He had a smaller shot as the sky darkened beyond the flat's single window crisscrossed with tape against bomb blowout.

And behind a key click she came into the room, coveralled and tin-hatted, swinging a lunch tin, so small and beautiful. Owen always felt there should be a trail of sparks behind her, for her trim, perfect body moved into any room with unseen but powerful snapping and popping.

"Cheerio, love." The sparks were within the brush of her lips.

Putting her hat aside, she leaned over the table. "Lovely, sinful food and cigarettes and enough gin to turn the Channel clear."

She loosed the top buttons of her coveralls, sorrel hair glinting, eyes of blue and green, always smoky. "I wasn't really expecting you. You said your unit was going into a difficult stage of training."

He touched her because he had to. "What's the use of command if I can't bend a rule or two? God—only three days away from you and I'm coming apart at the seams."

"Such a sweet lad." Her lips parted to his, and that special flavor of geraniums came to him on the light flicking on her tongue. Her naked breasts nudged his chest, magically freed of restraint. He kissed her hard, but she didn't respond. Her hands urged him back and down upon the couch that was a pull-out bed. Eyes closed, Owen gave himself up to her.

Fingertips and lips and the tingling net of her hair, velvet skin warm and slidy. Now he knew what men had told him, that some women have black magic woven through the fibers of their bodies, a special type of witchcraft that either drifts a man off to never-never land or hits him in the belly like a battering ram. Helene varied from sexual pile driver to the stroking of angel feathers, depending upon her mood.

She closed on him and it all went away from Owen—his unit, the war, the family—and duty was only a diminished whisper.

Outside, the air raid siren screamed, shattering the peace of twilight.

CHAPTER 3

INTERNATIONAL NEWS SERVICE—Washington, D.C., Nov. 26, 1943: The understaffed Office of Price Administration, aided by the FBI, has taken extensive measures to detect counterfeit gas coupons and stop the theft of them. In this city only, some 20 million gallons' worth was heisted. In San Francisco, bogus coupons caused 3 million gallons of gas to be sold illegally in the space of a few days.

Penny Belvale couldn't lie still in the hospital bed. Everything was clean and white and smelled of medicines. She was used to jungle stench and doing without showers. She had been thoroughly gone over by a team of Australian doctors and nurses, all of them kind and efficient. But when all her tests came back, would they know she was pregnant? Would they be disgusted or sympathetic, or—best of all—just not give a damn?

This foul thing in her body, this dark and awful parasite sucking away at her insides—there had to be a way to rid herself of Hideo Watanabe's child. She would find that way or die trying.

On the next cot, Stephanie Bartlett sat up. "Bloody awful, isn't it? After sleeping on those bare boards in camp, and worse, bedding down in

27

the jungle with spiders and snakes and the Dyaks, you'd think our bodies would welcome mattresses and sheets. I know we welcomed the food. Och! I may never stop eating."

Penny brushed back a wisp of hair. "It seems sinful. So much food, when the women left back in camp are suffering. God, I hope they don't take a worse beating because of our escape. I wouldn't put a damned thing past Watanabe, the miserable son of a bitch."

"Major Wobbly, yes. And there was the guard I . . . eliminated. Any woman would have leaped at the chance to escape. We mustn't blame ourselves. We are all dying slowly, anyhow." Stephanie lit a Players cigarette and offered one to Penny. "Do you ken that the very air here is clean? Even in the jungle with those evil mercenaries, the air was better in camp, because it was free, we were free. For a bit back there, I was half afraid those Dyaks might, as they say, work their will upon us."

"They wouldn't touch us; they knew they wouldn't get paid if they played games. Trust my military family to foolproof a maneuver as much as possible."

Stephanie smiled. "Oh, I don't know; our intrepid leader was so taken with you that he would have forgone his share of gold if you'd warmed his bed and become number whatever wife. He was so ugly he was kind of cute."

Penny pulled her knees up and thumped her pillow. "They were all deadly little men. I don't think the others would have let him break the contract by delivering only one of us. So many times I thought we'd never make it through the jungles, and then that scary boat trip. It's hard for me to believe I'm not dreaming."

Hesitating, she pressed one hand against her

belly. "And I don't want to believe this . . . this horrible thing I'm carrying."

"Not the bairn's fault."

"It's Japanese, damn it! Japanese, Japanese!"

Stephanie leaned over, and her warm fingers stroked the back of Penny's hand. "Hush, now; we will do what you want. After all, this is a ruddy hospital, staffed by doctors who have no love for the bloody Japs. It can be done before you fly home."

Shifting her bare feet over the side of the bed, Penny sat taller and pulled in a deep breath. "Damn it, I wished for a baby someday, one to walk the great halls of Kill Devil Hill and Sandhurst Keep, someone to keep the traditions strong. But never this thing." Her clenched fist pressed against her belly.

Stephanie said quietly, "If I get through this sodding war, if puir Dacey lives through the camp without his legs, I want naught more to do with wars and warriors."

Penny said, "And Chad Belvale?"

Stephanie shook her head. "After you'd rung up your general in America, you offered me the telephone. If Chad had been on the other end, I probably would have spoken to him. But he's not in America, and that gives me time to think proper. I could not say to a stranger what I must say to Chad himself. So I only said a polite thank-you for the rescue. The general must think I'm daft."

"Has Chad asked you to marry him?"

"He did; if ever we meet, he will again. Such a braw and lovely man." She stared at the smoke rising from her cigarette. "If I had no husband . . ."

Penny looked away. She understood; if her own husband had been behind the wire or all shot up, she would probably have acted the same. Dacey Bartlett lay without legs in a men's POW camp down the road from the women's camp. The odds were high against his survival.

She didn't even know where Farley was. General Belvale said he was doing okay. He had skipped over that before she could ask more questions. Penny figured that Farley had been wounded, possibly badly, and the general avoided details so she would not worry. Maybe he had said more, but some things were garbled by radio static. Penny drew in a puff of smoke and coughed. She felt guilty for not fretting more about Farley, for not even bringing him to mind over long stretches of time. It had been the POW camp, she thought, the strain of trying to survive.

And when captivity got easier because Major Watanabe made her his whore, she had pushed away any memory of Farley. What kind of woman would think about her husband while being screwed by another man? When she got home she would have a chance to clear her head.

"Come to the States with me, Stevie; come home with me for a good long rest. Both of us have to fill in an Army G-Two in Washington about the camps. Then I'm sure General Belvale can pull strings and arrange sick leave from your army."

Stephanie leaned over, and her hand was warm. "Dinna fash yourself. All in due time, I say. I'd best get back to Scotland the soonest I can and then to duty. Still Jerry planes to shoot down; still battles to be fought. As for Chad—I'll think hard upon him. If he's in Britain, I will find him. I have never loved anyone as intensely as I love this man."

"And do what? Say what?"

"I don't know, Penny. There is love and there is duty and there is honor. I just do not know what I shall say or how I shall say it."

CHAPTER 4

ASSOCIATED PRESS—London, Dec. 4, 1943: The USAAF has taken delivery of a long-range fighter which will provide an effective escort for American bomber fleets.

After significant losses for both Bomber Command and the 8th Air Force on raids over Germany this fall in the air "Battle for Berlin," fliers have welcomed the addition of the P-51B "Mustang," which has the range of a bomber and is superior in every way to the German fighters.

Gavin Scott arrived in London just as his promotion to captain came through SHAEF headquarters, and about goddamn time. One of the family's high brass had pushed through the orders when the first word of Gavin's escape flashed across the sea, and that was as it should be. The boost in rank was due him not only for his six kills in the air, but how many pilots walked away from two crashes? And to top it off, he had also escaped from a POW convoy in Italy and bought his way out of neutral Switzerland. There he could have sat out the war as an internee, living fat and sassy with a share of the family money conveniently at hand in a major Swiss bank.

However, with Chad Belvale as an uncle and General Preston Belvale for a grandfather, it wouldn't look good to sit on his butt while there was a war going on. Besides, he still had a lot to show Uncle Chad and his bitch girlfriend.

Too bad that the kid who escaped with him didn't make it. What was his name? Oh, yeah, Hillman, Joe Hillman; tough luck, kid. You have to be fast on your feet to make it these days, on land or in the sky.

Because Gavin had been spirited out of Switzerland via a couple of bribed officials, there had been no publicity, no photos in the newspapers. The appearance of neutrality had to be maintained. What the hell, after he found Lieutenant Stephanie Bartlett and paid her back for humiliating him, the press wouldn't matter. A lot of fighter pilots made their reputation through the newspapers. He wasn't sure just how he would punish the bitch, but he would find a painful way. He was just starting a ten-day leave, and although he'd run into several roadblocks as to her whereabouts, they had only made him more determined to find her.

First he had to get his mouth fixed; that lousy Kraut guard had knocked out three teeth with the butt of his rifle. So tonight he would follow military tradition and wet down his new set of railroad tracks. Find a good pub and buy drinks for the house, toast the gallant RAF. Drink one to Lieutenant Stephanie Bartlett, queen of the ack-ack guns. Somebody might know her or know where she was.

Where the hell was she, and why had the Limeys stamped SECRET on the duty station of a junior officer? After he got to Stephanie, he would go home, but not to mark time for the rest of the war. Gavin saw himself in the Pacific Theater splashing Jap Zeroes; he would become the only ace in both theaters. The U.S. had P-38s in the Pacific, too—forked lightning, his kind of plane.

How about that—little Jap flags painted on the fuselage beneath the small swastikas he would have marked on his new plane, signifying kills on both sides of the world. The Jerries had downed him twice, and three was a charm, one to screw up the half-ass Jap pilots. Banzai and good-bye, you little shits.

Here in Blighty his burned, scarred face was a plus. Here the girls said, "Such a terrible wound," one side of his handsome face practically gone, and him bravely going right on flying. By about the second "poor boy," he was in their pants.

What he wanted most was to get back into Stephanie Bartlett's pants. This time she wouldn't laugh. She would be too busy crying.

ASSOCIATED PRESS—The Pacific Theater, Dec. 18, 1943: General MacArthur ordered plans completed and forces detailed for the capture of Saidor in New Guinea. It is to be used as an air and naval base against Japanese forces both here and in New Britain.

Word has also come through from China, where Generalissimo Chiang Kai-shek has again asked President Roosevelt for substantial financial aid and for more aircraft.

Lieutenant Sloan Travis swung along the road ahead of his platoon, his muscles loosening and warming despite the damp cold that blanketed the English countryside. Wisps of fog drifted overhead, where a weak sun tried to disperse it. A good day for a hike, ten miles out and ten back; not cold and not hot. Because it was a good day, he pushed the pace a little, to about three miles an hour instead of the regulation two and a half. He

looked back at platoon Sergeant Jerry Pelkey and
the section leaders, Sergeant Parke and Sergeant
Poydock. Each man headed two squads of 30-cali-
ber machine guns, heavy weapons as opposed to
the air-cooled guns in rifle companies. These
Brownings were water-cooled, and the best defensive weapon the army had. When the air-cooled
weapon overheated, the water-cooled gun was just
warming up, and if it was fired long enough to
sizzle the barrel, you did a quick field strip and
replaced it with a spare. The army had even furnished asbestos gloves.

He had learned about all there was to know
about the gun, including how it felt to road-march
with the 51-pound tripod on his back. Better that
than the gun itself, clumsy at 37-plus pounds when
the water jacket was full and had to be moved
from shoulder to shoulder. The number one gunner
could walk with a good balance, front legs over his
shoulders and the trail leg down his back, looking
somewhat like a tall and humpbacked spider.

Checking his watch, Sloan raised his right hand
high, signaling a halt. "Take ten," he called out.

And Poydock said, "Smoke if you got them.
And one of you brownnosers better have some cigarettes, account of I'm fresh out."

Sergeant Pelkey joined Sloan to sit atop their
upended helmets on the sloping roadside. "Good
clip today; we're moving right along."

"Keeping our legs, Sergeant. Remember the
landing in Africa, after weeks on shipboard? We
could barely hike those thirty long miles to Oran,
even after that ambush by the Foreign Legion."

"Those bastards were tough. Ah . . . I might be
stepping out of line, but how come the company
commander hasn't been with us? Three or four
weekends—"

"He missed three," Sloan said. "I don't know
where the hell he goes. We have—he has relatives

here. He doesn't spend the time with his old man. In fact, I've covered for him. He had the colonel, a flyboy, and me for kinfolks here—me in a back-handed way. It might be a woman, although Owen isn't known as a cocksman."

Pelkey slid around on his butt until he could put his boots on higher ground, an old soldier trick to drain blood from the feet and keep them from swelling. "You really belong to that family? You hear a lot of latrine gossip about it—generals and such, loopier than bedbugs and going up to screw around on the front lines. If I wore stars I would be so far back I couldn't even hear the artillery."

Sliding his boots down and sitting up, he went on: "Latrine rumors have it that some higher brass say that the Belvales and Carlisles start wars for the hell of it, for glory. Kind of like those Jap guys and their long swords."

"The Samurai." Sloan said. "The holy warriors, the crusaders, the Maccabees, the dog soldiers of the Cheyenne and those gunfighters trained by the Mormons for their protection in the West. From what I know—and that's not much, because I'm the pariah who broke family traditions and didn't enlist but got myself drafted—when one war closes down, the family stays in readiness for the next war."

Pelkey nodded. "Sort of like Joe Louis keeping in shape for his next title defense?"

"I guess so. After I refused to go to West Point or Virginia Military Institute, I stayed away from the castles, Sandhurst Keep and Kill Devil Hill. I wanted to be a writer, not a soldier."

"Did you do any good writing?" Pelkey stood up and put on his helmet. "You make a pretty damn good soldier, field commission and Silver Star. At first I had you pegged as a Class A ass-hole. You think your genes have something to do with how you act under fire?"

"Watch how quick I shed the uniform when this

war's over." He stood up and put on his tin pot. "Get them up, Sergeant."

"Yes, sir. All right, ladies, off your dead asses and on your dying feet. Saddle up and move out smartly. Hey, Bowley—get with it, man; you don't show me anything!"

"I ain't in show business, Sarge."

Bowley swung his tripod up and around by one leg in an arc that spoke of long practice, the steel legs dropping just so upon his shoulders.

The burst of fire kicked over and through them, tracers skipping along the road before the roar of the Stuka reached them.

In reflex, men dived for cover; fifth and sixth squads leaped to set up the guns, but the plane was gone in an eye wink.

Sloan climbed out of the ditch. "Anybody hit?"

Nobody yelled back. Not until the Stuka screamed down for another strafing run at the column caught out in the open. Sloan saw Bowley when the ricochet hit and knocked him out from under his tripod.

UNITED PRESS—Shangri-La, Dec. 24, 1943: When President Roosevelt was asked where the planes that bombed Tokyo came from, his answer was Shangri-La, a mystical, magical place of dreams, not an aircraft carrier.

This time, after a meeting of heads of state, the president and Prime Minister Winston Churchill announced the appointment of General Dwight D. Eisenhower as commander-in-chief of Allied liberation forces in Europe. Churchill also announced that General Montgomery will command the 21st Army Group in place of General Oliver Leese.

Pacific Command sends Christmas greetings to all troops in the field and all ships at sea.

Keenan Carlisle stood quietly in his blue convales-
cent suit while Second Lieutenant Sueko Lokomaikai pinned silver oak leaves on the hospital garb
all ambulatory patients wore. Everybody on the
ward applauded—patients, nurses and the ward
boy. First Lieutenant Nancy Carlisle came up to
shake his hand. "Congratulations, Keenan. Best of
luck."

The moment ought to have made him uneasy, to
say the least; Nancy was his ex-wife and Susie his
girlfriend. That he didn't react foolishly must be a
sign of growing up, he thought, of a new maturity.

"Thanks," he said, and Nancy smiled. There
was a brightness about her, a glow that told him
she was in love. Long ago and far away, she had
looked at him in just that way. Had he ever been
like that with her?

Now it was Susie, dark eyes warm, midnight
hair pinned up according to regulations, the
nurse's cap perched upon it. Her white uniform set
off her dusky skin. Without lipstick, she could be
a fresher, younger copy of the woman he had lost
in China, Chang Yen Ling. The pain of her loss
hit him again, tightening his jaws and knotting his
gut. Fucking Japs and goddamn sharks; he saw
them vividly inside his head and inside his heart.
He might not live long enough to kill enough of
both animals, but he intended to try.

The bright moment of his new rank dissolved.
When he thought of Yen Ling, he remembered
who he had been and what he was now. He would
always be part of the family, but no longer as the
peacetime husband or a parade ground soldier. To
the Japs he had become *yonsei,* the fearsome ghost
of the jungle who feasted on human heads and kept
the Japs on the edge of panic. To the Kachin he
had become He Who Will Not Die.

"Come," Susie softly murmured, "you're halfway home, Keenan. Let me take you the rest of the way."

He let her steer him out of the ward and down the hallway to the PX coffee shop. Over steaming cups she said, "Has Nancy filled you in about your nephew? Farley Belvale will be going home soon to Letterman General in San Francisco. He's much better now, caring for himself and speaking rationally. He's still on the locked ward, and maybe you ought to visit him."

"I tried," Keenan said, "but he didn't want to see me. I think he feels guilty for crapping out in combat. Damn it; battle rattle is as much a wound as a shot in the belly. The family knows that and won't blame him. Even so, he's more rational than most of us.

"No, Nancy hasn't said much to me about Farley or anybody else; we don't carry on long conversations. For all the friendly, civilized-divorce attitude, there's always a tension between us. What would we talk about? Remember when, or make plans for tomorrow? In the jungle you don't think about tomorrow. It's enough to stay alive for the day."

She touched the hand resting on the table top. "Keenan, you can look ahead now. You're out of the jungle."

"The jungle is always with you, like the bastardly Japs; I see them in the night. I kill them, but they just keep coming. That's okay by me; I enjoy that."

His fists unclenched, and he said, "Sorry, Susie. I didn't mean to use you for a crying towel. Let's have dinner tonight in the best restaurant Honolulu has. Just as long as it's not some Jap sushi joint."

She looked down into her coffee cup, and Keenan saw a frown wrinkle her forehead.

He looked around the coffee shop and noted

Christmas lights strung over scraggly plants. Sure, eighty degrees outside and one was supposed to hark the herald angels. Yeah, palm trees and tinsel. The fact was, it was all wrong, and it wasn't just Santa and tropical islands. Where, tonight, was there any peace on earth?

CHAPTER 5

INTERNATIONAL NEWS SERVICE—Dec. 30, 1943: A book on the best-seller lists is creating an uproar in the publishing industry. Leading church figures and parent-teacher associations have called for a boycott of *A Lion Is in the Streets,* by Adria Locke Langley, a thinly masked story of Huey Long's lust for power and carnal appetites. Sexually explicit, say the detractors.

Kirstin trotted the Morgan, keeping him on a loose line and trailing the lunge whip behind him in the dust. Laddie Simbo kept one cautious eye on the popper, knowing exactly where it was at all times. The big gelding hated exercise, but he had to be worked, the edge taken off him before turning him over to any of her student riders, men from Harmon General Hospital, soldiers missing parts of themselves. Since she began the riding program, more than a few badly wounded GIs had gone from morose to proud, realizing they could adapt to missing limbs and go on living. Long ago some wise man said that the outside of a horse was good for the inside of a man.

She glanced at the Texas sun, weak with winter, and told herself to quit thinking. It didn't work. Sergeant Harlan Edgerton—the name and his bright image leaped vividly from her memory. So young and so depressed, thinking he was only half a man. One leg was gone as well as one hand, but the greatest loss was in his mind. He had worked horses on his father's ranch, and turned even more bitter when he couldn't leg one of Kirstin's horses into gait control.

And so she had taken him to bed, and finally had to say no when he asked her to marry him. Oh, Lord—first a divorce and then a widow, and a boy so glad that he remained a man despite his losses. Now she admitted that part of her charitable gesture had come out of her own need to reaffirm life.

Jim Shelby had been killed before they had time to become used to one another, and part of her had died with him. She had lost Chad and then Jim, and both her sons were in combat. Farley was safely on his way home, but Owen was still in danger, as was his father. Kirstin had needed proof that life was stronger than death, and so she made love.

She clucked to the gelding and flicked the line so he dropped from a trot into the swift, flat-footed walk of the true Morgan. She had proved to Harlan that he was no gelding, and to herself that she was still wanted.

There would be no riding for a few days; most of the ambulatory patients had been on leave from the start of the holiday season and wouldn't return until after New Year's. She flicked the whip along the ground, and Simbo grunted into a slow, rocking-horse canter, snorting as if Kirstin was torturing him.

"You big bum," she called out. "You could hold that gait all day long and barely work up a sweat."

It wasn't sweating time on the ranch; the wind had a bite to it, and the great oaks had given up all their leaves, limbs spread bony against the gray and mournful sky. She had come down to the stables to get out of the house and work off a fit of depression. She didn't feel any better.

"Ho," she said.

Surprised at such a light workout, Laddie Simbo stopped to face her at an angle. She popped the line so that the light throat chain snapped him under the jaw. "You know better than that," she said, and he immediately slid his hooves around to stare straight ahead. Her horses were trained to stop without turning in, and Simbo knew it, so she didn't pop him hard. He went sprightly into the stall when she lifted off the halter, head and tail high.

"I'm glad one of us feels snorty." She hung the gear in the tack room and tucked her chin into her woolen jacket as she walked toward the house.

Her foreman met her at the back door, wearing a heavy serape, his head snugged into a battered Stetson that had been rained out of shape long ago.

Gregorio Venegas said, "All is well at the stables? The horse can wait, señora. This is no weather to be outside, for horse or man."

"It's not that bad."

Head tilted, he sniffed the air like a good hound reading scents on the wind. "Pardon, but it will be bad very soon. With your permission, I will call in the hands and make certain that your horses will remain dry and not spook. There will be much thunder and lightning. Warm yourself, señora. It will not matter with the señor's quarter horses; they are safe in the big barn, and they are used to the weather."

She didn't answer, and Gregorio's leather face creased.

Twisting his hat in both hands, he said, "A thousand pardons, señora. At times, I think he is still with us, the señor. I do not wish to cause you pain."

"*De nada*. I have to remind myself every day that Jim's pickup won't come roaring up from the country road. Thank you, Gregorio; I'll ride out any other storm, even your Texas blue norther; happy New Year to you and the boys."

The cook had gone home early, leaving a pan of chili on the stove. Kirstin didn't turn on the heat. She passed through Jim Shelby's study. His presence was all around her in the room—leather smells, brass things gleaming softly, reflecting the flames in the fireplace, a certain peace.

She sighed and poured bourbon on the rocks. Bourbon and branch water had been her husband's drink, a good Texas drink. And he had been a good Texas man, truly a man for all seasons and reasons. He should not have rushed to join the army. Damned few senators and representatives did, and those few found cushy jobs a long way from danger.

Jim Shelby had died on a forsaken jungle island in the miserable goddamn infantry.

"And Chad?" His name jumped out loud and surprised her. Sipping whiskey, she thought that and a long marriage did that to you, kept the leftover memories in an old file that could never be totally closed. It was difficult not to compare one husband against the other, and Chad Belvale had his good points.

But of course he was infantry, also, and had led both their boys into the toughest part of the army. Chad used to say there's nobody ahead of the infantry but the enemy.

And there was Owen, a company commander in the European Theater of Operations, the good old ETO that covered about half the world. And there was Farley on the other side, the Pacific Theater. He had seen something in the jungles, something so horrible that his mind threw up roadblocks. He had always been gentle and somewhat subdued, different from his brother in many ways.

It had been a real break, Nancy Carlisle being stationed at Tripler Hospital to help Farley. And Nancy would soon be bringing him home.

She lifted her glass. "Farley, here's to you; you're coming home in one piece, and I thank God and Nancy and the entire Medical Corps for that."

Everything was working out for Farley; his wife would be in California to greet him. A lot of luck and the leverage of the family money, and Penny was freed from prisoner of war camp and ready to comfort Farley. It could be worse. One branch of the family had already lost its males—Lieutenant Walton Belvale and his father, Major Dan Belvale, KIA in the army's terse yellow telegrams bearing their canned message: "The War Department deeply regrets to inform you . . ."

Would telegrams come in for Chad and Owen?

INTERNATIONAL NEWS SERVICE—Washington, D.C., Jan. 5, 1944: President Roosevelt, planning to use his State of the Union address as the beginning of his re-election campaign, is calling for a second Bill of Rights which would guarantee security and prosperity for all.

Nurse Nancy Carlisle stroked his hair, and T/4 Fitzgerald Kaole DiGama sighed into the base of her throat.

He said, "I wish to hell you didn't have to go back to the mainland. You're so much on my mind that I walk into walls and the nurses have to tell me twice. What will I do after you're gone?"

His skin was warm and brown and she loved it, loved how Hawaiians made love, open and laughing and without any lingering of guilt, real or imagined. She was in love with Hawaii, and maybe in love with Fitz; he was so much a part of the islands, tasting of sun and frangipani blossoms and the soft winds that stroked the blue, blue sea. Fitz was solid, too—firm as the lava foundations upon which Hawaii had grown lush and beautiful.

Turning on the bed, Nancy eased a leg over him, kissing him lightly.

"Some kind of *haole,* you," he breathed. "More like a mama Pele. Sometime cool on top, but anybody mess around that volcano, here comes all that lava, burns up houses on the slope, everybody run like hell."

Nancy smiled down at him, filling her eyes and nostrils with him, moving her lower body to clasp him close. "You can't run like hell from me."

"Don't want to."

With another man between her thighs, she thought of Keenan. He was so changed from the man she had married. Rumors about him ran through the hospital—about this lone and deadly killer who had stalked the Japs through the jungle, beating them at their own game and adding grisly refinements of his own. The awed whispers told of head hunting.

She couldn't quite believe that of Keenan, although she had always been aware of a certain chilled core within him.

She said, "Fitz, do me a favor?"

"Stand on my head and pound salt, spit in mama Pele's eyes, play grab-ass with a shark, if you ask me."

"Nothing so drastic; I wouldn't spoil those lovely buns. I'd like it if you kind of kept an eye on my—on Major Carlisle."

He sat up. "You want me to keep an eye on your husband? For what—catch him playing around with *wahinis?* He's already got something going."

"Ex-husband, and I couldn't be happier for him and Susie. It's not that. Something is still coiled inside him, something dark. He's not the man I married; he's a stranger in many ways. If he should—if he goes berserk, please let me know right away. I'll give you a private number to Kill Devil Hill for General Belvale—"

"Hey, now—me and some big wheel general? How you salute on the phone?"

"Preston Belvale is family, and the call is always charged to the other end. The call will go straight through, top priority. I just don't want Keenan hurt anymore, or have him hurt anyone else."

Fitz said okay, sure, and she snuggled up to him again. Maybe she was worried without cause; Keenan hated the Japanese to the point of psychosis. He could be capable of anything when he found out that Susie Lokomaikai was at least half Japanese.

CHAPTER 6

SECRET to Kill Devil Hill, Lt. Gen. Preston Belvale—
The Italian front, Jan. 13, 1944: The Allied air offensive increases in preparation for a seaborne landing, date and place classified Top Secret, Need to Know only. Units of the 34th Infantry Division advanced beyond Cervara.

In the French sector, the 3rd Algerian Division on the left and the 2nd Moroccan Division on the right launched attacks upon Sant'Elia Fiumerapido.

Feldwebel Arno Hindemit squatted by the bedside of the man he had long called friend, Hauptmann Fritz Witzelei. Of all the scheissen officers who should be shot and never missed, it was bitter bad luck to have a good one hit, and hit badly. Arno looked down into the pale gray face and patiently waited for Witzelei to wake up. It was what an infantryman did best, wait.

He stood two tall bottles of liberated Italian wine beside the tied-together stable straw that served as a hospital bed. At least the straw was clean, but the odor of cow shit clung to the very walls of this big barn. He tried to blow another scent from his nostrils, the ugly smell of rot, the smell of death approaching or death departed.

47

Carefully he unwound his kerchief from a chunk of garlicky light-colored cheese. The line troops scavenged bits of food like this, when the Italians had any themselves, while aid stations farther back had to make do with whatever issue got trucked through the constant Ami strafing and bombing. This way, at least he could do a little for his captain, this cheese and sour wine and the understanding of a comrade.

Franz Witzelei, schoolteacher and onetime defender of the Third Reich goals; now he was a seasoned *landser* officer who would do his duty despite his complete loss of faith. True soldiers did not fight for faith or fame or medals. They were paid to fight, and little as that money might be, they fought to protect their family or squad or platoon or company; only then did they fight to save their own precious asses.

Down the line of makeshift beds and stretchers often touching, a man moaned and another man coughed wet and strangled. This dairy barn, luckily not bombed yet, held men so badly wounded that moving them would probably have been fatal. Here, if the Ami ground attacks could be held off, some patients might heal and get shipped back to Germany to undergo more air raids. The rest waited to die, and even those final moments would probably be in captivity. Fighting along this *verdammt* Gothic Line would not cease until every frozen ridge and every exploding valley was overrun by the Allies. Gott, if the Führer would pull the armies out of Italy and Russia, there might be a chance to defend Germany and perhaps gain a negotiated peace.

To the last man, to the last bullet, Hitler ordered over military radio; do not give up one inch of land. When the last men and last bullets were burned up, what was left to defend the fatherland? The bloodsucking Gestapo? If the Americans or

British reached here before the vengeful Polish Brigade, patients still living would be cared for. The Amis and Tommis were like that. Arno wasn't so sure about the Polish; they had come a long way from the bombing and starvation of Warsaw, but it was still on their minds. They blamed the entire Wehrmacht for the evil done by the SS and Gestapo, and much evil there had been. Word spread in the army despite cover-ups or, worse, the stone-cold attitude of who cares.

Blinking, Arno propped up his Schmeisser machine pistol and searched out a cigarette from the folds of his damp greatcoat. Carefully he drew three pairs of spectacles from an inner pocket; one had a cracked lens, like those blown off Witzelei. He had searched in the ruins of villages for two of them, gambling that the SS hadn't mined every fallen chimney. The other pair he took from the staring eyes of a *landser* who did not need them anymore. Witzelei was nearly blind without his glasses, finally shattered in the fight that had nearly killed them both, and the army was not prepared to test his eyes and issue new glasses. Even if it could do that while holding its collective ass in both hands and climbing one *verdammt* mountain after another, the army would consider Witzelei too badly wounded for the waste of new equipment.

It seemed a hundred years since 1939, since the blitzkrieg had thundered across Poland, and the crazy attack he had made upon a machine gun and received his first Iron Cross. That was before he turned much, much older and grew up into a type of sanity. What he had done by carrying his wounded captain out of that murderous shelling by Allied warships standing off the coast was done out of friendship, not for any military tactic. Glory was for ignorant Hitler Youth or the bastard *Panzertruppen* and the Luftwaffe, not tired old *landsers*.

Lighting his mildewed cigarette, Arno wished, almost prayed, that this aid station would not be taken by French Foreign Legion troops. The Moroccan goumiers delighted in slicing the ears off the wounded as well as the dead. It had been regulation that their monthly pay stopped when they went into combat. From then on, they were paid according to how many ears they turned in. German intelligence said that particular barbarism was no longer in practice, but then, German intelligence said a lot of things. Arno thought the ugly little goumiers had gotten into the habit of taking ears, official or not.

The Algerians were almost as bad, taking no prisoners when it was so much easier to pick over what small loot they could get from corpses. Drawing upon his cigarette, Arno gave silent thanks that no Senegalese units had been reported in the area. Those tall, shiny black savages, with teeth filed sharp and their great knives, tortured before they killed. The talk was that they would rape every man they captured, many times over. Arno shuddered.

"The war must be over." Witzelei's eyes were open. "The front line army could not spare you otherwise."

"Scheissen, schoolmaster. I was sent to gather malingering *landsers* to use in our next great and overwhelming victory."

Witzelei made a weak grin. "And you have yet to be cured of diarrhea of the mouth. Even here someone listens."

"Fuck them. What can they do—send me to the front?"

"They can execute you as a traitor."

"Fuck them twice, then; I won't be the only fool to go down. I lost my faithful Schmeisser to those great Ami shells, but this one is almost as trustworthy.''

Uncorking a bottle of wine, Arno said, ''Is it better by you now?''

Witzelei strained to lift his head from the rolled jacket that served as a pillow. Arno slipped one hand under and tilted the bottle. After gulping hard, Witzelei sank back, eyes closed briefly. When he looked up again, his voice was stronger.

''They say I am broken up inside. I hope I can return to you soon. I put you in for the Iron Cross, First Class, and I thank you for whatever time remains of my life.''

Arno pushed the spectacles into a limp hand. ''One of these might give you back your eyes, Hauptmann.'' He took a swallow of wine and grimaced. The farther up the Italian boot they retreated, the wine was more raw and heavier with resin. He said, ''One Iron Cross is more than enough, whatever class it may be. I just did not want to break in another *dummkopf* officer.''

Witzelei bit his lip and clutched the glass tightly. *''Danke.* Now I won't be blind as well as helpless.''

After he took another drink, this time on his own, some color touched his unshaven cheeks. ''Always the *landser* with the hard ass. Did you get new officers?''

''One—also more than enough. It is a catch-all company now. Cooks and truck drivers and typists. You and I are all that is left from Poland and France; three men from Tunisia, three more from Sicily. The rest are dregs, including this *Leutnant* with a cleaning rod up his ass.''

Propped up now upon one elbow and accepting a slice of cheese from Arno's knife blade, Witzelei said, ''What is this officer you love so much?''

''A bird turd, fresh from officer school; the pure

51

Aryan, blond and blue-eyed and as full of shit as a Christmas goose.''

Leutnant Junger was all of that, and to make up for not being one of the prestigious Prussian Vons, for being baby-faced and not getting into the war until it was almost over, he sneaked around looking for something to report to the Gestapo. At the moment the unit was off the line and resting between low-level air raids and long-range artillery barrages.

"Maybe he will grow up when we fight again. We miss you, *Hauptmann.*''

"Yes, I am ashamed to lie here. Is it as bad as I fear—the war?''

"They are everywhere, the Amis with so much equipment. We destroy ten tanks, fifteen come to take their places; if the Luftwaffe shoots down ten of those forked-tailed fighters, twenty fly in for revenge.''

He remembered that Tunisian day long ago when they discussed the fighting ability of the Americans. The Amis had just been badly beaten and panicked at Kasserine Pass, their first true blooding. Arno said then that they would learn in time. Now they were veterans who had learned their lessons too well and were rich in equipment and supplies of all kinds.

"*Hauptmann,*'' he said then, "I will hide this plunder beneath your jacket. I will visit you when you are moved closer to Germany, but now I must get back to the company. Perhaps we can be more ready this time.''

"*Feldwebel—* Arno, goddamn— I do not have the words. A poor schoolmaster, *nein?*'' A single tear beaded Witzelei's lashes.

"But a fine soldier and a better comrade.'' Arno touched his hand, then stood up and hurried down the narrow aisle between the straw piles and stretchers.

UNITED PRESS—Italian Front, Jan. 22, 1944: Operation Shingle, another massive seaborne strike, was launched here before dawn. Troops swarmed ashore at the harbors of Anzio and Nettuno, quickly overrunning two battalions of the German 29th *panzergrenadier* division. Within 24 hours, supported by four cruisers, 24 destroyers and six transports, the Allies landed more than 36,000 men.

Preston Belvale rubbed his bad leg. Somehow he had become the fond grandfather presiding at a family reunion, and after a fashion, that's what it was. Crusty Carlisle had lost weight and was darkly tanned; he looked good. You had to peer close to find the new lines grooved in the leathery face and the fatigue set deep behind his eyes. But Crusty had just put the time of his life behind him, and that showed, too.

His granddaughter stayed near, refilling his glass, touching him often. Pulling on his Cuban cigar, Belvale saw Gloria Carlisle-Donnely lightly acting out the much greater homecoming she would give Sergeant Eddie Donnely when he returned—if he returned. She knew there was a chance he wouldn't come home, or that he'd be trundled in as a basket case. She was family and could soldier through the tough times. Gloria would stand up to tragedy, even though she might not understand.

"Damn it," Crusty grunted, "settle somewhere, girl. I can pour my own booze. Tell you what—see if the cooks can sidestep Lady Minerva and make a decent dinner. No goddamn grits, souse, black-eyed peas or chitlins—something civilized. Hell, even the Japs wouldn't eat hog guts. I prefer raw shark and octopus. I never knew an octopus had a beak like a parrot. Son of a bitch bit me; with all those legs, hell to throw loose."

When she was gone, Crusty said, "Catch me up on the war. The Aussies are tight-lipped, especially when they wonder about somebody. I overheard one guy insisting that I must be an impostor of some kind; ungentlemanly, you know, certainly not the type for a general officer."

Belvale grinned. "And the Aussies are rough-edged, according to the English; the convicts, don't you know. I should have you roar into one of their private clubs in London and give them the granddaddy of all shocks. But after the war; they're our allies now, and they might not get over you. War news: General Lucas just screwed up the big landing at Anzio.

"Well, the landing itself went all right, and a big surprise for the Krauts, but Lucas dragged his feet. He had fifty thousand men, and sits on the beach-head instead of driving inland against undefended roads and railways that carry supplies and replacements for the German Gustav Line. He waited for tanks and heavy artillery to arrive. Kee-rist! He had it all going for him, numerical superiority and surprise. He has resistance now—more than he can handle. I think he's caught in a meat grinder."

Crusty drank off his bourbon and rolled a Bull Durham cigarette, licking the paper together. "Old Jittery Lucas never could play poker worth diddly squat. If he bet, you knew he had power up the gazoo, and he got bluffed out of many a pot. I could have made a good living off him, but he got shipped out of Benning."

"You could make a living off your uncanny luck. If you haven't used it up crossing that much ocean without getting lost, dying of thirst or being blown out of the water."

"Luck, hell. We made our own luck, loading up on coconuts and fish bait and anything that would hold water at any speck of coral and uncharted island worth about two bits on the open market. You'd be surprised to see how many juicy fish float up in shallow water when you drop a grenade, even a Jap grenade. One swabbie medic and the toughest goddamn marines I ever saw. We made our own luck, Preston, and we kicked some ass."

Belvale pulled on his cigar and ran his thumbnail over his mustache. "I guess we all make our own luck."

"Damned right. Look what a gamble you took, springing Penny and the Englishwoman from the POW camp."

"It was a gamble, all right, but the odds weren't all that bad once they made it out of the camp. From what the ladies told me, they probably wouldn't have made it through the war—bad food, little medicine and the typical Jap mistreatment."

Crusty nodded; smoke spiraled up from his roll-your-own. "The Englishwoman—wasn't there something between her and Chad? How come she hasn't gone home right away?"

"She might have, but she stayed in Washington for a thorough debriefing. Her husband is, or was, a POW close by her camp. She saw him once; no legs."

"Oh, shit, that would screw up most romances. What about Chad?"

"I filled you in on everybody else in the family, but not much about Chad. He's been playing games—assigning himself to different units as an observer while his battalion marks time in England. Maybe he and that Englishwoman can work out something if they think it over for a while. Chad wants back in Italy. I'll approve a TDY change of station for him, but not for long. A temporary duty transfer until his own outfit is ready to jump off."

Dropping his voice out of habit, Belvale continued: "All we have at the moment on the invasion of France or the Balkans is the title—Overlord. Stalin wants it right damn now to pull pressure off the Russian front. Churchill isn't a puff of cigar smoke behind him, but we're not ready. MacArthur is screaming for more landing craft in the Pacific, and he may be right. He has a lot more ocean landings."

Crusty grunted and poured bourbon. "Why doesn't he teach his troops to walk on water? He's pretty good at that."

The whiskey had a smooth and smoky flavor; Belvale waited until Crusty complimented it before mentioning that it was homemade bootleg and watching his expression. Crusty hated to compliment anything below the Mason-Dixon line. But he had come to the Hill before going home.

"Pretty good booze," Crusty said. "Did you import it? You know, I haven't seen much of Europe since our war to end all wars."

"Forget it, Charles; you're going on a long leave after G-Two is done with you."

"I got your Charles dangling," Crusty said, and held a forefinger out horizontally. "Jump up on this and crow. Or you can rotate on my thumb."

CHAPTER 7

Dark; it was so dark that the sun might have died in its far circling and would never bring back the light again. Crusty Carlisle stared up at the unrelieved blackness of the ceiling. Shifting in the big bed, he finally said the hell with it, and switched on a table light.

He suspected what was wrong: this comfort, the

safety, the soft quiet all around. His body, his alert system, wasn't geared to luxury now, and the sudden dreamless sleep of the old had passed him by. It was to be expected after the experience of the past months. An animal's body and mind were designed to fight or flee, and in times of great tension, a man was only another animal, a little smarter, a little more stupid. Here he had nothing to fight and no place to run.

Perching on the side of the bed, he rolled a Bull Durham and licked it into a cylinder. Scratching a kitchen match on a bronze ashtray scarred by many such lightings, he blew smoke at the ceiling and checked to see if the heavy oaken beams really passed high overhead. They hadn't lost themselves in the dark. No stars shone through, and the sky didn't rock. He wasn't aboard a leaky and wind-tossed ship. He was home; he sat here in the solid protection of Sandhurst Keep, the great logs, the fitted stones around him. He sat in the master bedroom where most of his ancestors were born, and where many of them had died. As many more were buried in the ridge north of the house.

Beyond that, the Keep was too damned quiet. Not enough young ones at home now; not that many young in any way. Keenan wasn't that young, and it appeared that no extension of the line would come from him. It would be good to sit with Keenan and share war stories. Gloria lived and worked at the Hill's operations center, married to an ornery sergeant who might just fit the family pattern. There were a few other Carlisles not far away, and the intramarried left to continue the line by name. That was important, damn it; it was the only promised immortality.

The old Keep could be freshened, its colors brightened and some of the hard edges smoothed away. Kill Devil Hill was closer to D.C. and the center of things, but Sandhurst Keep was just as important to the family and to history. Raised by grittier, no-frills generations, the great house wasn't as luxurious as the Hill, and its lands were harsh and stony in contrast to the Hill's gentle rolling hills.

"What the hell."

Winter-issue long drawers sagging, he rose and crossed the room for a bottle. He'd never liked the iodine taste of scotch, although it would get by in a sandstorm. The Irish whiskey, now—he drank that from the bottle and scorned a water chaser. Old Bushmills was what Preston Belvale would call sipping whiskey, its smooth brown flavor a fine blending of peat smoke and honey. He carried the bottle back to the bedside table.

He listened to the night and heard the dim belling of a coursing hound, heard the old house settle itself for the rest of the night with small creakings and whispered groanings. Like him, he thought, and rubbed some of the Irish whiskey into both shoulders, squinting around the cigarette smoke circling up into his eyes.

Two drinks later and the cigarette butt ground out, he left the light on and propped his back up against the carved head of the bed. They were centuries locked together, the Carlisles and Belvales. As one, they had fought beside kings and risen against tyrants. Almost from the first shots fired in the American Revolution, they were on line. They went shoulder to shoulder against the lobsterbacks, and their own lost scalps and hung in lodges and longhouses of the Five Nations. But they held on to their land and to their identity, no matter the war, to include the battles where they faced one another over gun barrels. They knew who they were and why they were. . . .

. . . Colonel Elijah Belvale bled at the mouth where a ricochet had driven a wooden splinter through one cheek. Peering through the storm slats of a first-floor window, he lined up the pistol on a careless Yank lounging his horse beyond one of the white porch pillars. Around him, his remaining few rifles fired sporadically, hanging smoke thick in the drawing room of Kill Devil Hill.

Squeezing gently the trigger of his Navy 36, Elijah caught a profile glimpse of the Yank and hesitated. The horseman passed from the line of fire, and the moment was gone. He might not have been a Carlisle known, but that shouldn't have meant anything. In this desperate, violent time, brother was likely to kill brother and might not realize what he had done. And perhaps the killing would happen anyway, there was so much hatred and duty boiling in the poisonous brew pouring across the land.

Elijah knew he should not have come to this particular spot on this day. Of course he knew the land, and had meant a short cavalry sweep to trap a small body of Yankees against the river. Of course he wanted to see for himself how Kill Devil Hill fared. Never a strong woman, the mistress of the Hill had passed away with lung fever in the first months of the war. Beulah Rose Belvale departed life as she had lived it, quietly, with hardly a ripple.

Since then, the Hill and what livestock could be hidden were managed by Auntie July, the black cook and lifetime maid-companion to Mistress Beulah. The hands-on work was done by black Roland, foreman and horse handler. Both had been born on the Hill, and it was home to them. Most of the slaves slipped away north after the first shots were fired. A few others remained, uneasy and bewildered. Their color protected them, and helped guard the Hill itself, helped vegetable gardens to grow where tobacco patches had once flourished.

The small body of Yankees turned out to be a large body, and its outriders drove Elijah's band to cover in the Hill. It was an ironic joke that with his volunteers, he should fall in his own house to the Yankees.

"Not by that one," he said, and shot a man running. He flung a burning torch away as he went down.

"They're after burning us out," he called. "The damned cowards."

Kill Devil Hill put to the torch? Banners and armor in the great hall burned or ruined; the precious records of antiquity, the lovely polished woods—oh, God!

One of the riflemen fired a Spencer repeating carbine captured from some blue belly in an earlier skirmish. The South had no such weapons in the beginning, and the North came equipped with the new gun that you loaded on Sunday and shot all week. Its sound was different from that of the Henrys and Springfields used by the Confederacy.

Elijah missed his next shot, but the Spencer knocked another torch carrier down. The pitch pine torch wrapped in burlap flared beside one more dead man.

A bullet slammed beside Elijah's head, coming from the back of the house. "Corporal! Guard the rear!"

A pane of stained glass shattered in the vestibule, and another one crashed in the great hall. A leaden .54-caliber rifle ball banged hard against the hand-shaped and colored stone of the fireplace. Coughing the brittle tang of powder smoke, Elijah knew the end was coming. His handful of men couldn't hold out against the mob outside. Bad luck and at least a full enemy company had trapped them there. And, he admitted, his selfish compulsion to see home, just for a moment.

Raising and cupping his hands, he yelled, "Get

out! Get out now! Surrender if they let you! Corporal—see to it!"

His troops had that much chance coming to them, an opportunity to live.

Corporal Crawford shouted back, "How about you, Colonel?"

Outside, a bugle sounded and a man with a bull voice called out something Elijah couldn't understand.

"I stay," he said, wiping at eyes smeared by gun smoke. "Kill Devil Hill is my home, and when they burn it, I go to hell with it."

Not alone, he thought. He had four more rounds in the revolver and would rush across the front porch firing.

"But, sir—"

"Go, damn it!"

When he heard yells out back around the empty horse stalls, Elijah kicked open the front door, bent his knees and lunged straight ahead. The first lick knocked the pistol out of his hand; the next, up side his head, spun him off the porch to land on his hands and knees. Be damned if he would remain there. A little wobbly, he rose and faced them, the blue soldiers who had knocked him down. It would have been better if they had shot him.

"Colonel Belvale?"

Elijah blinked. "Sir, who the hell—"

The man sat his black horse, wide and solid. He was the one who had slipped away from Elijah's gun muzzle. He said, "It's been a spell since I came to the Hill, cousin. I'm Jubal Carlisle, Major Carlisle now, and sad to meet you like this."

"J-Jubal—"

Another man pushed up to them, a lean pale rider on a pale horse. "Major, take the surrender and then fire the rat's nest of these rebels. I ordered that before you arrived on the scene."

Jubal Carlisle took off his hat and ran a kerchief around the seat band. "General Thornton, I'm afraid I can't do that. The fight's over and honor is served."

The pale face darkened. "You are refusing a direct order, Major?"

"Not a lawful order, sir. Major General Carlisle's orders on pillaging and needless destruction are quite clear on that, sir. Folks in these hills have long memories. Brutality will bring vengeance for decades, whereas an honorable defeat is acceptable."

"And, Major, although you constantly remind me of your political connections, I too have a long memory. Perhaps next time you will not stand before me unless it is to be hanged for insubordination and misconduct in the face of the enemy."

"This one doesn't have much of a face left, sir."

The general whirled his horse and spurred away.

"Silly bastard," Jubal said. "That mistreated horse will kill him someday. All right, Lige, to make it official—do you surrender your sword to me?"

"Threw the damned thing away a while back; a pain in the ass to tote."

Swinging to earth, Jubal said then, "Fix your face; it never was pretty, but some better than this. There's a skirmish brewing down the creek and I have to go. But before I ride, will you give me your parole as an officer, a gentleman and a Belvale that you will not again bear arms against the United States of America?"

There was really no choice if Elijah wanted to save the hill from burning, and he thanked God and a Carlisle for the chance.

"Upon my honor, I so pledge," he said, still tasting blood and black powder and the bitterness of defeat. . . .

CHAPTER 8

Press pool, wire services, radio, individual correspondents—CINPAC South Pacific, Feb. 4, 1944: The invasion of the Marshall Islands continues as Admiral Chester Nimitz assembled the biggest force so far employed in a single operation in the Pacific. Some 40,000 marines and soldiers struck at several targets in this far-flung and stategically important archipelago.

Other navy admirals are titular heads of sectional units, and the marines stormed ashore under one of their favorite commanders, Major General H. M. (Howling Mad) Smith.

The archipelago, made up of at least 2,000 islands and islets, is about 620 miles long and cannot be skipped by General Douglas MacArthur's recent island-hopping tactics. It is too big, too important and that much closer for Allied bombers to reach Japan proper.

Highly placed intelligence sources here said that the Japanese defense forces are under command of Rear Admiral Monzo Akiyama, who realizes he must be attacked and not bypassed. Landing troops have already run into stiff resistance by die-hard defenders in pillboxes, and U.S. pilots report enemy airstrips on several of the larger atolls.

Tech Sergeant Eddie Donnely was again out in front of his platoon, but not as point or listening post. Everybody took a turn, and leadership to him meant just that—leading, not pushing from the rear. With his BAR, he was a connecting file, halfway between the pair of .30-caliber water-cooled guns on loan from Mike Company and his rifle platoon. His own heavy weapons, two air-cooled 30s and a pair of 60mm mortars, were emplaced in the company command post, not far from the beach.

The trouble was, that command post and several others strung out along the rim of this little bay were set in piss-poor positions.

There had been no real fighting on the beach, only the occasional pop of Jap snipers' .25-caliber rifles. But unloading the ships brought on problems that hadn't been foreseen; there was confusion and the tide rising too soon, waters gone shallow and the threat of enemy submarines made the usual snafu—Situation Normal, All Fucked Up. The hatchet-swift nightfall in these islands caught people out in the open, the alligator landing craft bobbing and swaying offshore, and some of them immobile with their tracks dug deep in muddy sand. The companies moved a short way inland under the coconut trees and set up their headquarters, blending with battalions for a stronger perimeter.

Against the tracked sands of the beach, supplies bulked high and dark, a great richness of food, fuel, clothing and ammunition. The Japs would trade their sacred mountain for such a treasure, so they would be coming, and all out. If they stayed with their SOP, they had set their defenses inland, but not too far, where they would gather for a banzai charge in hopes of driving the troops back into the sea. It was possible; the outfit had no real depth. One breakthrough could curl right and left to their flanks and butcher a lot of feather merchants who would react with hurt surprise.

There should always be protection between the bad guys and the signalmen, the beach party and others of the gear in the rear pursuasion. Survivors would try to return to civilization soonest, and they knew the quickest was when the smoke cleared. They'd be right on top of the next manning level report, line 99, ready and eager for reassignment. With friends in Personnel, transfers were easy in peacetime. But here there could be a thousand authorizations and the only way a man would move was farther ahead, replacing the dead and wounded.

> (Barracks talk:
> I'm feeling fine
> on line 99,
> although treated shitty,
> I'm sitting pretty,
> And if things move apace,
> I'll shake this fucking place.)

Up ahead, the bolt of the heavy 30 on the left flank snicked almost without sound, eased from half load to full load with the latch cover cupped tight to muffle any metallic sound. Eddie would bet the bolt was overoiled to help protect the quiet. The M Company gunner knew his business. Eddie also hoped the gun was well dug in. The position faced a swift-water creek that had its own sickle-shaped beach, racing water about hip deep. It burbled across a front of ragged brush and splintery palm stumps chopped off at different heights by the ship-to-shore cannonading. In the night, that cover was too good. You couldn't see the buck-toothed bastards until they screamed in behind the long bayonets.

Clunk-clunk.

Holy shit—a Jap rapping a grenade against his tin helmet to jar the safety pin loose and arm it, ready to throw.

Whack, whack, whack!

The right flank gunner had found a target, and the near gun probed the dark with a longer burst. The Jap grenade arched over the machine gun and blew close to Eddie, stinging sand into his face. A fragment rang his helmet like an off-key bell.

Japs splashed loudly into the creek, shrieking that goddamn banzai horseshit to pump themselves up and scare the hell out of their enemies. The scare part worked.

Whackety-whackety-whack!

Lifting his chin from the sand, Eddie saw the halo of muzzle flashes flicker around the left gun. *"Banzai!"* the little shits screamed. The right gunner clung to his trigger, slamming through most of an ammo belt, 150 rounds. The muzzle blasts were too steady and held too long. It gave the shits time to zero in on the gun crew. A Jap grenade exploded, landing right in the gun pit and scattering hot water and warm blood.

Eddie yelled: "First platoon! Watch the right flank—the right!"

In blind answer, the M-1s of his riflemen probed the night now ripped and torn. The surviving gunner worked his weapon well, spacing short bursts and walking them into the creek to share with the charging Japs. His number-two and -three men, in the hole with him, banged away with carbines.

Aaaahh! That damned choked-off cry of a man badly wounded—aaahh! Jap banzais gobbled high-pitched over each other. On they came, right into the deadly muzzle of the machine gun.

Blam—aaahh!

Oh, Christ, they were at the gun squad with grenades and bayonets, and the deep whump of a GI .45 said they weren't getting in free. Eddie came to his knees, BAR poked ahead. Around the gun the ruckus died off, leaving Eddie's ears ringing and the tart flavor of gun smoke on his lips.

"Banzai! Banzai!"

Coming out of the CP, a white flare popped above the treetops and silhouetted a pair of Japs below. In the stark light they were puppets jerking up and down as they stabbed long bayonets into the machine gun position, and into the new dead there and searching out the wounded.

Eddie didn't know he was standing erect until the butt of the BAR kicked along his hip. Running crouched and firing, he slammed headlong into the Japs. One went down, so close that the muzzle blast of the BAR set his raggedy uniform ablaze.

In the drifting light of the flare, he saw the other one down on one knee with the long rifle raised protectively high and slanted across his chest. Enough light spilled through the jungle canopy for Eddie to see the bloodshine dark upon the bayonet steel. A low three-round burst jerked the Jap onto his back. Eddie propped his BAR butt down against his thigh. Then he snatched up the Jap's Arisaka, wheeled it up end for end and threw his shoulder weight behind the downward thrust.

The bayonet pinned the Jap to the earth like a fat bug. He jerked and twisted, both hands slipping in blood as he tried to pull the bayonet free of his body. Butt up, the rifle swayed tic-tock as Eddie slid into the gun position.

The flare hissed and bubbled out; the sudden lack of light was a sheet of deep and furry blackness holding a circled green echo behind his eyes.

"Eetai, eetai," the Jap moaned.

"Yeah, it hurts. Suffer, you son of a bitch."

Fumbling over the gunners in the dark, Eddie found what used to be life—blood, sticky and warm; so much blood. He lifted and rolled the gunner's corpse up in front of the hole. He stopped working with another body when he could find only one arm. Head up, he strained his eyes and ears into the dark and heard little rustlings.

"Eetai, eetai"—low and thin as the whimpering was, some Jap would pick up on it and come calling.

Why not? It was an old jungle trap. GIs on Guadalcanal had been drawn to their death by the fucking Japs pretending to be GIs wounded or lost and looking for a safe way home. Now they had learned.

"Eetai . . . eetai—"

Behind the gun Eddie braced himself on one knee and draped two fabric belts of ammo over the other. The rustlings grew louder in the dark, but they were still no louder than beetle clickings. If he'd thought it would do any good, Eddie would have prayed for another flare. Behind him the CP was spooked and alert; he hoped he and his riflemen wouldn't get caught in a shit storm of friendly fire.

As if to answer, the flare—no, two flares!— arched high in the air and turned the night into high noon. And there they were, splashing out of the little river, shrieking as they ran straight at Eddie's position.

Slapping the clamp with the heel of his hand, he loosed the pintle for free movement of the gun. The Japs shrilled and came on, waving bayonetted rifles, and out in front a guy whipped the air with his long sword. Using the forefinger-thumb grip, Eddie stroked the trigger and nailed the swordsman along with the first few squealing Japs in the short skirmish line.

A sudden silence halted noise and sudden movement; only the flares dipped and swung as they drifted earthward.

"Eetai, eetai!"

The wounded Jap's anguished cry keened into

the quiet that was a lie. Eddie tapped the trigger again and moved the gun muzzle slowly across the next staggered row of attackers. They fired as they came on, and when Eddie eased off, he heard bullets chopping into the dead GIs around the gun. They were brutal sounds, nasty sounds, and he closed them out by firing two short bursts—one into the splintered tree stumps on the other side of the river, and the other through the Japs lunging up out of the water.

The flares burned out. More Japs screamed in the blackness, coming on, always coming on. Carefully Eddie worked the gun in spaced bursts of four and five rounds, quartering his front, tapping the wooden pistol grip to give the gun vertical movement as well.

Wham!

Grenade—a sharp stick poked through both ears? Mouth full of dirt, anyway—some raked into his eyes. Christ—where was the gun?

He found the pistol grip, but the gun bucked only twice. Ammo. He felt the empty belt snaked out into his lap. On the left flank and right flank, erratic rifle fire hurried his search for ammunition. There! Raising the cover latch, he fed in the metal tip of another belt, slammed the latch and yanked the bolt handle twice. What the hell, noise meant nothing now; they knew exactly where he was.

That living whack-whackety-whack was beautiful music, a song out of hell for some. Tasting the night, tasting the flare-powder smoke blacker than the night and as heady as strong whiskey.

No more flares fired the heavens like Roman candles, but Eddie didn't need light now. He knew their attack route—across the river and straight to the little slope that Eddie's gun blocked. The dead Mike Company gunner had been sharp. Christ— Jap bullets jerked at the corpse. The gunner had it all but luck.

Loading another belt—the last belt—of .30-caliber ball into the gun, Eddie waited for the next onrush.

"Eetai . . . mizzu, mizzu . . . eetai!"

Yeah, Eddie could have used some water, too. Why didn't the bastard die? At first his moans were bait to draw his buddies—if Japs had buddies or friends who would search for their wounded. Licking at dry lips, Eddie knew he hadn't seen any Jap value life, including his own.

He said, "Okay, damn it," and used the BAR to kill off the poor bastard.

CHAPTER 9

Pravda—The Russian eastern front, Feb. 7, 1944: In the northern sector, troops of the Volkhov Front (General Meretskov) took the important railway junction of Batetskaya and reached the suburbs of Luga.

NORTH AMERICAN NEWSPAPER ALLIANCE—The Italian front, Feb. 7, 1944: General Freyberg's [home office: check first names, Army & Navy Directory; censors too busy here with personal mail; too busy anyhow] New Zealand Corps replaced the U.S. II Corps on the Cassino front. The sector of the U.S. 34th Infantry Division north of Cassino went to General Tuker's 4th Indian Division. General Freyberg announced that before another attack is made on Monte Cassino, the historic abbey will have to be bombed. (Home office scramble phone: I think it's bullshit; no Krauts ever seen within the walls; no shots coming out.)

                30 and ENDIT—Stackhouse

Lieutenant Sloan Travis trotted at the head of his platoon, catching a hint of spring in the moist air. The 2nd Platoon pounded after him like so many long-distance runners. They had left their heavy weapons back in the barracks for the day, which was more than anything else an endurance run.

The infantry legs; gas in the tank; feet cared for and problems with shoes or socks caught now.

Sloan was a believer in this kind of training. It helped keep you alive. Most make-work training the army dreamed up was more than an irritation; it was a frigging shame.

North Africa was still in his mind—Algeria and Tunisia—and memories of Sicily were even closer. He had expected more of North Africa—Arabs in burnooses, the Foreign Legion and colorful kepis, sultry-eyed maidens and Beau Geste.

Romance faded swiftly, exposed to reality; there were damned few burnooses and more Arabs with dirty asses hanging out of their rags. GI barracks bags—the old blue ones with drawstrings—were prized, and it wasn't unusual to see an Arab wearing a bag, leg holes cut in the bottom, the drawstring serving as a belt and somebody's serial number stretched across his scrawny butt. The Arabs believe their messiah will be born not to woman, but to man; therefore the baggy pantaloons of daily wear. GI mattress covers were good for trade in Malaga wine, eggs and wormy dates to break the C ration monotony. The troops had learned to trade quick; the Arabs could steal the cover without waking you and be blessed by Allah. Today's Foreign Legion had ambushed their allies-to-be and killed GIs for the sake of their "honor." Then they stacked arms and rushed to surrender so they could fight the true enemy, *le boche*. Americans who fell at Saint-Cloud and Oran didn't know the difference; they were just dead.

The sultry-eyed maidens staffed whorehouses where GIs were kept in line by MPs, and any woman molested—or even spoken to—on the streets could call forth savage vengeance—like bloody genitals crammed into a drunk's mouth.

And Beau Geste slept with bedbugs; he was a barely paid sadass who stole anything he could

carry and squirted cherry syrup into his beer.
Would any readers buy the brutal truth about their
own fantasies? Sloan might not ever write them.
He might not write anything, now or ever. Damn,
he had told the brass he didn't want the responsibility of rank; it was enough that he had to concentrate on protecting his personal ass, and never
mind an entire platoon. They pushed rank on
him—didn't he realize duty, honor and country
weighed heavier upon the family?

Sloan breathed deep and stepped the pace up
another notch. Getting in top physical condition
would save lives, because after the first rush of
adrenaline under fire, the body drove itself all out
for survival. Reaching beyond the body's—and the
mind's—normal capabilities made the comedown
abrupt and weakening. When the downside hit, the
body demanded rest and a return to sanity, and
everything ran just a little too fast for catching up.
The gas tank needed filling, and just when you
were too tired to run any farther or any faster,
there came the bad guys.

Then you were dead.

And Sicily? There hadn't been much reading
about Sicily in Sloan's background, only the Black
Hand and the Corsican Brothers, with asides on
Napoleon and wine grapes. Reality was grinding
poverty and old women in black, and little kids
with big, dark eyes hoping you would scrape any
leftovers from your mess kit into their held forth
cans.

England had not disappointed him: the fabled
castles, London Tower and the great city itself
spreading history and romance before him in a
great feast. The hallowed graves of Arthur and
Guinevere at the ruins of the ancient church; Plym-
outh, and there to stand where the Pilgrims stood
and looked out upon a trackless sea. He loved it

all. Protecting all that made some sense out of the war.

Trotting easily as a light sweat warmed him and the .45 on his hip nudged him in a slow rhythm, Sloan glanced often at the hazy sky. A frigging Stuka had dropped out of that sky a few days back. It had strafed the column and killed one bad-luck GI. Bowley was the kid's name; a moment before, he had laughed with Sergeant Pelkey—"I ain't in show business, Sarge."

Shit, should he have ordered the machine guns to be carried, just in case, and slowed the road march pace? The enemy planes were so fast that they were in and out before a gun could be set up. The BARs, he thought—only two in the company, and they weren't in the Table of Organization and Equipment. Nobody knew where those handy weapons came from, but leave it to soldiers to forage for themselves and damn TO&E. Next hike, Sloan's troopers would have all the firepower they could carry in comfort.

Next hike, next inspection, next payday—the United States army ran on credit and dreams, a jawbone army. He didn't know where or when the term originated, but it had probably been around since armies existed. Samson and the jawbone of an ass? One day—one jawbone day—somebody ought to compile a dictionary of such talk.

For what? Edification of civilians? Civilians didn't give a good goddamn about the army, the vocal mom and apple pie crowd, the "our boys" bullshit; buy savings bonds and win the war; loose lips sink ships.

"Sir?" Sergeant Pelkey trotted up beside him. "Break time?"

"Sorry, had my head up my ass, I guess." Sloan stretched his right arm over his head, signaling a halt. Out of habit he glanced down the line as the columns disintegrated to the roadsides left and right, when the men fell out for water and smokes.

REUTERS—Italian Front, Anzio sector, Feb. 8, 1944: German General von Mackensen's 14th Army carried out a second massive assault on this Anglo-American beachhead. This action pushed the Allies back almost to the line they had held on January 29.

German losses were too heavy for an exhausted army, and General Kesselring ordered the offensive to be suspended.

Owen Belvale stood in the London drizzle and tried to hail a cab. One after another was occupied, and he began to get angry. Goddamn, he didn't have all that much time to see her, and some of it was going to be wasted right here on the curb. He was wet, anxious about Helene and more than a little nervous about how far Major Langlois was going to stretch for him.

His last conversation with the executive officer hadn't gone very well, and Owen knew his leaning on a friend of the family might be reaching a limit.

"You better listen up," Langlois had said, his Cajun accent blurred by anger. "I've sidestepped and rerouted everything from training reports to orders that require both your attention and your signature. If your daddy ever finds out what's going on, your ass is sure enough going to be in a sling."

"Look, he's on a pretty loose rope himself." Owen didn't like the sound in his voice, the whine he couldn't stop. "He's out playing war games, having himself sent all over the place and sticking his neck out when he shouldn't be. You know he's doing things out of channels."

"And that's about all that's keeping you from

getting nailed good.'' Langlois threw his hands up in the air, waving away the burden of friendship. "Your old man catch you, he's gonna come down on you, and you gonna be able to hear the sound from now to Tuesday. I'm telling you, boy, you better turn down the heat with that woman."

"Damn it! It's not like I . . . Look, it's not that easy. God, do you know what it's like, having a woman who can make you burn? Just the touch of her skin . . ."

Langlois's lip curled and his dark eyes pinned Owen still. "I know all about having a *jolie fille*, and I also know when to keep my pecker in my pants."

Owen had left, walking out into the rain, intending to show Langlois how much he could get done when he put his mind to it. His strides faltered, then took him in an unintended direction. Briefly, he would just see her briefly, take a taxi and share a moment or two with her, no more.

Now there were no empty cabs, the rain was hardening, and his need to see her was growing. Damn it, damn it! He really would keep it short, and there was no need for his father to find out. He could manage it; all he had to do was see her.

The Times—London, Feb. 8, 1944: More and more Allied soldiers are seen on the busy streets here. The uniforms range from the American tailored look to the bizarre. Senegalese walk about barefoot, their feet so callused they can ignore rough ground and inclement weather. Wrap leggins and tasseled red fez complete their getup—if one can ignore teeth filed to points, and a huge sacred knife.

The public is advised to avoid being curious about the knife. It cannot be pulled from its sheath without drawing blood; that would dishonor the soul of a blade blessed by a witch doctor in Senegal. The blood will be yours, and be grateful that just a shallow slash and a drop from your thumb qualifies.

Chad Belvale stood tall and jumpy at the edge of the tarmac, lighting one smoke from the butt of another. This time they were Old Golds, PX leftovers ranked barely higher than Philip Morris. He wondered who had shortstopped the good smokes. Probably the same rear echelon clowns who'd pirated the best C rations.

Gleaming silver, the B-17s touched lightly down one after the other on the blacktop lanes of Heathrow airport. Chad fingered the sheaf of mimeographed orders tucked into his overcoat pocket. They damned near gave him a free hand. General Belvale had put just one sticker in them. Shrewd, the old man; that kicker set the departure date and return schedule.

On the radiophone General Belvale's voice had crackled: "In and out, Chad. I can't say much on open radio, but you may understand what time had to do with it. Lieutenant Bartlett has been debriefed here and is entrusted with a courier pouch. MI Five, British Intelligence, will be on hand. ETA oh nine hundred on the seventh."

So the big jump was coming off before too long, the Channel crossing into Hitler's backyard. Who but the Big Red One would lead it?

"Stephanie." Chad breathed hard and clamped the phone tight in his fist. "Thank you, General."

"Remember who you both are; remember where and when you are."

"Yes, sir; thank you, sir." He had never meant anything more.

Snapping back to now, Chad saw her—Stephanie Bartlett, moving small and tidy among British soldiers, the walking wounded. Beyond them he could see tiers of men on stretchers. He hurried toward Stephanie, and was cut off by medics moving back and forth, by wheelchairs.

When he passed through the blockades, Stephanie was gone.

Honolulu Star-Bulletin—Honolulu, Hawaii, Feb. 10, 1944: Shining white and marked with a big red cross, three hospital planes left Hickman Field today. Each plane is staffed by dedicated doctors and nurses.

They will touch down in San Francisco where their precious cargo will be offloaded to waiting ambulances. Each plane carries severely wounded servicemen who require extended medical treatment. Some are ambulatory, but must learn how to adapt to a changed life-style. Some are bedridden and will receive treatment from the best specialists in the country at Letterman General Hospital.

Lieutenant Farley Belvale tightened his grip on the armrests as the plane lifted off. Closing his eyes, he went through the prayers he knew: Our Father who art in heaven . . . Now I lay me down—

He flinched as Nancy Carlisle patted the back of his hand. "Easy," she murmured, barely heard above the sound of the engines. "I get nervous just driving by an airport. We'll level out in a minute."

He would not tell her he was afraid of flying; it would be one more aberration for the shrinks to Ping-Pong their theories with him at the net. First the flight to Hawaii, then this one to San Francisco and some army hospital. It never seemed to end. He forced his fingers to loosen their grip. "Okay, okay, okay."

Too many okays; he had to watch that. He had

learned many lessons on the locked ward, like how to stay out of the "five dollar rooms" where they stuck you with horse needles and kept you in isolation. When he got to where he was going, maybe they would let him use a knife and fork; eating steak with a spoon, a dull spoon, was a problem. And the answer wasn't eating with your fingers; the guys in white didn't like that. If Nancy was around, they let it go. After she left they reamed ass.

"All right, Farley?"

"Yes, sure . . ."

That's enough; don't repeat and don't count things, like making words come out even. Nancy was a nurse, and she was nice. Nancy was a nurse—4; and she was nice—4. Total—8. Good. He always felt better when the count was even. If it wasn't, he had to save back a word for next time. Then he might forget and everything would get muddled again.

The plane reached its ceiling and leveled off, the roar of its engines dropping to a drone. "There," Nancy said. "We can smoke now."

"Yes, sure."

He must be a smoker; there were cigarettes in his toilet articles kit. Of course he smoked. You could have cigarettes but not matches; the ward boys had lighters, and you had to beg a light. If you had a match of your own, you might set beds on fire and burn every son of a bitch in the world.

It was like the way they took the drawstring out of your pajama bottoms so you wouldn't hang yourself. And how the safety razor they gave you was locked so the blade couldn't come out. They made you shave every day and watched you do it. If you didn't want to shave, two of them did it for you; one sat on you and held your arms, and the other one scraped your face.

The plane bucked through an air pocket, and he held on to the seat arms. Anything sudden scared him these days, but he mustn't show fear. Holding to that family directive would help when he met his wife. He ought to practice before he came face to face with Pretty Penny.

CHAPTER 10

INTERNATIONAL NEWS SERVICE—Feb. 12, 1944: In the Anzio sector, German attacks on the Aprilia salient are opposed by the British 1st Division. In the southern sector of the Gustav Line the bridgehead established by units of the British X Corps has reached its maximum allowable depth and is dug in and hanging on despite fierce counterattacks.

Preston Belvale sighed as he pushed back from the table and sniffed the rich aroma of Creole coffee, the heavy chicory of Café du Mond shipped from New Orleans. Thanks to Dame Minerva's manipulations as lady of the mansion, the table at Kill Devil Hill was as good now as before the war. And without black market dealings, without extra ration books. Most of the food came from the land and out of storage in old-fashioned smokehouses, the salt-cured hams hung peg by wooden peg, the peppered slabs of bacon and the great sides of beef flavored by slow and lovingly careful hickory smoke. He lit a little cigar and sighed again, this time against the pressure of his belt. Relaxed, he rubbed his game leg.

Gloria Donnely scooped up platters and dishes. "Dessert?"

"I hope it's a light one."

"Continental—guava jelly and cheese. You, too, Gramps?"

Crusty said, "Gramps? I got your— God damn it, Preston, you put her up to that. Gramps, my aching a— Gloria, get the hell out of here so I can talk. Yeah, the jelly and cheese. Preston, what beats me is how you learned about civilized food, even if it's Frenchified."

"A crispy serving of catfish atop a slab of salt-cured and honeyed ham, home-canned garden peas, and corn bread so rough it scrapes your throat. Add the only coffee worth drinking and it's Eden grown up. If there were no other reason to fight this war, it would be to keep the enemy from hauling off this kind of food."

Belvale's cigar lifted blue and aromatic smoke. "Looks like we blew it at Anzio. They pinned us down, rather than us cutting off their armies in the south. By the grace of God, they haven't shoved us back into the sea. They keep trying and we hang on, despite heavy casualties. If we try to back out, they will chop us to little bloody ribbons."

Crusty Carlisle finished rolling his cigarette and nodded thanks to Gloria when she served the simple dessert. He smiled at her back as she returned to the kitchen. "There goes a good strong woman with brains. She kept the cook out of listening range. If there's no need for Gloria to know some bit of intelligence, she avoids knowing. Good training. She knew you and me would have our heads together."

Belvale said, "She's been cheery all day; she just heard from Sergeant Donnely—two V-mail letters."

Nodding, Crusty said, "He's doing right by her so far. No females running around the jungle, so he didn't collect a harem."

"Before you fault Donnely, give them time together, time to discover that orange blossoms cover warts. He didn't duck more duty in the Pacific, and he probably could have ridden his wounds to a ZI job. If Gloria asked, you'd have seen his orders got lost in the great paper shuffle.''

''Zone of Interior my aching ass; whatever else he is, Donnely is a line soldier, the only kind worth knowing. As far as me keeping him out of the line of fire, even if Gloria came crying to me—hell, no; maybe; I guess so. In his way, he probably belongs in the family. Let's go up to the war room and see if we can't ream a few fat asses about Anzio.''

NORTH AMERICAN NEWSPAPER ALLIANCE—Marshall Islands, Pacific Theater of Operations, Feb. 12, 1944: Fighting has been sporadic here, in the main concentrating on Kwajalein atoll. There are quiet stirrings beneath the surface operations, as is the case when American troops are readying for another assault. [Home office: on both scramblers—this is a hell of a place to scare up feature articles and not straight news copy. Didn't gripe much until the word filtered down today on Chiang Kai-shek's demands. Suppose you know the Gitmo wants money from the U.S. for our military personnel's pay and "maintenance," whatever the hell that means. Our people are protecting his ass and he charges us for it. He also wants another $500 million dollars Chinese money for building airstrips he should have finished months ago. If we give the old Baldy what he wants, I'm hanging it up and coming home because everybody back there is nuts.]

30 and ENDIT—Stackhouse

Eddie Donnely waited patiently behind a thorn tree, his BAR muzzle propped across the branches. Somewhere out there, hidden Jap snipers had a line of fire. The Jap score was two head-shot GIs and one lucky bastard who got nailed through both sides of his jaw. The million-dollar wound, the trip home and away from this bullshit forever. Hell, with the advances in medicine, the teeth could be replaced and the jaw rebuilt. Score three for the Japs; nothing for the troops.

He waited, eyes up and slow-scanning from left to right, then reversing the visual sweep as he lowered his stare. Big Mike Donnely would never be forgotten so long as his truisms lived. "God surely hated right angles," Eddie's father had said. "Watch close for them in and around trees and the brush."

Carefully, one by one, Eddie stretched his calf muscles and steeled himself as some kind of beetle felt its way over his face. Ahead lay a little clearing partly covered with broken branches knocked around by ground artillery and supporting fire from destroyers. The jagged stumps of coconut trees showed sickly white against a brown-green backdrop, and the suggestion of a breeze bore tastes of gunpowder and things burned and fried. Lightly among them came the strange purity of the sea, too soon blanketed by the furry stench of death.

Each dead thing had its own attar; the only smell that came close to matching that of a dead man was that of a gut-swollen rat. Maybe rats would inherit what was left of the earth; certainly they were survivors.

Creak! A movement loud and blundering—a ragged-assed rifleman from George Company on the left flank, lost and with his head up his ass.

"Hey!" Eddie hissed. "Sniper country. Get the hell back."

Rifle slung, the guy passed through half the clearing before he stopped, looked around and said, "Huh?"

"Run!" Eddie yelled. "Run, you flat-peter bastard—run!"

(Barracks talk: Flat peter, a soldier so stupid and so clumsy that he is always stepping on his dick.)

Damn! All this time spent waiting to pop a sniper, and this asshole loused it up. He stood uncertainly, peering around as if he could see any danger.

Prangg!

The guy fell forward, his legs jerking, his rifle clanking on the ground, shot in the back. The Jap lowered himself back into his spider hole, a hole dug straight down with only room enough for the sniper to bend his knees. He lifted a camouflaged circle of ground cover, fired once and pulled the lid back over his head. There was no way out, and sooner or later he'd be found. No matter to the Jap; with the first shovelful he knew he was digging his own grave and would be rewarded in his emperor's heaven.

The rifleman stopped kicking, and within minutes black flies came to swarm about his head and the blood spot glistening between his shoulders. The Jap in the spider hole didn't rise again and would not until he had another easy target.

The other sniper did. It was only the faintest rustle in the treetop movement that wasn't made by the clean salt fingerings of the sea close by. Eddie found him far up in the palm, tucked into the ribbon-fanned leaves like so much extra bark.

Balancing the BAR against a notch in the thorn tree limbs, Eddie lined up the sights just so. Then he cut loose a burst of five. The Jap fell as far as he could before his tie-down stopped him. His Arisaka rifle spun onto the floor of the clearing, and the Jap hung upside down without movement. Eddie gave him more time, in case; the bastards were good at playing dead.

Then he eased the BAR out of the tree and

waited a while longer. When he moved into the clearing, he went directly to the lid of the spider hole and forced the last of his clip into it. By habit, he heeled another magazine into his weapon.

"Too bad, you little shit," he said into the hole. "You didn't even get a chance to yell *'banzai.'* "

CHAPTER 11

War Department, Washington, D.C., Press Pool—
Eastern Front, Feb. 12, 1944: The first Ukrainian Front
(Russian General Vatutin) maintaining its pressure on
German General von Manstein's Army Group South,
captured the town of Shepetovka.

INTERNATIONAL NEWS SERVICE, Italian Front, Feb. 12,
1944: President Roosevelt describes the situation on
the Anzio beachhead as "very tense." A new attempt
by units of the U.S. II Corps to reach the Via Casilina
is still unsuccessful. North of Cassino the 166th Regiment of the 34th U.S. Division tried without success
to seize the abbey of Monte Cassino.

Burma: In the Arakan sector, the 26th and 5th Indian
divisions converged from north and south to free the
7th Indian Division from its encirclement. The move
jolted the timing for Japanese General Terauchi, who
was about to throw his troops into a finish-it attack.

Lieutenant Colonel Chad Belvale shifted his
weight in the hard straight-back chair. In England
formal waiting rooms were of a pattern—hand-
crafted wood waxed to a deep shine; on the walls,
dimmed fox hunting prints hung carefully at eye

level for short people, but too small for details unless you got up and peered closely at them. There was always a clean but nap-worn carpet, these chairs that did not invite lingering, the oak desk and the bespectacled secretary whose flinty eyes dared you to disturb her master with anything trivial. He felt her eyes follow him as he stood and crossed the anteroom to peer at a hunting print: red jackets and white horses with exaggerated flowing manes and tails. Something like Morgan horses in the show ring, and Kirstin tall and lithe in the saddle. Horses had enriched Kill Devil Hill for so many generations that it was natural for Chad to think of them as one, Kirstin and her favorite breed.

Recrossing the room, edgy while sweating out the closed office door, he remembered when his wife brought the first Morgans to the Hill. It had caused more than a ripple in that sea of long, lean thoroughbreds, but she stood her ground. Most owners bred for speed, she said, and didn't give a damn about the animal, just the money. Morgan breeders ever tried to improve the horse, in looks, performance and stamina. Like Kirstin herself.

He put a cigarette in his mouth, but the hard-eyed secretary stared him down; he stuck it back into the pack. Throwing his rank around and calling in some favors had gotten him this far; he had been on the transatlantic lines to the Hill and to the Keep, asking for help in reaching Stephanie. He had fought his way through a blizzard of red tape and passed spy-catcher traps to the sanctum sanctorum. He had been blocked from greeting her at the airport, but damned if he would be kept away from Stephanie much longer.

The discreet click of the office door spun him around. God! There she was in uniform, small, light on her feet, moving in that special way. Right behind her came men who might have been twins, but for the dim and differing colors of their suits. Their faces were bland, designed and trained to fade into most backgrounds and not be remembered. England's intelligence spooks: MI5.

Chad's long strides brought him to Stephanie; he folded her within his arms and buried his face in the exotic scent and silken feel of her hair. She trembled against him no less than he quivered with her.

One spook cleared his throat. "Umm . . . Colonel Belvale?" He might as well have added the "I presume." It was that formal.

Chad hated to release her, even for a moment. "Yes." He didn't look at the man, but down into Stephanie's brimming eyes. Gently he kissed her, savoring the tingling softness of her lips and her geranium breath.

"Colonel?"

"All right, damn it—what?"

It came out harsher than he intended. He was still touchy about the way MI5 had handled Stephanie's arrival. They had spirited her away from the airport and left him with his face hanging out. In any army, G-2 screwed up as often as it produced vital information on the enemy.

"Sorry, um . . ." The other spoke now. They even sounded alike. "Lieutenant Bartlett has been placed on furlough—a short one, I fear. We need more details regarding the camp and as many names as she can bring to mind, to include the Japanese guards. There should be more medical tests, but the medics say that waiting a day or two will not cause problems. Your, um, Lieutenant General Preston Belvale agrees with the timing and the operation. In time, one supposes this British officer will return to her duty with antiaircraft guns."

Okay, some of the family pressure had reached

this far. "How long? And what was all that razzle-dazzle at the airport?"

Stephanie touched his cheek, gentle fingertips, feather-stroking. He saw now that her face had thinned and her eyes were deeper set; her skin was sun darkened and the sun had bleached some color from her hair. She half turned toward the men.

"Permission to leave now, sir?" At the man's nod, she saluted sharply and then took Chad's hand. "I will explain all."

Small, sculptured and warm, her fingers were also strong, entwined with his; he felt calluses. The urge to hold and caress her was near to overpowering, but it was up to Stephanie now. She hip-brushed his lower thigh as they walked—no, quick-marched—down shady corridors that made abrupt turns. Sound was muffled here, and although no guard appeared, he had that watched sensation, feeling eyes upon them. Getting out of this MI5 station was almost as tough as getting in.

On the street, Stephanie slowed, but shook her head when the questions popped out of him. "In a bit, love; it will go better over tea."

"Stephanie, I tried to get to you the moment I heard from Kill Devil Hill. I wondered what the hell—"

"Tea, love. Since I got out of— Since I came back, it seems that I can't drink enough tea. If I don't stop eating, I shall be my own barrage balloon."

Pausing, she looked through a shop window that was X-ed by tape to protect the glass from bomb concussion.

Maybe that was the cause of Stephanie's tenseness; the Jap POW camp still gouged at her, and that near-impossible escape through dense jungle and over mile upon mile of dangerous ocean. He wouldn't hurry her, as much as he wanted to; he would give her time to dim the prison camp horrors and get over the tension. But he couldn't wait too long; his TDY orders to Italy gave him only two days with Stephanie; he needed years.

Reuters—London, Feb. 12, 1944: During the night more than 800 British bombers carried out yet another massive raid on Berlin and caused serious destruction in the city's industrial areas.

Captain Gavin Scott poured the blonde another shot of black market scotch. The hotel restaurant in Piccadilly had been a good choice; a fat tip doubled the rationed serving of duck for them both; not steak or even chicken, goddamn duck. Still, that impressed the blonde wren, already drawn to woozy pity by his severely scarred face and pilot's wings.

Londoners appreciated the RAF fighter pilots who had saved their collective ass during the heavy days of the blitz. The air raids had not gone away, but were only shadows of the fire bombings that razed so much of the historic city. What the hell; maybe the Krauts did England a great favor. Rebuilt, London could be brought up to date.

Old Adolf had screwed himself when he ordered his Luftwaffe to destroy the British population instead of sticking to their first objective, ripping up military airfields. The RAF would have been wiped out early on battered airstrips and so would have been unable to rise to meet the high-level bombers.

The blonde—Dolly? Polly?—said, "Ooh, eating this much is downright sinful; any more and I shall waddle like a duck. And marvelous scotch; I had forgotten the flavor."

Wiping his mouth with a clean but shabby napkin, Gavin lit Capstan smokes for both of them—lousy Limey tobacco. He said, "Later this evening

I'll have room service bring up steaks and chocolate.''

"Oh, dear, Yank, I . . . well, I'm married, and—''

"Bring him along.''

"Ooh! Aren't you the cheeky one? My lad would never so much as dream of an act so bawdy and illegal. This moment he is far out to sea and lonely. It is against the law—or just immoral?''

"Somebody's dumb law. Old bastards have tried to legislate sex for a hundred years; it doesn't work.''

Gavin refilled her glass and sipped his own drink. He tapped his cigarette into the ashtray and slowly scanned the crowd at the bar. Tomorrow he would pick up a few cartons of decent American cigarettes. "But you would consider joining a ménage à trois?''

Bet your ass she would. Right now she enjoyed the halo she wore; poor lass, caring for her man as if half his poor face isn't gone. English woman through and through.

Sure. For the hell of it, he might arrange a night for her to remember; maybe, if something better didn't come along. A secondary entrance door opened at the far end of the curved bar; a man and woman in uniform ducked through the blackout curtain. They came on a swirl of cool night air that spooned holes in the nimbus of cigarette smoke.

"Goddamn!''

When he snatched at his Capstan, the paper hung on his lower lip just enough to peel skin. "Shit!''

He had bumped heads with half the stuffed shirts in London and gotten shuffled from one know-nothing officer to another. Everywhere, her records had ended at Singapore.

Yet there she was at the bar; there stood Lieutenant goddamn Stephanie Bartlett.

And side by side with her, Chad Belvale. Son of a bitch Colonel Belvale.

They got only halfway to the tables before he blocked them in a narrow people-walled path between the bar and the tables. Her face went pale when she recognized him. Belvale didn't blink—the great stone face.

He was the same old bastard who had pulled rank on Gavin and stolen this bitch years ago from that same air raid shelter across the street.

Belvale said: "Something for you, Captain?"

He was doing it again, military as all hell.

"I'll have a flight check on your partner, Colonel. Didn't she tell you about our big night on the town? She's got a lot of mileage on her, but her model just keeps coming back for more."

He heard Stephanie say: "Chad, don't—"

The next thing Gavin remembered was the scarred half of his face slapping the floor, and he became aware of the bitterness and stench of his own vomit.

REUTERS—The Italian Front, Feb. 15, 1944: Battered so long in this bloody valley while the towering bulk of Monte Cassino frowned down at the troops. German artillery observers call down pinpoint firing on any movement below. General Freyberg, commander of the New Zealand Corps, again called for bombing the ancient monastery. Now his views are backed by British General Sir Henry Maitland Wilson who flew over the abbey and saw German soldiers in the courtyard.

Chad Belvale hunkered down on the raked-up stable straw, one of several men around a tiny fire. The straw kept some ground chill and dampness from tired asses. The fire was dug in and hidden behind the ruins of old stone houses that German artillery had blasted into rubble. The little stove—gasoline over sand in an inverted steel helmet—didn't give much warmth, but the light was a comfort. The black tea it heated was strong and bitter, but also a comfort.

His legs were growing numb; after backing away from the circle, warming his fingers around the canteen cup, Chad stood up and leaned against a slab of stone. Miserable; it was cold and muddy with a wet wind blowing. It was infantry weather, miserable.

He snuggled his head deeper into the hood of his field jacket; it was lined with dog fur. The Polish Brigade was made up of champion scroungers; they had used six years of wartime to perfect the art, and Chad was thankful for their gifts. In his own outfit—in his son Owen's company—there lived the king of hustlers, Corporal Weintraub. His machinations kept H Company fat and sassy. Here, every soldier worked to take care of his outfit because he had to. G-4 supplies got to provisional and bastardized units last, after American outfits were taken care of.

The dog fur was soft and warm; from the looks of the scrawny Italians they passed, Chad could well imagine what had happened to the dogs. He sipped the black tea cooling swiftly. The commanding officer of this group was also gifted: Colonel Jerzy Prasniewski looked as if he waited to step out smartly on the parade ground. His was a rare quality, to fight well and appear movie-good doing it. Prasniewski was a combat soldier and a half, and perhaps one of the last great swashbucklers. He didn't walk; he swaggered, eager for the next firefight. From his twirled mustache to boots only somewhat muddy, his men loved him, and according to reports, so did Italian women who crossed his path.

With a rifle he could group hits at two hundred yards that a silver dollar could cover. He had been at Lieutenant Walton Belvale's side when the boy was killed in Warsaw, the first family member to fall. That was before the United States was technically in the war, so Walt had a head start. He wouldn't be the last casualty, and if these brutal mountains were any portent, the war still had a long way to go.

The tea had cooled, but the rim of the canteen cup was still hot. Long ago some genius in Quartermaster had designed that rolled lip around the cup so it would hold enough heat to blister the mouth.

Chad drained the cup anyway. He had been an idiot in London; punching out Gavin Scott in public was a damn fool thing to do, but the smartass kid had brought it on himself, leaving Chad no option. Without rational thought, he had banged Gavin Scott in the belly and hooked him in the mouth.

And then put his shoulders against the wall, because the drinkers had turned silent and stared at him: "Lor, did you see that? Bashed the poor lad . . . and him so bad wounded. Oh, just look at his ruined face . . . and a fighter pilot at that. . . ."

Stephanie's voice was loud and sharp when she wanted it to sound that way. She hurled its cutting edge at uniforms and civilian jackets alike: "Let it rest! Leave it be! The captain is an ass who brought it upon himself. He insulted me and the British uniform. Him a bloody hero? Not likely. I know him well, and the best said of him is that he is only an ass. This time he overstepped."

The crowd stirred and muttered and swirled to help Gavin Scott to his feet.

"Let's get out of here," Stephanie said to Chad, "before the red caps come."

Mixing with military police wouldn't have been smart; Chad's orders cut the time too close. If he was picked up for brawling, he could have been grounded while the war passed him by. There would be double-barrel hell to pay when Preston Belvale and Crusty Carlisle heard he'd lost his head and gotten involved in a public brawl. The family chiefs flowed with the stream and bent with the prevailing winds, but only to a point. Behind the acceptance of today's mores and the growing power of its wives and women, the steel core of the family stood unflinching. It roused to protect the faithful, but would not show its face to those who disgraced the proud battle flags, the stained war axes and dented shields in the great hall at Kill Devil Hill and the honored headstones in the memorial grove.

He folded the handle of the canteen cup, slid the cup into its heavy felt carrier and fitted the canteen. Cold and muddy, infantry weather, but you kept a full canteen. Your mouth went dry under fire.

> *When it comes to slaughter*
> *you will do your work on water*
> *and lick the blooming boots*
> *of him that's got it. . . .*

No Gunga Din here; no scarlet jackets sweated through or darkening red where the belt buckle should have been. Indian troops, the Sikhs, Kurds and Pakistanis, British trained and equipped, were on the line. In the next war—and there would always be a next war, according to the holy family and the Holy Bible—these soldiers might be on the other side, bayonet to bayonet, as student confronted mentor. Even now there was a half-felt half-seen rambling of discontent among the colonial troops, and after this war was behind them, some men would be thinking of fighting in and for their own countries. The British Empire, weakened by the war, and the homeland, tired of sacrifice, would be in trouble.

Removing his helmet, Chad used it as cover to light and hide a cigarette. They never tasted good when you couldn't see the smoke or watch the tip glow and fade. He recognized his mood and tried to shake it, then gave up and went with the shuddering power of Stephanie—image and reality, the incomparable closeness at some moments flicked by a threat of subterranean chill.

She had snuggled up to him, but clutching, in a strange desperation. When he went beyond a gentle stroking, she stiffened against him.

"Baby?" he said.

She cried; her breath and her tears were soft and warm against the base of his throat. Tenderly he held her without questions, without strain. As she had never been before, here was the woman who had shown him how and why to make love of lasting value. She was the sprite who had taught him that laughter and love together were very special indeed.

Slowly she relaxed and in a little-girl voice spoke of the POW camp, its miseries and its small brave moments. And at last, in a whisper, she told him of being raped repeatedly by the Jap guard. He didn't question or say there-there to her. She was no child to be soothed by platitudes. She was Lieutenant Stephanie Bartlett, soldier and woman in her own right. He kissed her forehead. She said she killed Sergeant Katana.

The chill left her then, and although she didn't laugh, their lovemaking was deep and gratifying.

"Ahh . . . Colonel?" Prasniewski stood at Chad's elbow. "Dawn comes slowly, and many of us cannot sleep. I wonder if the Germans have sensed what is to occur. Much of the time their intelligence system is adequate."

The high, breathy shriek gained power as it arched down.

"Incoming!" Chad said.

"They know," Prasniewski said.

BLAAMM!

ASSOCIATED PRESS—The Italian Front, Feb. 15, 1944: This release should be bordered in black.

It has happened; the ancient and historic abbey of Monte Cassino has been bombed. This morning 147 B-17 Flying Fortresses led the air raid; 82 B-25s came in a second wave to drop their share of some 400 tons of bombs to destroy a shrine of Western Christian culture.

It was necessary, said the general, to shut down a German artillery observation post that has stalled Allied forces for months.

Even so, when the planes came, soldiers watching here made the sign of the cross.

It was dawn.

The earth shuddered and mountains leaped; between thrashings the earth moaned in pain and the mountains shook fire from their smoky crowns. The noise was hell squalling loose, rakes of massive horned talons across spinal ridges of granite; the seven thunders roared out a prophecy. Chad Belvale gripped field glasses, his chilled fingers tight on the metal. The abbey on Monte Cassino was obliterated by eruptions of raw earth and geysers of white smoke, of inky smoke.

In one of those strange quiet moments that flit through the most violent battles, Colonel Prasniewski said, "May God forgive us all. Two hours after the last bomb falls, the Americans will try to climb the mountain."

"But I thought the Poles—"

"So did we; a sudden change of orders. Perhaps for American good news headlines to offset the dreary reports of Anzio and so many casualties at the heavily defended Gothic Line."

"Damn it."

Prasniewski watched the skies for a moment, then focused his own glasses upon the smoldering abbey. "I do not think that the abbey will be easily taken. If once it was truly an observation post, it has by now been turned into a fortress. I do not believe that disciplined infantry can be bombed out of action. These men will burrow into the wreckage and have to be fought out by other determined infantrymen. This brigade will lead off and climb the mountain when the high command realizes that. It is our right, and we will do it."

There was no easy sparkle in Prasniewski's eyes now. They were slate, hard-edged and dedicated.

SECRET—War Department via Vatican City, Rome, Feb. 17, 1944: The bombing of Monte Cassino was a brutal mistake, according to high sources here. Officials said that Field Marshal Kesselring long ago notified the Vatican that none of his soldiers would set foot in the abbey; moreover, he had established a free zone radius of 300 meters around it where all soldiers were forbidden to enter.

The Germans themselves, as an extra precaution, took the priceless ancient documents kept in the abbey to the Vatican for safekeeping.

(This document SECRET. Repeat: SECRET.)

Preston Belvale held his cigar and sniffed at its smoke. "The news of this abbey screwup will get out, anyway; a matter of time until the press discovers how faulty our G-Two can be."

Crusty Carlisle sipped at his whiskey. "More the

fault of the damned Limeys; they kept pushing for the bombing. But what the hell? If I had been in command there, I would have probably gotten it done sooner. No civilians in a combat zone, and I'd rather kill off a potful of civilians—enemy civilians—than lose one sadass GI.''

"The monks were nobody's enemy, and the whole thing was screwed up from the start. We have word that the German Third Parachute Regiment moved into the rubble right after the raid. Now for certain they can look down on our slightest movement. And they're tough.''

He drew upon his cigar and thumbnailed his mustache. "Kee-rist, nobody even thought to coordinate the abbey bombing with the other operations. The Fourth Indian Division didn't know the time fixed for the bombardment, and their attack came too soon. They not only got bloody noses, but were hit by some of our own bombs.''

Crusty grunted. "Their General Tuker had them attack the wrong goddamn position. He didn't send them up Monte Cassino, but jumped of for Monte Calvario. What the hell is three-quarters of a mile off target? Fucking peanut.''

Reaching for the bourbon, he poured another drink. "Did you tell Gloria that Donnely is in the hospital?''

"No point withholding information. He's down with malaria, and she know that means he's doing time somewhere behind the lines. Safe, she calls it and hopes he stays sick for quite some while.''

"Damned near every soldier in the Pacific has malaria. They suffer and hang in. Donnely will, too.''

"Changing your opinion of him?''

Crusty finished his drink. "Hell, I never said he wasn't a goddamn good soldier. But he's also a major league cocksman. And for Gloria's sake—''

"She'll handle that if it becomes a problem.''

"Women, no matter how smart they are, just don't understand that a stiff dick has no conscience."

Belvale moved to the Pacific situation map. "Things are going well in the Caroline Islands. Admiral Spraunce caught a Jap task force cold at Truk. It's hard to believe the figures: 265 enemy planes destroyed, the light cruiser *Naka,* three auxiliary cruisers, destroyers, and tankers. Our casualties were a torpedo hit on the *Intrepid,* and the carrier shook it off."

Crusty said, "But the little bastards keep coming; they just keep on coming."

CHAPTER 12

REUTERS—Burma, Mar. 11, 1944: A Chinese and American attack on Japanese units cut off in the Wal-awbum area failed for lack of coordination. An armored group entered the village but did not get expected infantry support and had to withdraw.

Eddie Donnely shook in a puddle of his own sweat. Cold had him in a frozen fist, especially in his joints. Clenching his teeth, he held on to both sides of the canvas cot to keep from spasming off it. The real pain would soon come grinding long and mean. Dengue fever worked like that. First the sweats boiled the juice out of your body; then the ice came sliding in your veins; and then the unbelievable pressure gave dengue its other name: breakbone fever. Malaria but worse then malaria.

On the next cot a skinny kid ground his teeth, but the moans escaped anyhow. "Oh, God . . . Oh, my God . . ."

It could feel better being shot, Eddie knew. Prying his own teeth apart, he said, "Hang tough, buddy."

"A shot—can't they give us a shot? It hurts so much."

Morphine was rationed, and the badly wounded

needed it more, the guys with no hand or missing a leg; the poor son of a bitch with holes where his eyes used to be.

God damn. Clench your teeth and sweat it out. Concentrate on something else, anything else.

Gloria—he brought her face clearly to mind, deep and steady eyes; the honest strength of her, the comfort and the hot-bright inner flame of her. In passing, he had known only one or two like her, brass wives, officer material, but somehow not quite the same as Gloria, not as whole and complete.

It always started with officers' wives, the higher ranking the better. It had been a major's daughter who hurt Big Mike Donnely and damned near ruined his army career, and that would have meant his life as well. But the more involved Eddie got with a woman, the more tender he became, the more thoughtful.

The breakbone pain eased off his hips, and his tightly held breath hissed out. Women were made to be loved; they were beautiful, graceful and sleek; they smelled good and tasted better. They could sense love from afar and drew it nearer to them.

So many lovely women out there, needing love, needing to give it. The shakes broke, and he grunted up on one elbow to light a mildewed Old Gold cigarette.

So many beautiful women waiting out there with Gloria.

REUTERS—Burma, Mar. 14, 1944: Advance guards of the Special Force under General Wingate, the brilliant English commander of the Chindits, moved into Burma today. They constitute two brigades, the 77th and 111th, and three independent brigades of the British 70th Division.

Wingate's men have the task of dislodging Japanese from the area of Myitkyina to enable U.S. General Joseph "vinegar Joe" Stilwell to move his Chinese troops from Yunnan.

Major Keenan Carlisle sunned himself on the warm sand, one arm loosely about Susie's golden brown shoulders, his eyes closed against intrusion of the light, relaxed. He seemed lighter in body as well as in the pleasant drifting of his mind, detached from then and from when, leaving only now. And now should have been enough for any man in his right mind.

That was the trouble; at odd moments, a sudden shift of mental gears surprised him. He had been too long alone in the jungle, so that the dark spirit of the dread *yonsei* he had become there, the Japanese hobgoblin that feasted upon heads, would not completely leave him.

And when tidbits of information came in about Burma, Keenan grew uneasy. He had fought with the Chindits and marched side by side with Wingate himself. Anything complimentary said of the general wasn't enough; most derogatory sniping was bullshit. Offbeat and flamboyant as Wingate was, his men followed him gladly and he got the job done.

"Ummm," Susie murmured against his skin. "You taste good, *haole*."

He stroked her long, thick hair, so silken under his palm, tingling.

"You're beautiful."

"How you know? Your eyes are squinched shut."

"You shine right through my eyelids."

She chuckled and trailed the tip of her tongue across the base of his throat. "And you're one slick butterfly boy, no?"

"Butterfly boy?"

"Fly here, fly there, take a little sip of honey from a whole bunch of flowers; don't stop long enough to get your wings pinned."

He continued to stroke her hair, that thick, silken hair that blessed Hawaiian women. "You know better; your nectar can hold a man—or a butterfly—forever."

Poetic? Hell, he hadn't talked that way or felt that way since Chang Yen Ling died in those bloody shark-infested waters off the southern coast of her native China. The flavor and grace and throbbing music of Chang Yen Ling would ever remain with him, but it did not ride so painfully now. Because Susie Lokomaikai smoothed the sharp edges of memory.

Maybe time and Susie could still this need gnawing at him, this hunger to be sliding through the green darkness to find another Japanese victim, but he doubted that.

A cloud slid over the sun, for a moment chilling the little beach.

CHAPTER 13

European Theater of Operations information pool, all
press services—The Ardentine Caves, near Rome,
Mar. 24, 1944: Italian partisans smuggled out reports
by courier and clandestine radio containing the grim
details of a major war crime committed here.

By actual count, 335 civilians, many of them Jews,
were executed by German troops and their bodies
concealed in the caves. The slaughter was called a
reprisal for an attack by partisans that resulted in the
death of 32 German soldiers.

Oberfeldwebel Arno Hindemit raced toward the
captured Ami vehicle, a low, stubby workhorse
made only slightly uglier by messy camouflage
paint and careless German markings. The Americans called it beep, or jeep. Either way, a man in
one of these lost his brotherhood with the living
earth. A *landser* should be where he could dig for
protection, though it might turn out to be his
grave.

Blam!

Not too close, but damned if he would wait on
any officer who didn't get his pampered ass into
the car. Hauling headquarters officers about was
no duty for a senior infantry sergeant. Just now,

though, he couldn't think of any job that was. Sometimes he was just too tired to give a damn.

Besides, nothing was the same without Hauptmann Witzelei at his side, without the sharing that Fritz had taken with him, the steadiness and comradeship. Before the convoy of replacements took Arno north, he had managed to get back to the field hospital in the barn. Another man lay on Witzelei's straw pile, and the two pairs of spectacles, one with the lonely cracked lens, had been left behind. The man, the friend, was gone.

The war had reached the point of high stupidity after the captain died. The schoolmaster had become nearer to him than his father, become a brother in combat, and that was as close as men could be. Witzelei's slow change from schoolmaster who almost believed to cynical field officer and good comrade would always be mourned, at least for the rest of this *verdammt* war. Battles hadn't been fought intelligently for a long time, and after Sicily fell to the Allies, the end could be seen by anyone not infected with the "secret weapon" *scheissen* Herr Goebbels spread via radio.

Jagged mountain by windy mountain, the Gothic Line would fall back upon itself, eating its own tail as it was driven surely out of Italy. Any replacements would be drippy-nose young to creaky old and not all that ready to sacrifice all for the Führer and fatherland.

Wheeoo!

Incoming, all right, but zeroing in higher on the ridges. Here at the bottom of one more wet, rocky gulch between defensive positions dug into the steep mountainside, burned smells rode the air, and all too *verdammt* often the stench of rotten meat—mule or man. Once in a while the puny Italian sun nosed down through the high cloud layer and didn't stay long. Mercifully, the presentation

and promotion ceremony was cut short by more
Ami artillery fire.

Until the shells whistled in, they had been making a circus out of a formation that should have
been short and simple, photographers flashing
bulbs and asking idiot questions. At Arno's elbow,
die verfluchent panzer unteroffizier whispered:
"Berlin needs heroes just now. Try to look heroic,
Sergeant."

"Fuck you," Arno said. "Send me to the front."

And the muddy *landsers* watching slouched and
scratched while the adjutant hurried through the
reading of the orders, what Arno had done embel-
lished so that he didn't recognize it. And at last
the new officer presented the medal: "Iron Cross
First Class, Sergeant. The fatherland is proud of
its heroes."

Wheeoo!

"Take cover!"

Blam-blam!

Photographer and clerks scattered like headless
chickens, each trying to find the quickest way back
to Berlin.

Danke, mein Herr Colonel Rudolph Schmundt,
on rising so quickly to a rank you could not expect
until the Führer started running out of high-ranking
officers. Thank you for the medal and rank. And
since this is also your first time on any battle line,
you will soon discover why there is a shortage of
high officers. May God protect the rest of us.

Schmundt hit the front seat seconds ahead of his
adjutant, who piled in the back, boots dangling.
Arno crammed the accelerator to the floor and
wheeled the vehicle around for a run at the valley
mouth.

KA-WHAM!

This time the explosion was close enough to
slam a big hand behind the little car and hurl it
bouncing forward. From the corner of his eye,

Arno caught a flash of a face gone stark white. Colonel Schmundt had a death grip on his end of the lowered windscreen; it kept him from being spun out against a rocky slope as Arno skidded the jeep around a sharp angle.

He lost the adjutant there as the major lifted a fat bird and found a nest in the hillside. The valley narrowed at its end, and that end rose suddenly as a massive spear of granite aimed itself head-on at them.

Arno stamped on the brakes and twisted the wheel hard so the tires flung a spray of thin mud. Only by inches did the colonel's head miss the ragged slab.

They sat, while behind them the barrage lifted slowly, and waited until the last few explosions faded into the mountains. The adjutant limped to the jeep dirty and beaten up as any rifleman.

"Harassing fire," Arno said, bringing out one of those miserable Italian cigarettes. His hands did not shake when he lit it.

"Gott." Schmundt breathed fast; he needed time to get his own cigarette started. "You are a fine driver, Sergeant; fine, indeed. If you had not gotten us under cover so quickly . . ."

Looking at the shaken man, Arno watched the change take place as Schmundt realized he wasn't playing the Prussian game; he was humiliating himself before a lowly enlisted man.

"Ah, well done, Sergeant. You will report to my headquarters as my permanent driver, a just reward for a brave man."

"Yes, sir."

What did the bastard expect, Deutschland über Alles?

CHAPTER 14

REUTERS—The China-Burma-India Theater, April 1, 1944: Some American units are cut off by the Japanese in northeast Burma. In India the Japanese under General Mutaguchi blocked the Ukhrul-Imphal Road and surrounded the garrison at Imphal, which has to be supplied by air.

UNITED PRESS—San Francisco, Apr. 14, 1944: A patriotic group here, the Native Sons of the Golden West, today backed down from calling on legislators to deport all Japanese, whether citizens or not. Instead, they want Japanese internees separated by sexes in the detention camps.

"The camps will become breeding grounds," a spokesman said. "Everybody knows that Japs breed like rabbits."

Penny Belvale sat on a high stool at the bar in the reception hall at Kill Devil Hill. The homemade whiskey was better than anything to be found on the legal market, especially since wartime shortages hurried production and allowed more neutral spirits to be cut into even the best of brands.

She swallowed more than a sip. No raw taste in

this clear liquid, no burn going down; just smooth, warm and, she hoped, ultimately relaxing. In this part of the world whiskey-making had long since been developed into a fine art, improving with each generation.

The word caught in her mind like a leech on a wound. Generation—it implied life and continuity and future. It had nothing to do with the obscene mass that had grown cunningly day by day, refusing to dull or ease its pressure. Deep within her body it had continued to violate her—Major Watanabe's bastard child. The goddamn thing had been alive, and whenever she had thought she felt it move, she wanted to rip open her belly.

That had been part of the problem when she met Farley. Her poor, rattled, shell-shocked husband, more of a boy than ever, needing understanding and a gentle touch. Instead, she had been yet another rock for Farley to break himself on.

She was exhausted, thin and all raw nerve endings when she arrived in San Francisco. Coming out of the heat and insect-ridden air of Malaysia into the chill and damp of the Bay Area winter, she was made constantly aware of her body, both inside and out. Already she had tried old wives' solutions—jumping up and down, straining parts of her womb, drinking evil mixtures that only made her throw up. Nothing had worked, and she couldn't bear the idea of the family knowing her shame.

Several times during the ride to Letterman General at the Presidio she thought she would scream—the traffic, the noise, the jerking start and stop of the taxi. When it all edged up to overwhelming, she had to clench her fists and lock her teeth together. She was taking deep breaths and talking to herself when they wheeled Farley in.

Her first unstoppable response was resentment:

he's healthy; his cheeks are round and pink, and he's well fed. She tried to banish the feeling.

"Hello, dear." She reached him in two strides, took his hand, bent to kiss him, a quick brush. "You're looking well."

"Hello, Penny." His eyes were shy, his voice quiet. "I'm so glad to see you. They say you've been away, and you've lost weight. Yes."

She realized he hadn't been told about her capture, the prison camp, anything. Of course, it made sense. Why wouldn't he be protected? Then why did it make her angry? "It's been a little hectic lately, Farley. Not much time to relax. I came as soon as I could."

"Did you miss me? I don't write much." His words were slow and careful. He seemed a little disconnected.

Penny pulled a chair up next to him, held his hand in both of hers. "It doesn't matter. Everyone travels so much lately, the mail is months behind. Listen, you can walk, can't you?"

"Oh, yes, but they prefer not. No strain, they say."

The words dropped like separate little stones. She looked away, willing herself to remember he was broken in places she couldn't see. But he was round instead of angular, and he was pushed when he could walk. If he had cracked under pressure, was it more than she had had to bear? She could swear she felt something in her belly move in answer. No, it couldn't have been as bad as what was put on her, not by a long shot.

"Right Farley, no strain. But you have to try sometime. You could use the exercise, you know."

He flinched at both the words and the tone. His fingers spasmed on hers, and he removed his hand. "You sound like a reporter. No, wait—you sound like a silly reporter."

"What are you talking about?"

"The words. The words have to be even."

"What words? Farley, what the hell are you talking about?"

He began to cry. She was stunned, and part of her instantly wanted to hold him. But there was also a part of her that wanted to slap him silly.

The tap of General Preston Belvale's cane brought her back to the present, and she drained the whiskey from the bottom of her glass. He came around the other side of the ornately carved bar, and she smelled the soft blue smoke of his cigar.

"You look to be wound tighter than a two-dollar watch, girl. What is it?"

"Thinking of Farley, and feeling guilty again. Some way to treat a husband."

"One thing at a time. Make sure you're recovered from your—uh, surgery—first, before going on to the next thing. My grandson is in good hands at the moment."

"You can call it what it was. I had an abortion. I was pregnant by a goddamn Jap, and I had an abortion." It had taken everything she had to tell the family that she was—how had Minerva put it?—with child. The reaction had been calm and swift, and the doctors quietly arranged for. Only Preston Belvale, the stiffest of them all, had asked if she was sure—that she would have no recriminations.

He drew slowly upon his cigar. "No cause to go jumpy. You couldn't avoid it. I should think we've outgrown the western frontier attitude that blames the captive women for Indian rape." He poured himself a shot of clear corn whiskey. "What were you supposed to do, kill yourself? That strikes me as a wasteful and stupid thing to do."

"And ineffective. That's not the way to get even. General, I'm still an air service pilot and there's still a war on. I want to go back to ferrying planes. I have to do something; I can't just sit it out.''

Preston studied her, his expression a mixture of doubt and pride. ''Are you sure?''

''Completely.'' She had to get back in the air. By all that she was and all she hoped to be, she had to be there when Major Watanabe paid the price. And pay he would.

FLEET NEWS SERVICES—For immediate release, April 28, 1944: An Allied naval squadron commanded by Admiral Sommerville of the Royal Navy, consisting mostly of British ships, also including the American aircraft carrier *Saratoga* and three U.S. destroyers, bombarded Japanese positions at Sabang, north of Sumatra.

Intelligence reported that Japanese Imperial Headquarters was alarmed, since high officers thought Allied naval presence in the Indian Ocean had been eliminated.

Captain Gavin Scott settled deep into the embracing seat of the P-38, enjoying the rush of air beyond the cockpit, the lift of air beneath his wings. Different air, tropic, sunny; none of the chill fog and a feel of being locked into a small space. The Pacific was broad and the Pacific was wide, and a fine hunting ground for someone about to become a double ace, an ace on both sides of the world.

Scanning to his front, then high and low, with a quick glance rearward, Gavin grinned. When goddamn Chad Belvale punched him out, he did Gavin a big favor. Of course Kill Devil Hill and Sandhurst Keep, with their widespread intelligence web, knew about it at once and had the colonel shipped out of London and out of England before a scandal could arise.

In the same vein, off went Gavin on emergency orders to the busy South Pacific. He would deal with Colonel Belvale and wait for revenge on Stephanie Bartlett. Here and now he had been given the opportunity to be the best-known pilot of the war. Flying off some nameless coral strip, courtesy of mid-rank brass who didn't know what the hell to do with a hot-dog pilot with all-powerful connections behind him. So they let him call his own shots. He chose to be a hunter-killer, going out alone and looking for trouble. If they wanted him to screen bombers, that was all right, too; bombers drew Japs like flies.

There!

A Zero come sight-seeing, idling near the only cloud in the bright sky. A photo mission, Gavin guessed, pictures of little islands below, of American naval movements.

Making the P-38 claw for height, he put the cloud between him and the Zero with its red meat-ball markings. Then, nosing carefully through the mist, he dived straight down on the unsuspecting Jap.

One long burst from his guns and pieces flew from the enemy plane; a shorter burst as the Zero grew big in his sights, and the fiery explosion was a thing of beauty. Gavin hurtled through scattering wreckage, yelling.

What a way to fight the war.

AGENCE FRANCE PRESSE in exile—Italian Front, April 28, 1944: Today the Polish II Corps took over the Monte Cassino sector from the British XIII Corps.

First Lieutenant Sloan Travis closed the office door behind him. "You look terrible, but at least you're here to look at."

Captain Owen Belvale put his feet up on his desk. "My old man back?"

"Be happy he's not, and that Major Langlois is close to your father. You're pushing it, Owen. You've been pushing your luck."

"I know, but what the hell has the company been doing? Roadwork, hup-two, hup-two—reading the Articles of War, getting some of our boozier brawlers away from the local constabulary."

Sloan lit a Chesterfield and offered him one. Owen's hand shook. Sloan said, "Speaking of which . . ."

"I'm just a little hung over; it heals and everybody does it, don't they?"

"To a point."

Looking up, Owen said, "I already have a father, Sloan."

"Okay. I signed for you and returned some division and regimental directives, training schedules and the like. Major Langlois shortstopped anything heavier."

Owen pulled in smoke and coughed. "Any word on my old man?"

Walking to the window, Sloan looked out and down on the narrow cobblestone street below. Two women in long skirts rattled bicycles, pushing them uphill beside the old stone building. He thought of coming back after the war and fitting himself into the calm, accepting way of life here. To write? He had written nothing since putting on the uniform, nothing on paper and very little in his mind.

Bridport housed H Company of the 16th in three municipal buildings emptied by wartime evacuation. One had been turned into a mess hall, another set up for showers and laundry, bunks in the other, which was as open and big as a gym and might once have been one. The company liked the setup; what wasn't to like? Training was tough and time-consuming, but when they came out of the field, the troops returned to a slower place in time, a different frame of reference. And to women here and real, touchable; the girls back home got farther away.

There had already been three marriages to Brid-port women; there would be more, and if the company stayed here much longer, babies. And divorces?

Sloan said to Owen, "Time's getting short and we're building up for invasion. The colonel will come in from Italy soon and put the final edge on the battalion. Everyone's staying close to home."

"Except me? God damn it, man, I'm handling things."

"Do what you damned well please, Owen. I'm the draftee, the handcuff volunteer who hates the service and the whole concept of the Hill, the Keep, and their holy warriors. What's your excuse?"

Owen ground out his cigarette in the ashtray, the sawed-off base of a 60mm mortar shell. "Damned if I know, Sloan. Maybe I do know, and then I don't understand. I—it's what she is, more than who; I feel like a raccoon with a leg in a steel trap. It hurts like hell, but I can't make up my mind to chew off my foot. She—damn it!—it's as if I never had sex before and never will again. Yet it's not all sex, difficult as that may be to shake free."

"You never had a steady shack job?"

"No, but . . . no other woman could have gotten so deep inside me. When Helene just comes into the room . . . I can't keep up with her, and the booze helps. When I'm with her, I don't give a damn about the army or my family or whatever. When I'm away from her . . ."

Sloan heard desperation in Owen's voice. He said, "Does she know who you are, anything about the family money?"

"N-no, I don't think so."

"Keep it quiet."

"Money doesn't mean anything to her." Owen slid a hand into the middle desk drawer and brought out a flat half pint. When Sloan shook his head, he took a long swallow.

"Anybody talking marriage?"

Owen shook his head. "But any time she wants."

Looking away, Sloan said, "As best you can, you should stay away from her for a while. I think you'd better sharpen up and let your troops have a look at you."

Owen took another drink.

Later Owen found himself reaching for the bottle beside the bed. The movement was reflexive, as without thought as picking up a cigarette.

Sooner or later they were going to send him back to war, and he would have to leave the warm, silken body beside him. He was so tired; twilight lay heavy in the room and he dearly wanted sleep. She stirred against him, and the friction lit memories of quick tongue and searching hands.

Damn the war, damn the family. He hadn't been shot at for more than four months, and he wouldn't mind if it stretched into forever. He took a pull from the bottle. His troops were training all over the English countryside, and he managed to put in an appearance once in a while, when he knew he had to. Owen snuggled deeper into the covers, and smiled when he heard a break in her breathing. With a giggle he turned to her, hands eager.

CHAPTER 15

UNITED PRESS—Caroline Islands, Apr. 29, 1944: A two-day series of air attacks ended today as American planes from 12 carriers pounded the huge Japanese base at Truk. Shipping, fuel, ammunition depots and airfields were wiped out.

Of 104 Japanese aircraft on the atoll before the attack, at least 91 have been shot down or destroyed on the ground. With this blow, Admiral Nimitz obliterated any danger to the Allied New Guinea operations.

First Sergeant Eddie Donnely hunkered down in the platoon command post. The hole had been scraped out of sand, tree roots, vicious little shards of coral and strengthened by slabs of shell-ripped trees. During the night its forward rim had been built up with palm trunks scarred by bullets. An occasional sniper's pop kept everyone's head down. Last night's smells clung inside the hole—frightened urine, the lingering stench of vomit, powder smoke ground into the sandy walls, a stain that might be blood. The floor grated metallic underfoot, composed of layers of empty brass from two nights of firing at dark shadows.

Eddie said, "Are you serious? You're the best noncom I have."

Sergeant Rodger Young said, "Might used to be; I just can't see worth a good goddamn no more. I about walked my patrol into an ambush I should've seen a mile off."

"You check with the medics? Maybe some stuff for your eyes . . ."

Small and sandy-haired, Young said, "They want to ship me out."

"What's wrong with that?"

Young rubbed his eyes. "Reckon you know that well as me. This here is my family, and a man don't run out on his family. How come you didn't stay in the hospital with that fever? You look like you been standing too close to the fireplace."

"Because I'm dumb. You want to turn in your stripes? I think that's dumber, and maybe an officer ought to handle—"

"Kind of short of officers, ain't we? Now, if you was to give my stripes to Coporal Lopez. I could kind of hang around and lend him a hand—"

"Okay, your choice, soldier. But if— Oh hell, I understand why you're staying. That doesn't mean there's not at least two crazy men in this hole."

Boof Hardin squashed a bug on his cheek and hissed his trademark: "Boof! Mash one of these little bastards and their juice burns you. You got three crazy men here; and, First Shirt Donnely, you better get some other eight ball to mess with this phone. Come sundown, I'd just as soon be in my nice deep hole instead of baiting them Japs with a phone line that'll draw them straight to my ever-loving ass."

"This is your hole. You think I've got runners and clerks and a bunch of rear echelon troopers here?"

It was one of those sweaty nights when the air was almost too thick to breathe and clogged your throat. The night hung black velvet curtains around the defense perimeter and noises faded. The long, taut time of listening began.

Ex-Sergeant Young was now out there with his squad, no longer in command, a fighter who couldn't fight as well anymore, a man with guts and ideals and under great stress. And there was nowhere to go; they were between the rock and the hard place, come nightfall.

(Barracks talk: Somewhere between shit and syphilis . . .)

The firefight broke suddenly, the evil whack-whack of .25-caliber Nambus and the ka-chung of M1s, the lighter spitting of carbines. There—*rap! rap!rap!*—the solid and steady fire from .30-caliber machine guns, the air-cooled and heavier water-cooled weapons.

Breaking above the skeletal fronds on the palm trees, the intense white light of a flare did little more than blind the watchers. Dug in just behind the platoon CO, the 60mm mortars belched quick flashes of muzzle blast and the cough that thinned as the finned shells climbed high.

"Banzai! Banzai!"

Direct to the company front, and off to the left flank where Fox Company was also under attack, the Japs continued to shriek, but Young's squad was taking the brunt of the attack. They needed help.

Over the noise, Eddie took the handset and yelled into it, "Company! Company! Young's squad is in trouble; Platoon CO going in."

"I'm coming with you," Boof Hardin said.

"No shit."

"Banzai! Banzai!"

"Banzai my swinging dick." Eddie climbed out of the hole, his BAR ready. It was ripped out of his hand and his helmet went *clang!* As he got off his knees, a hot wasp stung his cheek and sat him down again. It was crossfire low to the ground, machine guns perfectly positioned to sweep the jungle floor.

Fumbling around, Eddie found his BAR with a long gouge in its stock. He flinched when the Jap guns chopped the air no higher than a man's head, when they plowed sand geysers across the area to keep anything else from moving.

Rodger Young and his advance squad were in deep trouble, and from here, nobody could reach him.

Eddie slid back into the hole and called for mortar fire, bringing it in beyond the attacking Japs and hoping to shake up their rear. Otherwise they were just too damned close. The fury grew, the explosions mixing and tumbling one over the other, now blending in a string, now a series of deeper crumps that meant grenades from both sides.

Again Eddie started out of the platoon CP to help; again the intensity and accuracy of Jap fire drove him back. Spitting sand, he pictured what was happening: Jap after Jap rising from the primeval dark and charging behind long bayonets; GIs firing until their holes were overrun, until they fought it out belly to belly.

The higher-pitched Nimu sounds rose as the friendly fire dwindled. Only the thumping of a water-cooled .30 continued, firing the short bursts of an experienced gunner.

And then that stopped, too.

Yelling into the phone, Eddie pleaded for more mortar fire, for warm bodies to come up and give fire support.

At the other end of the line Captain Bobby Cullis said, "I have nothing to send you. About all we can do is pray for that squad."

(*Barracks talk: Tell your troubles to Jesus; the chaplain's on pass.*)

It was well past daylight before the flanking Japs

ceased fire and slithered back to their daytime lairs. Up front a pair of snipers made up the rear guard and got off a few rounds before dying for their holy emperor and their slice of eternity in tempura heaven.

When Eddie reached the forward position, nothing moved, nothing lived. To make certain, he killed each Jap again, a bullet through every head.

And found Rodger Young slumped over behind his machine gun. Twenty-eight good Japs were piled before him, this man whose conscience would not allow him to continue leading his squad. He had been an honest man, a brave man. Eddie would start the ball rolling for Young to receive the Medal of Honor. He damn well deserved it.

A posthumous award, of course. Weren't most of them?

UNITED PRESS—San Francisco, Apr. 30, 1944: The Marinship assembly line has begun launching Liberty Ships at the rate of four a month, bringing the average delivery time to one T2 tanker every ten days.

Penny Belvale could see a long way from this second-floor bedroom, and picked out a line of flowering dogwood trees. Beyond them in a poplar grove was the family burial ground, with graves filled and unfilled, the memorial garden of most Belvales and some Carlisles. She intended to take a good-bye walk there, now that her orders had come through.

Turning her head at the sound of the door opening, she smiled at Nancy Carlisle. "You look pretty in uniform."

Nancy did a half-turn and lifted two bottles. "Feel up to an icy beer? I raided the general's private stock."

Penny stared at the bottle. "Jax beer?"

Nancy took a chair and crossed her legs. "Imported stuff, all the way from New Orleans. The general could buy his own European brewery, but he likes his Jax."

"Pretty good," Penny said, the crisp flavor in the back of her throat. "How is Farley?" With Nancy stationed at Letterman, she had no choice but to ask.

"The official diagnosis is 'progressing.' I think he'll come out of it just fine, given time and care. He's a nice kid."

"Nice kid," Penny repeated.

"Part of the problem; he's too nice and too gentle to be an effective combat leader."

Penny swallowed beer; now it tasted bitter. "That doesn't fit with the family."

Nodding, Nancy said, "The family will find him a useful slot." She frowned. "I didn't know the family included a chaplain. He seemed kind of—I don't know—weird. Very interested in Farley's condition, pretty damned nosy, in fact."

CHAPTER 16

NORTH AMERICAN NEWSPAPER ALLIANCE—The Italian Front, May 29, 1944: Since the Polish II Corps took over the Monte Cassino front from the British XIII Corps, the fighting in this rugged terrain has been vicious and bloody. Little ground has been lost or gained by either side.

Field Marshal Albert Kesselring has seven first-rate German divisions dug into the ruins of Monte Cassino Abbey and defending prepared positions on flanking ridges. According to G-2 sources, Kesselring is determined to hang on to the abbey ruins, buying time in order to prepare more and deeper defense lines to his rear.

This hints of a pullout, but word filtering down from on high wants to know why 16 Allied divisions cannot seize ground pulverized by bombs and raked by countless tons of artillery shells.

[Home office: If this gets by, the censor was hung over; poured a keg of wine into him last night. There were no—repeat: no—Germans in the abbey at any time before the original air strike. American officers warned that battering the mountaintop into a jumble of massive stone slabs would only make defense easier. So who listened?]

—Stackhouse, NANA

Owen Belvale eased his arm out from under Helene's head a listened for any break in the rhythm of her breathing. Moving slowly in the dark he found the table and the bottles upon it. He needed a drink and took a big swallow of gin, eyes watering as he downed a chaser of flat warm English beer. Was there any other kind?

Remembering that cigarettes had also been left on the table, he searched for the Players and flicked his Ronson at one. Practically every male in the family was given a gold Ronson lighter at graduation, engraved with symbol of West Point or VMI. Then there were the diamond cuff links.

A few close members of the family who did not attend those holy schools received Zippos and smaller diamonds. But they all remained on notice that they were family, in whatever degree.

Outside, the damp wind picked up and moaned across the mooring wires of barrage balloons, a ghost sound of sorrow, of mourning to come. He drank more gin and pulled on his cigarette. Every time he came to Helene, he was the hunter home from the hill, bearing food and fancies. When it was time to leave her, a nagging sadness grew within him, a vague threat.

Why shouldn't he make it permanent, keep her always with him as far as whatever law and the U.S. Army allowed?

The bedside light clicked on. Helene slept cat-like, coming awake fully and gracefully alert. He could almost hear her purring.

"Darling . . . not sleepy? A bit to eat? I can put something together in a flash."

He shook his head. "I have to get the jeep back to the motor pool; some sort of early inspection."

Sliding out of bed, she flowed to him, a tiny Venus still aglow from such long lovemaking, the depths of her eyes smoldering, her rich lips damp. The things she had done with and to him—there were times when he couldn't believe it, and other times when the memories overwhelmed him.

Only Helene could have gotten so deep into his soul and uncovered every dark desire he had ever dreamed. Some of those fantasies ought to have remained hidden; a few drained him entirely of himself. Without ego, helpless, he became anything she wanted, everything she wanted.

He saluted her with a drink. She headed naked into his arms and sat on his lap, so little weight for so much woman, so much power. He put down his beer chaser to stroke her hair, silken tingles against his palm.

"Well," she breathed, "if you really must go . . ."

"Helene," he said, "will you marry me?"

She drew back to look him in the face. "What, luv? Is it the gin?"

"I'm serious; I've never been more serious. I love you."

A tiny frown marked her forehead but was quickly gone. "Oh, you're a lovely, lovely Yank, but . . . this bloody war and everything topsy-turvy the way it is—"

"Helene, I can buy you grand pianos, jewels, furs and cars and whatever you want. We can cruise around the world. My family is loaded."

"Loaded—does that mean wealthy?"

"A shade beyond wealthy."

Rising from his knees, she walked across the room and put her back to him, sculptured back, lovely buttocks. "We English avoid planning many tomorrows. One of Hitler's bombs can find us any time and blow us into bloody tatters. It would be nice to know I could live the war out safely in the United States, and live richly at that. But money doesn't mean so much to me."

She turned then. "But would you be there with me? God, all of Europe knows your army will be attacking France soon, and you have about used up your good fortune on other landings.''

"Helene, damn it—''

Eyes dark, she said, "Today is how I live, and I try to live it to the full, loving and being loved. If I gave you any other impression, I'm dreadfully sorry."

He wanted to say many things but couldn't put them in order. He had made a bigger fool of himself by sweetening the pot with money. Dressing in silence, he started for the door. When he turned, she came to kiss his lips and hand him his cap and the bottle of gin.

"Of course you know I do love you—in my fashion."

Lt. Gen. Preston Belvale; Maj. Gen. Charles Carlisle: EYES ONLY—SHAEF G-2, London, May 30, 1944: Reports are reaching here of increased and systematic measures against Jews. During the past 12 days 62 boxcars laden with Jewish children have been moved from Hungary to death camps in Poland. Mass atrocities against Jews take place in every German-held territory in Europe.

Crusty Carlisle said, "We better be keeping track of every son of a bitch involved in murder, no matter what breed he is—Kraut, Polack, Austrian or whatever. I hereby volunteer to pull on the rope."

"All Europe will be in chaos during the invasion, much less after the war, but we'll have G-Five people right behind the combat troops." Preston Belvale tapped the ash from his long Cuban cigar. "A new outfit, this G-Five; it's military government and the like, to put things together and keep the civilians straight. They're meant to spread a net of sorts early on, and scoop up war criminals, military and civilian. It all waits on the success of the landings."

Crusty grunted. "When, God damn it? There's been so much crap about when and where to land. Italy is a costly fiasco. 'Soft underbelly of Europe' my ass. We have kept Kraut divisions out of France, maybe an army corps, but it's bleeding us dry. It's a goddamn wonder Mark Clark didn't get shafted for that mess at Salerno. Didn't he screw that one up?"

Sighing, Belvale picked up a bottle of Virginia white lightning, the bootleg whiskey so carefully aged. He inspected the clear liquor for color and beading. "If it was up to Churchill, we'd have gone in a year ago—southern France, or even Norway."

"And left our balls on the beach or in the snow. Pass the bottle, Preston."

"Stalin didn't care where we hit or how badly we got hurt, just so the pressure was pulled off him. He's still growling about a second front." Belvale took back the bottle and poured himself a drink.

"There's not even a rumor in Washington about when and where, unless you want to go with those who change day by day. Ike Eisenhower has to make the heavy decisions, but I'd say the invasion will come pretty soon, depending upon the weather on the Channel. I'd pick Pas-de-Calais or Normandy: if they're waiting for us to come ashore, either one will be concentrated hell."

Sitting erect, Crusty said, "Let's go over and sit in."

"You'd try to go in with the first wave?"

"What's wrong with that?"

"Have another drink, Charles."

"Charles? Charles?"

"Sorry. Let's relax and think on it. Here we can

shake up Quartermasters and see that plenty of supplies get where they're going, and in time. We can influence promotions, keep the losers down and boost the good leaders. Maybe we can see that no more coal miner strikes cause mortar shells to be rationed on the front lines."

"Hang John L. Lewis by his own bushy eyebrows."

Belvale rubbed his game leg. "Over there we'd just get in the way."

"Okay, okay, shut up and don't make a prisoner of that bottle."

In the night, across the summer fields beyond the house a whippoorwill cried: *Chip married a widow! Chip married a widow!* And closer in, near the stables, a bullbat sounded its bass note as it dipped wide-mouth for insects. Memories came with the night. . . .

. . . The earth was sick and breathed in pain. A lonely tree stood against the night with mangled limbs pleading in silence. The man pleaded, too, moaning broken beyond the trench. The sound gnawed at the men standing on firing steps, the duck boards at the parapet, Springfield bolt action rifles ready and bayonets fixed. When they moved, their flat helmets made dull chunking sounds.

"For the sake of God," the replacement officer said, "why doesn't somebody go out there and help him?"

The captain's voice was tired. "Lieutenant Belvale, you've been up here how long—two, three hours? You won't last much longer being stupid. That's one of our sergeants about fifty yards out in no-man's-land, and he's hung up on the barbed wire, shot up and hung on the wire. We left him there in the last goddamn stupid attack when we had to retreat. The Heinies know exactly where he is and have him covered with a Spandau machine gun."

Second Lieutenant Preston Belvale said, "You're going to leave him out there to die in agony?"

"If he's lucky, he'll die before daylight. If he stays lucky, one of our sharpshooters can give him mercy, come daylight. That's what he's begging for now—death."

"Be damned!" Belvale said. "Is he straight ahead? I can guide in on the sounds."

"What?" the captain's helmet clanked. "You're not going after him—"

"The hell I'm not. Where's some wire cutters?"

Preston shed his light pack, helmet and web belt with canteen, first aid pouch and holstered .45. Then he freed the Colt and crawled up to the forward firing step, cutters in his other hand. Far to the right flank, a star shell burst high in the leaden sky. A dark wind lifted from the battlefield, heavy with rot. The sergeant's moan drifted to the trench.

Preston went over the top, belly down and snaking low in the churned and muddy field. Black. The night was black and he blessed it. He kept from gasping when he put a hand on a soft arm not attached to a body, and crawled over a stinking pile of bones. The sergeant moaned, much nearer now.

Listening closely, Preston heard guttural murmurs in German and smelled cigarette smoke. Reaching carefully out in the blackness, he ran slow fingers along a strand of barbed wire. It was slippery—blood? He touched the man's arm and then a stubbled cheek.

"Easy," he whispered, "easy, Sergeant. I've come to take you back."

"W-watch it. They're too close. Oh, God . . ."

"Where are you hit?"

"Ch-chest . . . takes my breath when I fight the wire."

Working as quietly as he could, Preston clipped wire, pulled and pushed and finally worked the sergeant's limp body off the tangle. Lips at the man's ear, he hissed: "Moan. Make them think you're still there."

"Achtung! Wer di."

The machine gun clattered, but fired two or three clicks high. Inch by inch at first, and then foot by muddy, stinking foot, Preston dragged the sergeant back, sliding into a shell hole bottomed with fetid water. The machine gun followed them, tracers streaking bright in the darkness. The only sound the sergeant made was the hiss of breath between his clenched teeth.

Preston heard a rattle of equipment and turned to trigger two shots at a German sent to follow them. It took three shots to drop the next one. Then all at once it seemed, other hands reached out and took the weight.

"Goddamn fool," the captain said. "Is he alive? Sergeant Carlisle, are you making it? Charlie, damn it, answer me."

His voice worn thin by pain, propped up against the side of the trench, the man said, "Damned right, no thanks to you guys. But this man—whoever you are, I thank you. . . ."

. . . Shaking his head and opening his eyes, Preston Belvale glanced at the ash grown long and gray upon his cigar, then over at Crusty Carlisle slumped, comfortable and nodding, in the deep leather chair. Were they too old now to be of much help?

CHAPTER 17

ASSOCIATED PRESS—Detroit, June 1, 1944: About three million women have entered the wartime labor force, adding a million to agricultural help, although most went into war plants.

These women working because of the war, who would not be working in peacetime, who are they?

They are 56% married, and their husbands are away in the services. A bare majority are between twenty and forty-four years. In smaller cities they have sometimes taken over their husband's jobs and done as well or better. War, statistical sources point out, has a way of sweeping aside old habits and prejudices of thought. Women have become possibly the most important secret weapon of the production war.

Major Keenan Carlisle shifted foot to foot. By a damn sight, he was no kid trying to win approval from the girl's family for another date. He wasn't even sure what he was doing on this one, except to make Susie Lokomaikai happier. She was such a happy person already that she was making him over in her image, dimming the mean and hurting things set so deep within him. He was going from He Who Will Not Die, from the *yonsei* that eats heads, to a man being healed in spirit as well as in body.

There was a plain wooden door set into a high wooden fence; it opened into a tiny patch of raked gravel and grass strips. The house was small and neat, with a tiny-windowed entrance porch where Susie sat to remove her shoes and help him with his. Keenan had heard of the custom, but didn't think it was Hawaiian. Inside, the floors were tatami mats, and the sliding doors were rice paper. The sparse furnishings were more than neat, only a few things placed about, but eye-holding against open space and bare walls.

Before he could ask questions, Susie brought in a short, chunky Hawaiian with crisp silvering hair. He wore a flowered aloha shirt, shorts and thong sandals. "Daddy, this is Keenan. Keenan, this is my father, Henry Lokomaikai."

"Hey, soldier. We been hearing about you, hearing much, man."

"Sir."

Two steps behind him, bowing as she followed her husband into the room, came a tiny woman with a porcelain face, a woman wearing a silk formal kimono.

"Mom," Susie said, "this is Major Keenan."

A Japanese woman! A goddamn Jap!

Jaws clamped hard, he tensed all over his body and a great pressure slammed into his mind. He knew that Hawaiians were a mixed lot, but Susie—her name, so mainland-beach-girl quick with a quip, so easy to laugh with, so goddamn easy to love—a Jap?

He didn't recognize his own strangled voice: "Susie, you—you're Japanese?"

Grinning at her father, she hadn't looked Keenan's way; she said, "About three-fourths, I'd say. Is that about right, Daddy? I mean, your mother—"

"Something like," Henry Lokomaikai said. "Ain't nobody keeps count after a while. One kahuna pineapple much like another pineapple. Hey, Sueko, more better you get your soldier a beer."

She looked at him then, and Keenan couldn't hide it, didn't want to hide it. He whispered, "What, Sueko, no goddamn sake?"

"Keenan?"

"No goddamn samurai sword hanging on the wall?"

She moved toward him, reaching out one small hand. "Keenan, I don't understand. What . . . Why . . . ?"

Her eyes looked different, more heavily slanted; a suggestion of buckteeth pressed out against her lips; her hair—thick and wiry, offering a good handhold to draw back her head and slice right through the neck.

Wheeling, he walked into a rice paper door and kicked it apart. Stooping to snatch up his garrison shoes, and shaking her voice away, he slammed out onto the street in stockinged feet, not knowing where he was going, and not giving a damn.

She wasn't Hawaiian, but a goddamn fucking Jap. Oh, good Christ—forgive me, Chang Yen Ling.

Fleet HQ, South Pacific, (RESTRICTED)—New Guinea Theater, June 1, 1944: On Biak Island, Americans tried again to break out of their beleaguered beachhead. The 163rd Infantry remains to man the beachhead while the 186th, supported by artillery and tanks, moved north toward the plateau in the center of the island. Several vigorous Japanese counterattacks from north and south have been repulsed.

Eddie Donnely was forced to watch the torture. Half buried in the fetid jungle floor, he stared out into an open clearing, a Jap headquarters of sorts. It was what he had scouted a long way to find, but he hadn't expected to find GI prisoners here.

Three guys in tattered fatigues knelt with their hands tied behind their backs. Behind them strutted a Jap junior officer wearing black-rimmed glasses and flicking a samurai sword so that the sun flashed off its blade. Drawn up behind him in a semicircle stood or hunkered a dozen or so of his men, some in new uniforms. Those had to be replacements slipped through the naval blockade. Stacked ammo and ration boxes were propped against native huts behind them.

Squirming, Eddie peered back over his shoulder to find Boof Hardin, the connecting file of this eight-man patrol. Hardin lifted a hand, the palm pale against the green darkness of the jungle. Eddie hesitated, then turned to stare again at the execution scene.

His orders were to find and pinpoint the Jap headquarters, avoiding firefights if possible, and then to report the location. Artillery and air strikes would take over then.

The Jap spraddled his short legs and posed with his sword swung high. Avoid firefights, the captain had said; don't let them know we know their position or they'll move it on us.

Three GIs on their knees, their necks bared to the executioner's sword.

"Fuck it," Eddie said, and rose up on his elbows.

His first shot caught the Jap just as the sword began its downward slash. It knocked the little shit over onto his back. Eddie fired into the circle of watchers and came to his knees to shout, "Bring them up on line, Boof!"

Then he yelled at the GI prisoners. "This way. Jump up and run this way!"

Off balance because of their bound wrists, they struggled up and tried for it. The center man went down before he took six steps; the guy on the left staggered, fell and fought to his knees again before the side of his head splashed and he went down to stay.

Beside Eddie, Hardin's rifle hammered steadily as Japs spun and shrieked. The third GI came that close to making it. Crashing into the brush, he lunged toward Eddie, blue eyes popped wide and mouth gaped open. A bullet hit him in the back of the head, stumbling him forward as his mouth geysered blood.

Eddie's patrol came up on line, spreading left and right, firing as they came, good soldiers clicking into place. Surprised Japs ran back and forth, some falling to the rifle fire that flailed them. Other Japs poured out of the huts and a Nambu machine gun went into action.

"I'm hit!" The kid on Eddie's left said, "Oh, shit," and fell over.

"Haul ass?" Boof Hardin yelled.

"You got it!" Eddie checked the kid and found him dead, a close-to-the-heart shot. DeLaura? Delgado? Eddie ripped away the dog tags and jammed them into a pocket. The kids came and went so damned fast you didn't get used to their names. Most of the time you didn't want to that much.

The rest of the patrol took off for the rear, crashing through the underbrush while Eddie and Hardin acted as rear guard, hanging back just far enough to slow the Japs with a few quick shots or a warning grenade. Then they trotted off after the others. The Japs didn't drop pursuit until the patrol staggered by a forward observer post and Eddie panted for help. The 81mm mortars farther back in the perimeter responded; the deep thump of exploding shells threw a curtain of fire and steel across the path.

Sitting on the ground, knees lifted and his head propped on them, Eddie sucked for breath in the soggy hot air.

"Well, God damn it? You had a firefight." Lieutenant Sullivan stood braced before Eddie, fists on his hips. He wasn't exactly a fresh replacement; his fatigues had started to rot, but were still new enough to mark him. He had been on line what—three weeks?

"Well, what? Here—I'll mark the Jap headquarters on the map, if I can dry this son of a bitch."

"Against orders, you started a firefight." It hadn't taken Sullivan long to acquire an Atabrine tan; his eyes were almost as yellow as his skin.

Eddie blinked up at him. "The Japs were about to take the heads off three GIs. We popped them. It was a judgment call. Here's the HQ location."

Sullivan passed the map to his runner, who took off for the artillery, bayonetted carbine slung over his shoulder. Sullivan said, "If the target isn't five miles off by now. God damn it, what's a first sergeant doing leading a patrol, anyway?"

(Barracks talk: If you ain't chickenshit, you sure got henhouse ways.)

Palming sweat off his face, Eddie said, "I led out because I was the best man handy while we're here in some sort of reserve. The old man get evacuated while I was gone? Did Bobby Cullis make it out okay?"

"Captain Cullis probably won't come back; his intestines are shot. That puts me in command, Sergeant."

Straightening out a mildewed cigarette, Eddie dried a match by rubbing it briskly through his hair. "I don't doubt it, Lieutenant."

"You say you attacked the Japs to save American prisoners. Where are they and did you have any casualties?"

It happened every time; if the company sat long

enough in reserve, along came some cherry asshole heaven-sent to rearrange the war and play by the book. "They're dead; crossfire from the Japs when they tried to run to us. And yeah, I lost a man: DeLaura or Delgado; got his dog tags."

"So your attack was not only a violation of orders but useless bravado that got the prisoners killed anyhow."

Boof Hardin limped over to plop down beside Eddie. "What?"

"Beats me," Eddie said. "Wild hair up his ass."

"Sergeant! Both you sergeants! God damn it, when you realize that you don't run the army and especially this outfit, you'll be better off. The casualty that you didn't have to lose, the prisoners killed . . ."

(Barracks talk: Don't let your mouth write a check that your ass can't cash.)

Eddie blew cigarette smoke. "Lieutenant, when you realize that it's better to die on your feet than to live on your knees, we'll all be better off. Those GIs—they tried; they gave it all they had. The fucking Jap didn't get to chop off their heads."

"Watch it!" Sullivan said. "I'm just about an inch away from bringing you up for court-martial."

"Boof!" Hardin grunted. "Ain't this a bitch? Pay attention, first soldier. Let us be sure to salute this officer every time we see him coming or going. I mean, sharp and happy garrison highballs. Everybody will see that he's a sure-enough leader of men—including those Jap snipers. I hear they'll wait all day for a shot at an officer."

He stood up at a reasonable facsimile of attention and saluted. "Here you go, Lieutenant; all due respect, sir."

A rifle popped, too far away to be a Japanese sniper, but Sullivan still flinched.

CHAPTER 18

Wire Services Pool—SHAEF HQ, London, on the Eastern Front, June 2, 1944: Heavy fighting continues to rage on the Rumanian front, but the Germans can make little headway against fierce Russian resistance.

The Allied advance continues along the whole Italian front. Albano, Lanuvio and Frascati are among the towns that fell while units of the American 3rd Division and the French Expeditionary Corps advance along Highway 6.

In the British 8th Army sector, the Canadian I Corps reached Anagni.

Kirstin Shelby stood away from the horse trailer and watched another one of Jim Shelby's prize quarter horses go down the road behind a dusty pickup truck. Some were not trustworthy as schooling horses, and some were a natural breeding surplus. She had gotten a fair price, and the young stud was headed for a good home. One problem with running a breeding farm is that you wanted to keep every foal born on the place. But no horse farm could afford to expand like that, and Kirstin's horses had to meet an additional qualification: they could not be flighty and so possibly hurt an uncertain horseman.

The older geldings and a few mares worked okay with the sensible Morgans at Harmon General Hospital up at Longview. The ranch hands put in a lot of volunteer time helping the severely wounded men there. The riding school program worked general good with those amputees trying to put their lives together again. Some didn't even want to try, and there was the damned shame, the utter waste of lives.

Earlier, she had become personally involved with a patient, and since then had tried to hold herself a little apart. That was difficult, because she wanted to hug every one of those badly hurt kids to her heart, to lavish upon them her pent-up love and affection. Not, she reminded herself, by taking any of the young men to bed to prove to them that a woman could still want them.

She admitted that her short affair with Sergeant Harlan Edgerton had been born partly from her own needs, her sense of loss and loneliness after Jim Shelby was killed in the Pacific Theater and one of her sons was hurt in his mind there. Now her other son and his father were in the middle of the war, overseas in the European Theater of Operations.

Why the hell did the army call them theaters? Did somebody write the scripts for the millions of actors on a big bloody stage? Generals were the directors, of course, and no matter how many of the cast unwittingly fluffed their lines or marched off the dark end of the stage, the show must go on. But when did the curtain come down on a happy ending?

Turning for the house, she became conscious of the summer heat, the air like a damp bath towel. Texas heat high-polished the leaves on scrub oak and warned jackrabbits and digger squirrels to hunt a cool place. She smelled baked dust and the resin of pine needles cooking in the sun. This time of a brilliantly sunny day even the big diamondback rattlers holed up in the shade, unable to absorb such direct heat. They would slither out after sundown to hunt meadow mice or anything not too big to swallow.

She would bet that her son received his most severe shock at night, the final ugliness that caused him to be classified as psychotic. Farley had always been uneasy with the dark, needing the small assurance of a night-light while his brother Owen scoffed.

The army had sent Farley into the blackness of a reptilian jungle. According to the newspapers the Japs were poisonous fighters, but without the courtesy of a rattled warning.

They had asked her not to go immediately to Farley when he came back. They said that seeing her might cause him to lose the progress he had made so far. Colonel Farrand had called her in person to explain. She remembered that she hadn't seen Luther C. Farrand often at major gatherings at the Hill, and never in family-only meetings. So he wasn't that close a blood relation, but still a relation and the man was a chaplain, a man of God who was taking a personal interest in Farley's problems. She was glad for that.

Kirstin went into the screened back porch and past the small chandeliers of waxy red and green chili peppers drying, the white woven ropes of elephant garlic and some bright gourds of yellow and green. How often had she breakfasted out here with Jim, looking out at the start of the hill country and its small, neatly rolling hills? The other way lay a cowboy town with traces of an early Spanish settlement, a frontier town proud of its beginnings and pleased with its present, a content and solid town.

Jim Shelby had been like that, a man of substance, reliable. And before Jim, if she looked close enough, there had been some of that in Chad Belvale, but much of that was due to family tradition and influence. He was solid enough there, more than enough. But in his relations with her . . . if Chad hadn't gotten so far out of step with whiskey and sex . . .

The hell with that; she had a future as well as a past. Spinning, she went back on the porch and rang the big triangle, banging its inside loop with a long iron bolt. Gregorio Venegas had never accepted radio intercom but if he was within earshot, he would come to the main house. If not, her foreman would appear at suppertime and she would tell him that he was to run the ranch while she was gone.

Everything else could wait; she would use her name or the family name or any other method that would get her air or train priority to the Coast. If necessary, she'd drive, however many gas ration coupons that might take.

She was going to see Farley, despite hell, high water, the U.S. Army and Chaplain (Col.) Luther C. Farrand.

REUTERS—The Italian Front, June 4, 1944: Rome fell today. The U.S. 9th Army drove in for the kill this evening. As the last rear guard German units left this capital city, the first of General Mark Clark's troops entered the suburbs to the south. The hard-driving American 88th Division reached the Piazza Venezia.

Oberfeldwebel Arno Hindemit kept his wine bottle hidden. He had come across a small flat bottle that was easy to conceal. The regular long-necked kind was too easily seen, and high-ranking officers had a habit of drinking up a soldier's supply with no thought of replacing it. He didn't let them get a smell of the knockwurst, either. No fool, this fattened *landser* sergeant.

His job was something any loafer could do as well. But since he had lost the good Captain Witzelei and the army had given up Rome, he saw there was no use whipping another infantry company into shape. That took time, and Germany no longer had that luxury.

As for the reconstituted regiment, truly not more than battalion strength, it got by in a drag-foot sort of way, without spirit. It still had a certain amount of discipline, and so it would remain on line. No major German unit had broken under fire; not yet. But with the Italian troops turning their coats and their rifles on their former ally, and harassed by newly formed partisan groups, anything could happen.

And the Amis never stopped. They were badly beaten at the Salerno landings, but they did not panic. They went to earth like frightened moles or good *landsers* and clung to their hard-won strip of sandy soil. Their planes strafed and bombed ahead of them, and flew close protection above them, challenging the Luftwaffe. Fat Meier's Messerschmitts stayed away, held back to guard Berlin, and rumor had it that they were not doing a good job of it.

Arno looked off at another mountain ridge, and another rising higher beyond it. *Gott,* what a miserable country for fighting a war, no better than Tunisia or Sicily. Wars were never meant to take place in a soft terrain and good climate. That would take away too much of the misery. There was a worse area, Arno admitted—the Russian front—but when the moment came, it did not matter where a soldier died. Now it did not seem to matter how, but only when.

Treating himself to a long swallow of wine, he could wish for schnapps. But wish quietly, he thought, because the devil that played with the future of *landsers* might hear, laugh, and turn the wine sour.

"Sergeant?" The colonel's orderly had done a shaky job of shaving him; little red nicks rode both high cheekbones. The chubby major grunted into the back seat.

"Sir!"

"An inspection trip today. I start with the unit on the right flank."

Arno wanted to tell him to walk the narrow twisting valley. It would take time and effort, but it would be much safer. The Ami artillery observers were good.

"Yes, sir," he said. Sergeants did not advise colonels.

But the enemy artillery didn't pick up the jeep. The Ami plane found them with the first burst of .50-caliber bullets punching holes in the rocky path and in the hood of the jeep; it careened sharply to the left and Arno's chest banged into the wheel.

The plane circled high, turned and came back, four guns blazing.

CHAPTER 19

UNITED PRESS—The Italian Front, June 5, 1944: The triumphal entry into Rome by Allied troops has been given a rapturous welcome by the populace.

Passing through this "open city," the Allies took up pursuit of the German 14th Army, now commanded by General Lemelsen. One of the advance flying columns is the Polish Brigade, the unit that finally fought its way into the stubbornly defended rubble of the bombed-out Monte Cassino abbey.

King Victor Emmanuel III, in accordance with his earlier statements, while retaining the symbolic crown, left the guidance of his kingdom in the hands of his son, Umberto of Savoy. A few Italians units have remained in action beside the Germans, but most have disappeared into the civilian population and some have joined small parties of partisans.

President Roosevelt was quoted as saying, "One down, two to go"—meaning the occupation of Axis capital cities, Berlin and Tokyo.

ASSOCIATED PRESS—London, SHAEF HQ, June 6, 1944: This is D day, the long-awaited Allied landings in France, the talked about "Second Front" that Stalin has pushed for. Despite bad weather in the English Channel, the largest armada in history crossed over to France during the night. Thousands of combat vessels and troopships were covered by a swarm of fighter planes as wave after thundering wave of heavy bombers cruised ahead to soften the targets.

Making the official announcement of Operation Overlord, Gen. Dwight D. Eisenhower included a message to the nations of occupied Europe, promising liberation and asking French civilians to evacuate a 22-mile strip of coast to hold down their casualties.

English Field Marshal Bernard Montgomery of North Africa fame was given overall command of all troops, but he is subject to the orders of General Eisenhower. The massive landing forces, spearheaded by an elite American infantry division, maintain a toehold on bloody "Omaha Beach Red" despite fanatical Nazi resistance and carefully prepared defensive positions of the vaunted Atlantic Wall.

During the night and farther inland around Caen, American and English airborne and glider troops dropped to capture vital road junctions and block routes to the beach for German reinforcements.

"Well, cousin, you ready for this?" Owen Belvale tried to sound casual, but his stomach heaved. The gray of the troopship matched the gray of the sea, the gray of the sky, the skin color of most of the men around him. Swells moved in rows from the channel toward the French beach, and dozens of suddenly small-looking LSTs cut continual white-foam circles between the lines of ships strung out to a horizon hidden in the breaking dawn.

"No one is ever ready," Sloan Travis answered, lifting the straps of his pack to ease some weight off his shoulders. "I don't like being on this ship, but I like even less the idea of getting off this bastard. I bet we lose people just climbing down the rigging."

"When are you scheduled?" Owen looked pale, the roll of the ship making him stand stiff and spread-legged.

"Twenty minutes," Sloan said. "Third station down. I just wanted to wish you luck." He held out his hand to his cousin, and as they shook he remembered something General Carlisle said years before. "Luck," Crusty had intoned to a group of kids, punching the air with his cigar, "luck is for rabbits."

Captain Owen Belvale thought his stomach was empty. He was wrong; green furry stuff choked up painfully as he braced in the bucking LST to hold his head over the side. Wet metal banged his chin and cold salt water sprayed his face.

Other men heaved; he could hear them fore and aft and damned the high brass that had picked this gray and blowing day to make a run at Normandy. The sea was so choppy that some small craft might go under. Lifting his head, he peered after the other boats leading this wave, the first wave. He found one by its crooked white wake and guessed that the other, filled with the battalion riflemen, was farther on toward the beach.

The shore wasn't hard to find. Ship's artillery blasted the beach and rolled barrages inland, the huge shells sending great gouts of flame soaring high into the air. Through the smoke, almost impervious to the shelling, loomed the Kraut super pillboxes, massive things firing 88s, and machine guns using interlocking fields of fire. From reinforced steel and concrete positions anchored deep into rock, supporting mortars arched a deadly rain of finned projectiles into the sea, seeking landing craft.

The noise was hell kicked over and stirred with a stick—hammering, yowling and sharp slaps. Motor upon motor roared; planes screamed low overhead; ships wheeled to deliver deafening broadsides. In small, swift quiets the put-put of landing craft and thin shrieks of pain wafted up to fill in the gigantic cacophony. Behind Owen and to the right, an LCP took a direct hit and exploded. Still choking back nausea, he weaved through thirty or so hunkered and groaning GIs and caught the arm of Second Lieutenant Matthew Cooper. He was a brand-new replacement who hadn't been given time to adjust to anything, much less to leading an invasion boat.

Lips at Cooper's ear, Owen said, "Get them off the beach ASAP. We can't set up supporting fire with the guns anywhere near here; it's suicide. The mortars—"

A shell blew up and slapped a geyser of seawater against the boat, and men cursed. The boat rocked. A handful of bullets slammed into the ramp and went keening off. The men stopped cursing. Somebody said, "Our Father . . ."

Owen's mouth went dry on his sickness. Swallowing hard, he hung onto Cooper's arm as the boat yawed and pitched. "Place your mortars behind a knocked-out pillbox; there will be some; your OP won't lack targets. Company headquarters and our other guns will try to move up behind the rifle companies—if we can."

Try, hell. Any man left on his feet had to keep grinding up that slope or die where he went to earth. The Krauts churned the beach sand and rock with small arms fire. Lightning ripped the air and the god-awful noise beat against Owen's head and bulged his eyes. He tasted salt and vomit.

What the hell, Dad? Yes, sir Colonel. I'm your chastened soldier boy. I would have been here anyway. You didn't have to drag me back to barracks. I would have been here; I wouldn't have gone AWOL and let my company land without me. Now Helene thinks . . .

Oh, shit—Helene. He had to make it back and fix things with Helene. Already it felt as if part of him had been ripped away. He would persuade her to marry him this time. The boat shoved its flat nose closer to shore and rammed into something that wrenched it violently off course and almost capsized it.

"Goddamn! Goddamn!" they screamed. "We're sinking! Jump—jump!"

"Hang tight!" Owen yelled. "Hear me, you bastards! We're okay; the boat's not sinking. If you go over the side, you'll never come up. You're carrying too much weight. Hang tight, damn you."

"It's a stake!" Cooper yelled. "Long stakes lined up damned thick and angled to rip out the bottom of the boat. And right over there—hedgehogs made out of railroad tracks and mines, damn it! Mines! I see big antitank mines wired to hedgehogs."

Another boat blew up, a big Landing Craft, Tank, erupting so close that body parts and shattered steel rained over into Owen's boat. Goddamn. Heavy casualties before they hit the beach. Peering through the spray and smoke, he made out roll after extended roll of concertina wire stretched wide along the beach, the double apron farther back. There would be more tangles of barbed wire around the bunkers and gun emplacements.

"No choice," Owen said. "There's no way back, so we're going in."

INTERNATIONAL NEWS SERVICE—Rome, June 6, 1944: The capture of Rome was a sweet but briefly noticed victory, overshadowed by today's invasion of France.

But veterans here are being reinforced by new blood from Britain, America, France, New Zealand, South Africa, Greece and Brazil. In the American 5th Army there are even Japanese fighting against the Germans in the mountains.

Crusty Carlisle snorted. "See, I told you we'd hit Normandy. All that action in north England was just for show—Limey troops moving here and there, those rubber blowup trucks and tanks. Fooled the goddamn Krauts."

"Not by much," Preston Belvale said. "I hope those panzer divisions stay put in Pas-de-Calais. By rights, they should have come smashing down the coast to take us on the flank and shoot us up."

Crusty stood with feet apart, watching the clack-clack printout of a Teletype machine across yellow paper. He rubbed his left shoulder; since his aborted tour of the Pacific, the arthritis had crept back. "Could be that the boss-bastard is having one of his heaven-sent visions. There are times when Hitler is the best weapon on our side. Any first-year cadet knows you don't split your forces to fight on two fronts. That peanut with a mustache screwed it up worse; he had North Africa going, too. Now he's got Italy and, at long range, England."

Preston nodded. "Even without those tanks, it's not a soft landing. The last walkover was at Arzew in Algeria; not Sicily, Anzio and not Salerno. Every TWX I get tells me that this time we're hanging on tooth and nail; if they push us off Omaha Beach the other landings will be rolled up, Sword and Juno, Utah and Gold. God only knows when—or if—we can try again. Eisenhower is going all out on Overlord; everything he has is in the pot, and he wishes he had more."

The Teletype stopped clacking. Another one dinged twice and began its printout. A phone rang and Gloria Carlisle—ah, Donnely—answered it.

Crusty said, "It's almost all conjecture; some on-scene G-Two is okay at first, but coming back it gets garbled all to hell. Some is bullshit for starters."

"We lucked out getting any advance news. If Ben Alexander hadn't stayed on top of things in the War Department—"

"Good old cousin Ben, holding down a Washington desk and working his two stars."

"For the good. He's put in for a ZI infantry command. Ben admits his lungs won't let him go overseas, so he opted for the Zone of Interior. He feels he can do better training troops. I'm sure he can."

Crusty crossed the war room in search of bootleg whiskey. Preston was right; the pure corn liquor was far better than the wartime commercial stuff.

"He can; Ben knows how to be tough when its needed. Hey, do you know what other peanut zipped into town and then right back to the Coast? That f—Gloria, how long are you going to hang on to that phone?—that lousy sky pilot, the great Luther C. Farrand. How did a bastard like him ever get into the family?"

Luther Farrand was part of the family tree, but a root grown far to one side and turned bitter. A soldier who avoided war, a chaplain seldom seen in church, Luther was a man who loved rank and power. Political connections were more important to him than blood ties, a fact often made clear when he stood on the same side of conference rooms as did family enemies. His resentment of family influence—and its refusal to exercise that influence for his personal upward climb—had shown itself more than once in religious lectures and biblical platitudes. But he had made the mistake of admonishing Crusty for taking the Lord's name in vain, and after a tongue-lashing of legendary proportions, Luther had stayed clear of both Sandhurst Keep and Kill Devil Hill.

Preston frowned and answered Crusty's question. "By being born a bastard, the story goes. Luther has been pissed ever since. He's got too much rank for his job, and he's bucking for a star as chief of chaplains. If he hangs around Washington, that's understandable, but staying out on the Coast—"

Crusty found the bottle and poured drinks, sniffing the light aroma of whiskey and eyeing the way it beaded inside the glass. "Farley Belvale is out there, at Letterman General. I think Luther is about to stir up trouble and come east to touch base with Tom Skelton, another peanut who just got his third star. We should have kicked his ass long ago. He's got some kind of Senate protection, or maybe somebody in the White House, but we've outflanked guys like that before."

"Farley is carried as battle fatigue," Preston said. "Kirstin called from Texas; she went out to stay with him, and Nancy is already there. Luther spends duty time between there, Fort Ord and Fort Lewis as the Sixth Army chaplain. Maybe he's sticking his nose in."

Gloria said, "That was Nancy on the phone. She says that Colonel Farrand is demanding Farley's medical records. He wants to bring in civilian shrinks to verify Farley's condition."

Preston said, "He's up to something. What, damn it?"

The bad guys, in this case, preferred to sneak up from behind, and usually tried to strike fatal blows with memos and subcommittee votes. Bureaucrats, Bible-thumpers and political weasels; sometimes the skin was different, but the smell was always the same. General Skelton, a textbook example of a paper soldier, had long fought administrative battles with both Preston and Crusty, often over the use of manpower and budget. Skelton won just enough of these engagements to keep easing up in the ranks, and his position had been solidified by some astute political alliances. Skelton might be constantly stupid about soldiering—it was he who declared in a general staff meeting that the Japanese couldn't fight, and any war could quickly be settled by a handful of good old American troops—but he was also damnably cunning about the chessboard of Washington power pieces.

"Boss" Kawley, a congressional politician so arrogant as to laughingly wear his derogatory nickname with pride, was one of the dark bishops on the board. His dislike for the generals came from having a couple of his personal pork barrels broken open, and he was more than willing to aid Skelton by pulling a political string or two. Kawley was powerful enough to be dangerous to the family, and like most politicians, he never came at you from the front, where you could actually see him.

And now Luther, the rank-happy part-time preacher, was being seen too often in the company of the bad guys.

Crusty said, "Call her back in half an hour. I'll find out what that Holy Joe is up to and bend his beak for him. It's like we have nothing else to do, right? Damn, but it's so much simpler out where the fighting is; you can tell the good guys from the bad guys. The good guys help out; the bad guys shoot at you."

The liquor was smooth and warming. Crusty sipped at it, this "sipping whiskey" of Preston's, of the South, and wondered if the lives of the family would have been much different if both ancestors had settled in the South. Not too much, he decided; some higher plan had separated them early on, so they could balance each other. But that developed into northerners and southerners spilling each other's blood.

He said, "Back to the war. Will Montgomery drag his ass and blame Ike? He really wanted supreme command of Operation Overlord."

"Later," Preston said, "he'll probably squeal to be elected top dog after we move inland a good way."

Crusty eyed his whiskey glass. "*If* we get inland, the peanuts should say. But damned right we will."

"It's going to cost."

Drawing a deep breath, Crusty said, "That, too."

COMCON TWX—Senior staff, EYES ONLY, June 6, 1944: The 200-foot cliffs at Omaha Beach are proving an obstacle more formidable than anticipated. The German 352nd Infantry Division is now known to be in the area. Heavy cloud cover has caused bombers to miss coastal defenses, with the only reported casualties a number of French cows.

Chest deep in the chill water, Lieutenant Sloan Travis clung to a crossarm of an iron hedgehog while the water washed him up and down. A Kraut mortar shell sledged into the sea and exploded. He felt the shock in his legs, in his back. Closer in, the burst could kill; although the fragments probably wouldn't reach you, the shock waves would.

Spinggg!

A bullet whined off the hedgehog, and Sloan's hands slipped on the wet steel. Above his head and attached to the spider arm of the beach obstacle a round metal mine glistened. He saw why Eisenhower had sent them ashore at low tide; it stretched the exposed run to dry land, but if they had come in higher water, the beach obstacles would have taken a heavy toll. Now was bad enough; high tide would have been a horror.

Sloan was glad he didn't have to make decisions involving hundreds of thousands of lives. It was tough being responsible for a single platoon, and he began to see the weight that higher command carried, a burden that could break a man's soul. He didn't want that kind of responsibility. Salt water splashed his face. A line of spouts whipped across between him and the beach, a machine gunner firing along a predetermined line.

"Lieutenant? Lieutenant!"

The boy dragged himself through the water to catch Sloan's arm. "Oh, Christ, Lieutenant, I'm hit—I'm hit bad."

Catching the collar of the kid's field jacket, Sloan dragged him closer. The enemy machine gun was stitching the water again. A bright flare arched above the beach, and the ship-to-shore barrage lifted immediately. According to schedule, Sloan thought, except that the bunkers hadn't all been knocked out. Through a clearing in the smoke, he saw the beach itself, too wide and rising gradually from the water to a seawall too far away.

"Lieutenant—"

"Hang on, mac. I'll get you to land."

Unbidden, lines from another war rang through his head: "I have a rendezvous with death . . . at some disputed barricade. . . ."

"Hang on," he repeated and, with a firmer grip on the jacket, shoved off from the hedgehog to bounce up and down on his toes, keeping his head above water. The sand firmed beneath his feet and the water grew shallower. Dragging the limp GI, he plodded forward, head down and panting. He had lost his helmet somewhere along the way and possibly lost part of himself.

The kid he dragged through the sandy shallows seemed so damned young, but a glimpse of the pale, watery face told him they were about the same age.

"Lieutenant— Oh, God . . ."

Command turned you old, Sloan thought; command and something called duty. Stooping lower, water sloshing in his boot tops, he dragged the kid higher up on the beach. A mine had gone off and left a smoked depression in the sand. He placed the kid in it and rolled him over as bullets beat the air overhead.

He was dead, a great hole in his chest. Most of the blood had washed out.

"Shit," Sloan said.

Lifting himself erect, water-soaked clothing dragging at him, he wobbled across the beach and went to ground in the cover of the stone seawall. He joined three other men crouched there. Correction: two men and another corpse.

Kraut machine guns chipped rock from the top of the wall.

CHAPTER 20

His radioman went down, bobbed up once, bloody face against graying and bloody hair, and sank when Chad reached for him. The weighty radio pulled him back into the tide, and Chad was cut off from communication with his battalion. He waded to the beach, his eyes sweeping back and forth, registering the casualty count and flinching at the sight of burning landing craft, of firecracker tanks and blazing trucks. A pall of stinking smoke hung choking across the beach, but not enough for cover.

There were far too many human losses. Men could see only so much before the deaths affected them. Even the hardened veterans of the 16th Infantry could fold upon themselves and stop moving.

The rising tide seesawed men who were facedown in the shallows; some men lay sprawled on the sand, singly or in small groups, marking fatal movement up the beach. Beyond the sad and flattened dead huddled the wounded, and the live men seemed to hang somewhere between. There was a crumpled line of dead stretching to the shingle bank that offered some protection, and farther up, an ancient seawall with the highwater mark dirty green and mossy. The sand was an off yellow marked with dark spots where shells and mines had gone off.

Out of habit Chad carried the .45 pistol on his right hip next to the canteen, but for firepower, he held an M-2 carbine shoulder high in both hands as he splashed ashore. Neither helped him across the open sand and through the endless two hundred yards of direct exposure to enemy guns, but he made it.

Reaching the seawall, he knelt among a line of men hiding out from the fire storm lashing the beach and probing the wall. Six-set loads of long rockets shrieked overhead, fired from the gunships cruising offshore. Heavy guns on the battlewagons and destroyers hurled their thunder farther inland, seeking out other lines of defense and working over supply routes. Friendly planes wheeled the sky, so thick there must have been traffic control and collision problems for the flyboys. They were doing a hell of a job of keeping the Luftwaffe in check and busy back in Germany.

Seeing a man he recognized, he called out, "Sergeant Pelkey! Is this the rest of your company? And where is Captain Owen Belvale?"

"Begging the colonel's pardon, sir—we're scattered all to hell, two of the guns are on the bottom of the ocean and I'm missing the captain and my lieutenant. What the fuck do I know?"

Turning on his haunches, Pelkey pointed. "Goddamn! Ain't that the colonel himself, the regimental CO? Look at him, strolling along like he's bulletproof!"

Good, Chad thought; Colonel George Taylor wouldn't ream ass because field grade officers played cowboy—not if he did it himself.

In one of those weird moments of quiet, Colonel Taylor's voice rose loud and clear: "There are two kinds of men on this beach—the dead and those about to die. Let's get the hell off this beach." Turning, he faced inland and walked erect and proud.

And they moved. The battered, wounded and pinned-down infantrymen climbed from behind meager shelters and moved, however slowly, through the firing lines. They pointed themselves into the paths through the barbed wire and minefields that the Special Engineer units had blown at such cost. They moved inland under devastating fire, and some of them fell; the rest kept going, firing as they went. Through the fire storm, over the tangled barbed wire and through exploding mines, they kept going.

"Oh, you beautiful bastards!" Chad yelled, and followed.

A massive bunker loomed before him, and he emptied half a clip at a firing slit. Then he was safely beneath its field of fire and moving toward other bunkers, some of them twisted and hammered by big shells and heavy bombs. A few shattered vacation beach houses lifted spider arms of broken boards and water pipes farther back. From within them German riflemen took the attackers under fire. A water-cooled .30 opened up, its deeper staccato announcing an H Company gun. H

Company meant Owen; even in such chaos, Owen would be near his guns. Chad needed to see him, just see him.

Pranngg!

Sniper zeroing in from the ruins. Christ, the Krauts had everything set, every detail planned, even to harassing fire. They were good at that. Had Owen made it this far, or had he been caught in that flotsam and jetsam on the beach? Was he down among the wrecks of tanks and trucks and LCVP boats; smashed DUKWs and the wrecks of men? If Owen had been killed, how would Chad tell Kirstin? What to say beyond the terse War Department telegram that "deeply regrets to inform you"?

In her agony, she would blame Chad. That might not be too far from wrong.

Chad shook off a sense of impending gloom; his son was a soldier, a good one but for his morbid attachment to that Limey super bitch in Southampton. Owen had neglected his command and had been technically AWOL at least a dozen times to be with her; he had signed out jeeps against standing orders. Worse, at other times he'd called on a driver to deliver him and pick him up, using enlisted men to further his affair, men who could not refuse. . . .

When word had reached Chad on his hasty return from the Italian front, Owen wasn't with his company, but gone again. One of the drivers remembered the way to Helene Lyons's flat and drove Chad there. Maybe he should have been easier on the boy; maybe he should have been tougher. He knew what he would have done if the miscreant hadn't been his son, and that made it worse.

He had probably embarrassed Owen beyond any hope of reconciliation, but at the moment he was too pissed to care. The naked woman behind him on the bed didn't panic or cover herself; hands behind her head, back arched, she just looked on. In his OD drawers, Owen struggled furiously until Chad put a hammerlock on him and shoved him down the steps to the jeep waiting with its top up. He threw Owen's uniform in first, and then Owen himself.

Twisting himself up on the back seat, Owen clenched his fists and threw a punch at Chad. Maybe he missed on purpose; maybe he just missed.

Chad said, "Son or no son, your ass is one thin goddamn inch from a court-martial right now. People are wondering when I'll stretch your hide to dry. Don't push me."

"God damn it," Owen said, "I'm going to marry her."

"Your problem and on your own time, not on the army's."

"What I do is my—"

"You're not a civilian, God damn it! You do what you're ordered to do, Captain."

Owen had been smart enough to shut up, and as the sergeant drove, he stared straight ahead, seeing nothing, hearing nothing—an experienced regular-army trooper.

And then the armada had to be loaded for D day, for the 16th Infantry's H hour, and there was no time for personal problems, unless you counted survival as personal. . . .

Chad picked a fat pile of rubble and knelt behind it. As the tribe gathered, this would be the battalion command post, if the forward movement didn't get too far ahead. It was slowing already, pushed back and down by withering enemy fire. Men dug in, and Chad knew then that, barring an overwhelming counterattack by heavy armor, the regiment meant to stay and hold the beachhead secure.

That mood was something that could not be ordered, a thing that rose from the guts.

On the right flank, the 29th Division's 116th Infantry Regiment was taking the same sort of beating, a new outfit coming into their baptism of fire, the poor bastards. A hell of a way to get introduced to war.

A man slammed to the ground beside Chad; the SCR 300 radio he carried banged into stone. "Holy shit—I mean, Corporal Weintraub, sir, H Company commo."

"Howe Company? Have you seen Captain Belvale?"

"No, sir. This operation is as full of shit as a Christmas goose. This here boat landed a mile off; that boat unloaded men in deep water and under they went. No, sir, I never laid eyes on the captain once the ramp went down."

"The radio," Chad said. "In working order? My radio went down with its operator."

"Old Jellicoe? That don't hardly seem right. He was kind of old and stove up, and Colonel Taylor moved him back where he'd be safe. What a fucked-up war."

Pranngg!

"My radio work? Did until that peckerhead sniped it. Look at that goddamn bullet crease. Wait up—yeah, sure, me and my radio can stay on the band if you want. What say we get off right?"

Holy of holies, the flat bottle of whiskey glistened as if it awaited sanctification. Chad said, "Now I know who you are. The regiment's number-one scrounger, the man who brought home an English army motorcycle with its sidecar full of fish and chips. Of course—Weintraub."

He drank, and it was smoky scotch to flow warm and mellow down Chad's throat.

Weintraub said, "I've had better fish, catfish from

the bottom of the mud pond, and it was a fair trade. Who you want me to try and reach, Colonel?''

"Fox Company is the point. If you can't raise Captain Mulich there, try George Company and Captain Guist. I need to know if we've got anything near a battalion left.''

New York Times—June 7, 1944: Today the War Labor Board ordered the American Federation of Musicians to end the ban it put on production of phonograph records in August 1942. The Board directly named the union leader James Petrillo as the directive stressed the importance of the entertainment industry and the vital relaxation of war workers.

UNITED PRESS—With the Pacific Fleet, June 7, 1944: American troops who fought their way ashore on Saipan Island in the Marianas have firmly established their beachhead and are making good progress advancing inland against heavy opposition.

Admiral Chester Nimitz said, "This landing is not as big as the one in Europe, but it is as important to this part of the world."

The Japs did it again, pulled back from the beach proper to prepared positions in the jungle and on higher ground. They give you the beach, Eddie Donnely thought, just to get you out in the open where they can work you over good. They had every inch of land on their range cards for accuracy with their mortars and Nambus. G-2 had passed word that some Jap artillery was planted on the high ground. No landing had turned out to be a snap, but all in all, this one gave signs of becoming a hairy bitch.

Following the advance platoons, Eddie led part

of company headquarters off the Alligator—that seagoing, beach-climbing chunk of steel and guns. He slogged up on the coral sand, ears tuned to sniper fire. There was none, but there would be. He hurried into the semi-opening edge of the brush, where palm trees swayed, some of them chopped up by naval gunfire, some untouched and holding to their crop of coconuts.

It would depend upon how the fighting went as to how the coconuts went. If the battle was tough, the coconuts would be shot down to be drunk and eaten. If things were easy, somebody would climb the trees and be careful not to break the thick husks.

Those coconuts could be turned into a kind of bootleg whiskey, aged for an anxious while after a hole was punched in the shell. Sugar was added for fermentation and a whittled plug jammed in. Sometimes the things exploded, scaring the holy shit out of CP personnel, but usually the coconut treatment furnished some fair booze, something on the line of Hawaii's pineapple okolehao. Back in the ZI or on the old overseas posts—Panama, China, the Philippines—a run to town followed boozing.

(*Barracks talk: Go get screwed, blewed and tattooed after you take a shower, shit, shave and get a shoeshine.*)

Not here, and maybe not ever again for the old doggies. The young ones wouldn't even remember the words.

He lifted one hand, circled it several times and then pointed down, the signal for "join me here." A few more paces into the shade and the front opened onto newly created fields where shells and dive-bombers had changed the face of the jungle. Some palm logs crisscrossed here. It was a fair place for company command post, not far behind the attack companies and close enough to seaborne supplies. But if a Jap combat patrol came banzaing close to the sea and around on either flank, the CP would be in deep shit.

(Barracks talk: What the hell—it all counts for twenty.)

Rap! Rap! Rap!

Japanese Namus, reaching from the jungle to work through the men and boats unloading along the beach. The defense was starting; the bloodletting was beginning. Muscles tightened in Eddie's neck and across his shoulders.

Stooping, he carefully examined the log pile. The setup was perfect for booby traps, but probing with a bayonet didn't find any. Still, he made the people wait while he ran his hands over and under each log, feeling along the hairy bark. It was like petting a big, dangerous bear, and he was getting tired of bears.

Then he said, "Clear, I guess," and stepped through to find a fire step while men behind him set up the radio and sound power phones. There was room for the CO and commo crew and two medics.

The first artillery shell whistled in—*KA-BLAM!*—to throw shreds of trees and churned sand over the command post.

"Early start," Eddie said, and settled into an Oriental squat to wait out the barrage. This was another sign that he was going Asiatic, like the old soldiers from the 15th Infantry in prewar China.

He thought of Gloria, almost tasting the sweetness of her, tingling at memories of satin skin and damply seeking mouth.

He was still smiling when the next shell blasted into the logs and scattered them like Tinkertoys. He spun up with them.

CHAPTER 21

AGENCE FRANCE PRESSE—Washington, D.C., June 8, 1944: Frenchmen here and around the world continue to celebrate as more news of the Normandy landings reaches them. Information from SHAEF in London announced that General Charles de Gaulle is waiting to lead his Free French volunteers ashore as soon as the beachhead is secure.

Fighting is still hectic just beyond the beach, and the thickly woven hedgerows of Normandy will soon offer near impregnable cover for German troops.

Lieutenant General Preston Belvale lowered his right hand; Gloria did the same. Belvale said, "Congratulations, you are now a second lieutenant on active duty with the army of the United States. Carry on."

Gloria Donnely saluted, and Preston smiled as he returned it. "You look wonderful in uniform."

She did, the WAC insignia and new gold bars gleaming, her hair cut to regulation length, eyes shiny with pride and anticipation. The Minerva of the family would sniff and pretend she didn't see the uniform; the very idea—women soldiers.

When Gloria approached Preston with the idea of enlisting, he had agreed to a point, which was to arrange a direct commission. What the hell, if the navy could make Jack Dempsey a lieutenant commander, and if the air corps could hang officer rank on Clark Gable, Jimmy Stewart and other Hollywood notables . . .

At least this girl had a solid military background, being an army brat from birth. She could quote general orders and pertinent regulations and would be a good soldier, as good as most men. As she half-marched, half-skipped from the war room at Kill Devil Hill, Preston wondered if the army would continue the Women's Army Corps when this war was over. There were signs. Originally it had been WAAC—Auxiliary Corps—and its member were doing a fine job of releasing men for active duty, meaning to combat zones.

Lighting a cigar, Preston frowned. There was also the possibility of women in foxholes; however remote, the chance was there. Russian women flew fighter planes and were feared as snipers; the Chinese used them as medics with line troops; women were numbered among the French Maquis, and British women had long operated antiaircraft guns and barrage balloons.

What was that about the female being deadlier than the male?

Something else he had not thought of—women outranking their men: Lieutenant Gloria Donnely and First Sergeant Eddie Donnely; technically, they could not fraternize. But all the regulations together would play hell trying to stop that.

Belvale stroked his mustache. There was more to think about than Donnely's injured feelings. Crusty Carlisle was on his way to Letterman General Hospital in San Francisco to look into something stirring there. It had to do with Farley, and Nancy Carlisle's furious phone call pointed to Chaplain Luther Farrand as the troublemaker. The sanctimonious son of a bitch had been shot down for his brigadier's star and the Chief of Chaplain's job in Washington. Although the family had nothing to do with blocking him, Luther didn't see it that way.

A Teletype clanged three bells, and Belvale went to read the TWX. It was casualty reports and material loss, the figures staggering and still incomplete. A thousand men of the 16th Infantry Regiment down within the first hour; tanks and their crews drowned without firing a shot; ugly numbers, but the stubborn survivors drove on inch by bloody inch to hammer their way up the beach. With direct air support from a thousand planes, and with bombardments from the warships rocking in the choppy Channel, troops of Operation Overlord should reach their objectives.

But would they? Messages coming through here and at the War Department showed a strong hint of panic.

The machine binged and binged again, and Belvale glanced down at revised casualty figures: 3,408 killed, wounded or missing from the U.S. 1st, 2nd, 9th and 29th divisions. Nothing yet on the British and Canadians.

And they were still on the beach. Would it become a vast graveyard?

NORTH AMERICAN NEWSPAPER ALLIANCE—Omaha Beach, Normandy, June 8, 1944: They did it. Allied soldiers crawled over their own dead and wounded to fight their way off the terrible beach and onto higher ground.

General Omar N. Bradley, out on the cruiser *Augusta*, could do nothing at that stage of the battle to influence events. He said the fight "had run beyond the reach of its admirals and generals."

Worried over alarming and confused details coming in, he sent an observer close inshore on a fast patrol boat. Firsthand reports were not reassuring: the beach was a shambles; casualties were tremendous; boats laden with more men and supplies circled at sea, piling up and unable to land.

A further radio report told Bradley that the situation was still critical. The general contemplated diverting support from Omaha to Utah and the British beaches. Abandoning the troops already ashore would mean death or capture for them all.

The message came: "Troops formerly pinned down now advancing up heights behind beaches."

It was that close.

_____

Oberfeldwebel Arno Hindemit wanted to pull his helmet down over his shoulders and hide. Perhaps for the first time, he envied the bastard panzer grenadiers their steel foxholes. Peering through a firing slit in a support bunker high above the loose crescent of the beach, he could not believe there were that many ships in all the combined navies of the world. They milled around in the English Channel, every so often spitting a string of water bugs at the beach where so much wreckage exploded and burned. Daybreak was not long past, and the raw entrails of the great invasion were already ripped and bleeding.

The German 352nd Division headquarters announced only hours ago that the Normandy landing had been repulsed and that no doubt the Führer's intuition was correct: this was a feint and the major attack was coming at Pas-de-Calais. That news, and the fact that the 352nd was an elite unit, had brought Colonel Schmundt to the Wall for a firsthand look.

Here an artillery crew sent 88mm shells whiplashing down onto the mess upon the beach and at times reaching out for the ships and boats. Arno squeezed the palms of his hands against his ears and swallowed to lessen the air pressure from the muzzle blasts. A pair of MG-42s reached out right and left, automatic weapons sweeping to overlap the next bunker's field of fire.

All *landsers* died deaf, Arno decided, and wished that the colonel and his sausage major would get enough of these and let him return to the jeep. Whatever the division commander thought, Arno knew that the Amis were too *verdammt* close. For all the hellfire rained upon them, they crept closer. And at full daylight, the enemy planes would arrive, and arrive again, while the Luftwaffe hid in Berlin, beneath Fat Meier's belly.

Colonel Rudolph Schmundt scraped his boots against the damp concrete floor; his aide, Major Hans Werner, lit a cigarette, the match glow picking out sweat on his porker cheeks. Because Schmundt had some kind of contact with high party functionaries, he had been able to engineer a staff transfer from the shaky Gothic Line in Italy to the Atlantic Wall. He brought Arno along, happy to show off his decorated driver so men would assume that they were line soldiers together.

Now he was not that happy. He said to bunker commander Leutnant Schosser, barely hidden worry thinning his voice, "They are defeated, those Amis? Herr Feldmarschall von Rundstedt swore to the Führer himself that these defenses cannot be penetrated."

Sandy hair protruding beyond the earpiece of his glasses, Schosser spread his thin hands. He reminded Arno of Captain Wetzelei; perhaps he was also a schoolmaster who would never return to the classroom.

He said, "Feldmarschall Rommel did not say that, and he is in more immediate command. He took leave yesterday, for his wife's birthday, after announcing that the weather was too bad for a Channel crossing. He is at home in Ulm.''

CRRAACCK!!

Scheissen—dust and flakes of concrete rained down on them in the deafening thunderclap. The bunker was wide and thick, but Arno felt it shift. Something that big had to be—

CRRAACCKK!!

—one of those battleship shells from a sixteen-inch gun that hurled a packet of high explosive and steel about the size of the Führer's automobile of the future, the People's Car. It would be a miracle if anyone ever saw a Volkswagen.

The crew at the 88 bounced off their weapon and off the walls. One gunner screamed, and a machine gunner's shriek answered. The bunker rocked, and a slab of concrete shattered down from the roof, narrowly missing Colonel Schmundt.

"Sir," Arno said, ears throbbing and numb-lipped as the dust settled.

"Quite right, Sergeant. Division headquarters should know of this immediately."

Arno bent to turn over Leutnant Schosser; he was as dead as Germany's hope of stopping the landings on the beach. *Scheissen*—his glasses were cracked, as Wetzelei's had been. Poor fucking schoolmasters, so far from their classrooms.

CHAPTER 22

INTERNATIONAL NEWS SERVICE—With the U.S. 1st Infantry Division, the Big Red One, in Normandy, D day plus two, June 8, 1944: Barely off the hard-won beaches, men of this veteran outfit faced German heavy panzers and mobile artillery rushed up to block farther advance. A dread Tiger tank, at 65 tons said to be the largest and most thickly armored in the world, fought many American tanks to a standstill.

The single Tiger destroyed [count censored] Sherman tanks before being knocked out by an act of incredible bravery.

[Home Office: 2 kum: name, hometown of hero, guess at decoration, sidebar on medals 3 kum—Ferrero, INS]

Lieutenant Sloan Travis hugged the earth, took the soil of France to himself and tried to flatten his body, to become invisible. Heat waves shimmered around and over him, caused not by the clouded sun of Normandy but by the fires of burning tanks—American tanks. Scattered behind him, they blazed and popped like popcorn machines at full blast as fire reached the machine gun ammunition.

Holy Christ, that lone Tiger tank had knocked

out at least twenty Shermans, zeroing in on most of them with bull's-eye shots from its 88mm gun. Had he seen only a few late-arriving Mark VI Tigers in Tunisia and Sicily and knew them to be the deadliest German tanks of the war. The gunner of this was pinwheel accurate, hurling his AP and HE perfectly into American tanks. Along this tight little bulge of the line above Omaha Beach, he was holding up any advance by this mixed-up bag of lost souls separated from their units, stopping the advance and killing people.

Hull down behind the corner of a stone wall, building wreckage acting as camouflage, the Tiger waited. If more U.S. Shermans and half-tracks came up from the beach and around the corner, this terror would kill them off as well. Maybe somebody was contacting the warships for supporting fire. If so, this chunk of earth was about to turn into the hottest corner of hell, and not only for the gutsy crew of Krauts. Shells would fall among all of the men, and any short rounds would land in the rear area.

WHAM—BANG!

Ears ringing, Sloan wiped loose dirt from his mouth. The 88 was the best weapon to come out of the war so far; a high-speed, flat trajectory weapon, its sound was distinctive, the muzzle blast followed quickly by the explosion of the projectile.

Projectile, trajectory—all that army technical garbage; more of it stuck to him than he realized. All right, because he lived the army now, it would hang on. Once he threw off the uniform, the rest of the junk would go with it.

Head on, Sloan lay not fifty yards from the Tiger, partially hidden by churned earth and stone and boards, the remains of a vacation house. Each time the 88 fired, he was bounced up and down.

WHAM-BANG!

In the echo, Sloan's tortured ears picked up the

sob of a wounded man. The guy needed help, but it wouldn't come easy. Sloan had seen three medics and a pair of litter-bearers struck down among their patients. It was so frigging open here; if anybody showed he was alive, the Tiger's machine gunners would work him over, and probe more ground. Several bodies had fallen close upon each other to prove that. Stronger proof was the advance stopped cold as soldiers refused to move ahead into the fire.

The wounded GI sobbed, a desperate, gurgling sound that fed itself between things popping and things blowing up with deeper booms. Sloan carefully moved his head, trying to spot the man. Where the hell was his platoon and Sergeant Pelkey? Why had so much of the warship shelling overshot the main line of resistance here? Most of the bunkers were unscarred. Now the ship-to-shore barrage was more on target, but the friendly fire was also more dangerous.

Rap-rap-rap-rap!

The machine gun chopped at a tumbled wall, and the tortured GI cried again. A rifleman lay behind Sloan, close enough to be touched on the helmet by a boot toe. Sloan reached back and nudged the steel pot.

Waiting for a moment of quiet, Sloan hissed, "Got any grenades?"

The hiss came back: "Yeah, but they won't scratch that goddamn thing. I got two Willy Peters and two frags. Let me know before you fuck with that big bastard so I can haul my ass and try to save it."

White phosphorous grenades—they might do it. He couldn't lie here until the Tiger went away; it might stay right there and fight to the death. It was doing a hell of a job exactly where it sat awaiting more fat targets.

"Pass me the Willy Peter," he said.

"Oh, shit," the rifleman said. "You're going to try it, ain't you?"

And the wounded man's sobs trailed off into moans. The machine gun searched for him again. "Goddamn," Sloan said, "shut up, shut up!"

A WP cylinder in either hand, the pins pulled and spoons held tightly down, he lunged up at the Tiger tank, arms pumping, stumbling over broken stone and catching himself. The machine gun caught up with him and knocked him down. He clung desperately to the grenades and wobbled to his feet.

"Shut up, God damn it!"

He was almost to the big bastard when the 88 went off and knocked him on his ass again. Not all that sure of direction, blinded by the muzzle blast, he rose to his knees and reached up, tapping the grenade. There—there was the nose of the iron monster amid the stink of burned powder. Pulling himself higher with an effort, he crawled up on the panzer, his wounded legs beginning to knot up.

Firing slit—where was the frigging slit? There—he shoved the grenade at it and let go of the spoon. It didn't fit into the slit.

Son of a bitch! Sloan rolled off the front deck of the tank as the thing went off and threw bright white liquid all over the turret. Maybe some of it burned into his legs. He couldn't tell the difference; they were pretty numb.

Yet he staggered around the track and away from the sizzling phosphorous. His free hand helped him climb the rear deck of the tank, he would slide back and lay the other grenade on the engine breather or the extra gas cans. It should burn into something there, and the smoke would drive the crew out into the open.

Too late, he heard the hatch crack open. He didn't see the pistol either, but the bullet creased his head and knocked him sideways. He held on, his head spinning and blood in his eyes. With the last of his strength, he underhanded the grenade at the Kraut in the opened turret as the bastard triggered the Walther again.

ASSOCIATED PRESS—Somewhere in France, July 8, 1944: Adolf Hitler made a personal broadcast today to prove to all Germany that he is alive and still in command of his beleaguered Third Reich.

Earlier stories filtered out of Berlin said the Führer escaped death by inches when a bomb planted at his conference table killed and wounded several high-ranking Nazis. Broadcasting from his "Wolf's Lair" in Rastenburg, Hitler characterized unnamed "usurpers" as the same kind of defeatist officer clique that wanted to repeat the 1918 "stab in the back."

A bloody purge of the professional military is expected as Nazi SS leader Heinrich Himmler was also named commander-in-chief of the home army.

First Lieutenant Farley Belvale laced his fingers so they would stop registering his count. The count went on, of course. It usually did when somebody was talking, but it was difficult to make the words come out even on both hands; too many sevens and nines.

"Farley," Nancy Carlisle said, smelling all fresh and crisp in her nurse's whites, smelling of green soap and the hint of perfume. "Farley, your mother is on her way up to the ward. This time you will see her. She flew all the way out from Texas."

Losing the count, he unwound his fingers. He hated to miss the count. Nancy ought to talk slower and be more careful to say short paragraphs.

"Mother," he said. "Today. Sure, why not?" Odd count, damn it; so he added another "sure."

"Hold that thought," Nancy said. "You're in good shape and getting better."

"Better than that. The colonel says there was nothing wrong with me in the first place."

Nancy's face looked funny. "What colonel? The chief of staff here?"

"Uh-uh, the chaplain. He says I'm fine, that I just got homesick."

"Chaplain? Colonel Luther Farrand? When did he see you? Was anybody with him?"

His head hurt. "Some general, I think; I was sleepy."

"Bastards," Nancy said. "Oh, those bastards."

Her hand was warm and soft on his. "Farley, please don't talk to those people again. Send them to me."

"General—how do you send a general anywhere?"

Patting his hand, she said, "Just don't talk to them or listen to them; I have a hunch what that goddamn Farrand has in mind."

He smiled. That was a long sentence, but it came out just right. In a kind of celebration he said, "Is Penny coming with Mother? I'd really like to see my wife."

He could do evens, too.

"Good for you. That's the first time you've mentioned her name. You're remembering more."

Turning his head, he wrapped his fingers around hers. Then he squeezed very hard and watched Nancy's face change.

"Why are you hiding her from me?" he asked. Shit, a seven. He squeezed harder.

UNITED PRESS—The South Pacific via Pearl Harbor, July 21, 1944: Assault troops and sea forces yesterday began the long-awaited invasion of the big island of Guam. Good beachheads have been established against light opposition. Resistance increased as marines and soldiers drove hard inland.

Dispatches from the front reported the landings were made on either side of Port Apra. From the shore areas, where Japanese defenses had been blown to pieces, the invaders drove swiftly toward a range of hills in the interior.

Major Keenan Carlisle crouched as he waded through blue-green water, feeling far more naked than he ever had in the poisonous cloak of the jungle. The sea was calm, and he saw only one Alligator tractor knocked out and smoking on the sand. Not often, and usually high, snipers fired. They must be eight balls left behind to die, poor soldiers that their brass wouldn't miss, while the better troops took cover. There were some in every army.

The barely opposed landing was standard operating procedure for the Japs; back off from the beach and hole up in well-prepared defenses inland, the coconut log and concrete bunkers staggered and zigzagged so that the fields of fire interlocked with each other. They would also be dug in behind the bunkers, in rat holes and snake pits to fit the little turds who were not afraid to die for their emperor. At least, they said so and put on a public show.

He remembered a number of them not so anxious to go to Jap paradise. It was when they looked into the eyes of the *yonsei* who ate heads, the one known as He Who Will Not Die. That *yonsei* was out of place as a battalion CO in the forefront of a conventional seaborne attack, but there had been no other way to get quickly back to combat. Away from Hawaii, away from Susie Lokomaikai.

For shipping orders, he'd had to argue briefly

with Crusty Carlisle, but the old hard-nose had finally given in. General Belvale would have been tougher to bypass.

Crunching coral sand beneath his dripping boots, he strode up to the thin and leafless trunks of trees toothpicked bare by the pre-landing barrage. The area stank of burned things—black powder, bark, maybe a Jap cooked by a flamethrower and not yet swollen out of his raggedy uniform.

His radioman panted up beneath the SCR-300, and Keenan reached out to help the kid with his load. "We set up battalion CP here—for now."

A company commander—Flynn? Finn?—sloshed up, wet to his belly button. Keenan hadn't had time to print all the names of his officers on his mind. "Straight ahead, Captain, until you run into serious opposition. Don't try to bull your way through. Dig in and wait for Baker and Charley companies to come up on your flanks. Let me know when you're in position."

"You got it, sir."

They came past him then, sloshing and dog-trotting, fresh-faced kids tasting their first combat and worn veterans of other landings, their cynical eyes hooded in faces of Atabrine tan. Appointed company runners dropped off and used their entrenching tools to start a perimeter. Battalion medics moved close on the right flank to set up the aid station. Their men dug in and checked their weapons, too. They knew that Japs didn't respect the Red Cross armband, and they recalled the grisly stories about them slaughtering wounded men in other aid stations. In his own way, Keenan accepted the Jap point of view: you killed the little shits anytime and anywhere you could, the sick, lame and lazy included. Hell, they expected it.

Going down on one knee, Keenan slid back the bolt of his M-1 and blew sand off it, possibly imaginary sand. He was a little tense, too conscious of the hairs on his forearms as individual drops of sweat gathered at their roots. Unhooking one canteen from his web belt, he burrowed it into loose, damp sand to cool. A stray bullet whined high, and the new guys pulled in their heads. Without glancing up, the older ones continued to dig.

Keenan drew in a great breath of soggy air. Try as he might, he couldn't keep Susie out of his mind. Her name was Hawaiian, and she hadn't told him she was a Jap; neither had Nancy mentioned it, like it wasn't important. What the hell did they think they were doing, hiding something that vital? Maybe Susie didn't believe she'd done anything wrong. He remembered that stricken look on her face when he slammed out of her house. Through her Jap-style house with its paper doors, through the ghosts of her kind, the shades of other Japs without heads.

Prang!

Light caliber, a sniper too scared to zero in properly, firing quickly and ducking back into cover. He would be shot out of his nest before long. Keenan made sure that the CP was as solid as it could be made by nightfall—one 81mm mortar and two 60mms settled in, radio and sound power phones protected by sandbags, communication established with the line companies and with the regiment, passwords and signals set with the aid station on his right.

Night came suddenly, a sheet of humid blackness flung across the island, further blinding troops already drawn tight as piano wires. The first panic firing began in Fox Company—the single pop of a carbine; then the ka-chungs of M-1s as other jittery riflemen joined in. The Japs wanted that, so they could easily mark GI positions for a night attack.

He touched his radioman on the shoulder. "All companies cease firing except for clear sight targets."

It would be a hell of a good time for an attack, catching line units not yet safely dug in, confusing green troops into climbing from their foxholes or trying to hide deep and passive.

They screamed down the beach—*"Banzai! Banzai!"*—not expected from that direction, and overran a startled beach party.

Keenan shouted, "Left flank! Turn those machine guns this way. Mortars, hang tight! Too many GIs over there."

Too damned many Japs, too. So black that the muzzle flashes didn't show who was who. A formless shadow shrilled out of the dark and slammed Keenan to the ground. The Jap stank, his sweat greasy. Keenan's grip tore away the shirt, and the Jap bit him on the shoulder. No goddamn bayonet or samurai sword; whichever, it must have been dropped when the bastard banged into him. Then they had each other by the wrists, twisting and straining as they kicked the ground of the CP.

With a surge of power Keenan got his thumb hooked into an eye socket and bore down. The Jap shrieked and bit him again, this time locking on to the soft flesh of his throat. It hurt like hell and might reach the carotid. He jabbed hard with his thumb and jerked the other hand free. Both hands on the little bastard's head, Keenan pried him off his throat and rolled over to jam his knee into the crotch.

Both knees braced on the squirming body, Keenan kept twisting the head to the right and up. The Jap's hands flailed at him, then fell away as he jerked sharply and the neck broke with a wet pop. Keenan rolled the body aside. They were all over the CP, screaming and firing. In a close-up muzzle flash, he saw a peaked cap and used the butt of his M-1 to smash the head it rode.

Almost as swiftly as it had begun, the CP firefight stopped. Keenan gave it a few minutes before rising to his feet and calling for a head count. "Yo," they came back at him, "yo!" Not enough answers, the response thinned by losses.

Climbing from his hole, Keenan made a slow and careful tour of his defenses, hissing the night's password, the one with all the *l*'s that Japs weren't supposed to be able to pronounce: "la-la-pa-loo-za."

At the left limit of the perimeter the brush thickened. Keenan helped a GI roll two more sandbags to the lip of his hole. Then he turned back, moving quickly until he suddenly crouched as his old jungle warning system kicked in.

Too late.

CHAPTER 23

REUTERS—Guam, July 23, 1944: Refusing to acknowledge the inevitable, Japanese forces have attacked American lines with pitchforks, empty bottles and baseball bats.

American officers described the results as carnage.

Keenan Carlisle's head throbbed him about half awake, worse than any hangover. He lay in a natural dip in the ground, its size enlarged by the strike of a 4.2 mortar shell or something bigger from the ship guns. He tasted smoke and blood. His helmet was gone and when he tried to sit up, he found the heavy trunk of a splintered tree pressing him back.

"It is better not to move."

Keenan's body spasmed end to end as a chill came over him. Somebody in this pile with him? He had no weapon—no rifle, no pistol—and he didn't know where he was on the assault map.

Low and reedy, the voice came again: "You all right, Joe?"

Hell, no, but he had six inches of sharp steel tucked into his left leggin, if he could work it free.

A Jap! He was pinned in this shit pile with a fucking Jap, an English-speaking Jap. He felt the man's knee touch him from behind.

"I have my officer's small pistol," the Jap said. "I will not use it unless you attempt to call out to your patrols."

The guy was hurt; how badly, there was no way of knowing for sure. Dark, it was so damned dark. Keenan tried again to lift the load across him. He strained until withheld air burst from him and he fell back panting.

Why hadn't the Jap blown a hole in him? Maybe he didn't have a pistol, as he claimed. The way Keenan was pinned, he couldn't twist around far enough to find out. At times he could feel the hot breath of the Jap on the nape of his neck. Tensing all over, he thought that this was a chickenshit way to die.

Maybe he could strangle the bastard. He tried to roll toward the man this time, a move that would put them belly to belly. Only partially turned, he felt a broken stub threaten his throat. Pinned down again, he made out some of the Jap's face, blurred by closeness. Damn, he was married to the son of a bitch.

The Jap said, "It is strange. We can only kill each other, and according to which army comes along. I would expect no mercy if you are alive when your army come; the same would apply to my soldiers."

Worming an aching shoulder deeper into the sand, Keenan said, "Mercy, my ass; as merciful as a samurai sword. My men will blow off your head. Educated in the States, you little shit? And you pay us back this way."

"I returned to Hiroshima for the death of my father. I was not allowed to leave."

The man stirred, and Keenan tried a slow contracting of his upper body. He could almost reach the shaft of his fighting knife. Almost.

Wiggling again, Keenan felt the cold mouth of a gun nuzzle his neck. The Jap wasn't bluffing; he had a grip on one of the 8mm Shiki Kenjus, some-times carried by high-ranking Japs in addition to the long samurai blade.

Keenan said, "Whether I'm dead or alive won't make a difference. My men will kill you either way."

"Ahh," sighed the Jap, and Keenan thought he could hear pain in the sound. Maybe the guy was hurt inside, crushed beneath Keenan and the weight of the fallen tree.

"Ahh, as your men are trained to do. As mine are trained. Is this not of some importance to you and me?"

Keenan's shoulder ached, but he moved it an-other half inch, nostrils flared at the musky odor of the man. "My job is to kill Japs."

"As mine is to die for my emperor."

"Be glad to help you."

It was a chuckle; Keenan couldn't believe it, but the Jap had laughed. Everything was screwed up: he was crammed helplessly into this hole with an English-speaking Jap, a Jap with a sense of humor.

And one holding a pistol?

The man said, "I have water, ahh—if I can reach around . . ."

Water would be good. Keenan lay twisted and hurting and thought of cold, clear water; he thought of lying still on the beach with Susie Lolo-maikai as soft, cooling wind kissed along their bod-ies. He thought of this goddamn Jap acting human while trying to get his pistol into position to shoot Keenan in the heart. But he already had a perfect head shot. What the hell? Sighing a gob of released air, Kennan stretched his arm, trying to touch the shaft of the knife in his leggin. He could almost grip it in his extended fingers.

"Ahh, here it is. If you will turn your head . . ."

Mouth distorted and tongue stretched, Keenan lapped at the trickle of sour water as if it were the finest champagne. What was with this little bastard? Was he fattening him for the kill?

The guy quivered and Keenan said, "Are you hit?"

"Ahh, I think so. I cannot feel my leg."

"Your legs are still there. Probably just numb."

By a quirk of shell burst, they had become body-connected Siamese brothers, drawn mentally closer by their weapons. Tired and aching, Keenan dozed off now and again, only to jerk awake in a sweat of fear. The Jap hadn't moved. Maybe he couldn't. Was that gun blocked somehow? The little bastard could be using this enforced truce as an exquisite modification of slow torture.

Keenan reached his finger farther around the hilt of his fighting knife. A sudden desperate lunge and he might pull it free before the Jap fired.

Scratchy voiced, and as if he were talking to himself, the Jap said, "I was to bring a prisoner for information. I can—ahh—never become an officer because I was educated by my country's enemies and because my father was only a poor—ahh—fisherman, and so I found you . . . before the shelling."

The man stopped whispering, and Keenan heard something else: the muffled tread of a patrol slipping through the jungle. He scrambled for his knife and fought it loose.

The Jap murmured, "Imperial troops. Remain very quiet."

"You," Keenan hissed. "You must stay quiet or I'll cut off your goddamn head."

A lame threat and the Jap must have known it. Any second now he would yell or shoot or both. Either way, Keenan's ass was grass.

Good-bye, Chang Yen Ling. Sorry Susie. . . . Soft noise by muted sound, the patrol passed, so close that he smelled them, the different kind of man-sweat on the Japs, the stench of their jungle-rotted uniforms. One peep from Keenan's Jap and they would be all over him, slashing and stabbing. The man didn't try to call out a warning, and the patrol slid away in the night.

"Joe—ahh, Joe . . ."

"They're gone. What the hell? Why didn't you yell and have them kill me or shoot me yourself?"

Smaller than Keenan had expected, the Jap shuddered and worked his narrow chest for air.

"I wish I could have remained in San . . . Francisco. Ahh . . . but there is always duty."

The voice shriveled away to threads, and the body seemed flatter. "Duty leads me to my death. Ahh, but this is not so for you. *Mizzu*—water; my *sayonara* gift. . . ."

Then his words slid off and he stopped talking, stopped everything.

Scratching and twisting, Keenan struggled to free himself. It bothered him to think that the Jap had been almost human. Because the pistol was real, cupped in the small-boned hand.

NORTH AMERICAN NEWSPAPER ALLIANCE—The South Pacific, August 10, 1944: American troops completed their occupation of Guam today, sweeping enemy resistance before them. Guam is one of the largest Japanese positions anywhere, and a giant step closer to Tokyo.

Prior to the landings nearly three weeks ago, American planes dropped 627 tons of bombs and 176 rockets on the enemy fortifications. Spokesmen said the Japanese still had pockets of resistance.

Gavin Scott brought his P-38 Lightning to a stop on the runway, feather light because of the case of beer on his lap. Take it up pee-warm and bring it down icy from 20,000 feet, and everybody loved you for it.

That was about all this jungle-happy outfit liked about him. Well, screw them; it was their jealousy of the hottest pilot in the theater, not counting Pappy Boyington of the U.S. Marines. If the Japs lasted long enough, Gavin would catch up with him, too. The word was that Boyington was a roaring drunk, so his reflexes must be slowing by now and some sharp Zero pilot would nail him.

Setting the plane down with the lightest of touches, he rolled it close to the so-called tower, a jury-rigged construction of light logs. The strip itself was a mess, damned near inoperable after a rainstorm, turning to a bottomless mud that dragged heavily upon wheels and slowed liftoff.

When Gavin first arrived out here, nobody warned him of anything or offered little tips on surviving. The other pilots acted as if he had come to them through some kind of game preserve, some spit-shined and upholstered field for the pampered few seeking win-the-war publicity.

He slid his canopy back as two mechanics, shirtless and burned brown over their shoulder tattoos, climbed in tandem to relieve him of the beer.

"Thanks, Captain. Better drink yours now; it heats up real quick."

A church key popped a hole in the lid on the cold sweating Schlitz, and Gavin couldn't make himself go slow; it was so damned good, so cold. For a moment he wished himself back in civilization. The muggy green heat and cloying stench of the jungle closed around him when he lifted from the cockpit. A reporter from *Stars & Stripes, Pacific* was supposed to interview him today, if he could make all connections to get through to this forward field.

The other pilots wouldn't like it, of course, any more than they liked him operating more or less as his own command. He should give a damn? He wasn't here to shoot up troop barges or strafe plodding freighters; he had come here to shoot down Japs, to have little Rising Sun emblems painted beneath the swastikas already there. Only two red assholes so far, and he'd had to search far afield for those.

Striding across the now dusty field, he again thanked Colonel Luther Farrand for arranging his transfer. "Tell it to the chaplain" was no joke when that sky pilot had a connection in the War Department almost as powerful as the Belvales and Carlisles and, in time, maybe more so. Something political was stirring in Washington, and it would pay to be on the winning side when the smoke of an ancient feud cleared.

CHAPTER 24

Berliner Illustrierte Zeitung—Aug. 7, 1944: Among the proud ranks of heroes of the Third Reich a new name has risen—that of Oberfeldwebel Arno Hindemit.

The *feldwebel* has more than once, above and beyond the call of duty, risked his life in order to save officers important to the Führer's military plans. This time the officer whose life was preserved is Colonel Rudolph Schmundt, from a financially powerful family that has stood always at Führer's elbow in time of need.

Departing from army tradition, the presentation of the Knight's Cross to Oberfeldwebel Hindemit, is a decoration usually reserved for officers. For his bravery and loyalty the senior sergeant has been returned to Berlin to take his place among the Führer's personal guards.

No bomb or artillery devastation he had seen before prepared Arno for the battered look of Berlin: the rail cars and their iron lines twisted among the high-piled rubble that blocked the lengths of the entire streets. Old *landser* that he was, he might have expected the ruins, but heretofore the damage had always been in someone else's city, the destruction done to someone else's home. He could only feel that this would get worse. The lin-

gering pall of smoke was sour, greasy and somehow dusty. Ragged carpets of shattered glass
reflected the dimmed sun.

Fat Hermann's great invisible Luftwaffe allowed
the Tommis and Amis to bomb Berlin by day and
night. And since the Allies were now dug in on a
solid line across half of France and Italy, could
invasion of the fatherland be far away?

Scheissen! This was sliding quickly on the downhill side of time, but what was a man of honor to
do about that? Arno must hold to himself or become less a man. Even if he was tempted to run,
there was no place to go.

He was awkward in a black uniform that stank
of mothballs, mold and perhaps some residue of
the former owner. Luckily there were no bullet
holes. Slinging his field gear over one shoulder,
Arno followed the SS *leutnant* along a path that
snaked through small hills of bricks and masonry.
Here was the holy of holies, the Führer's bastion
in the rubble of Berlin. Hitler's command bunker
was somewhere above this patch of battered land,
policed and tightly guarded in ring after defensive
ring. Where Arno walked now was the outer perimeter. He would probably never see Germany's
leader. He had never seen Hitler in the flesh, and
it had not bothered him.

He had gotten along without that so far.

The guard barracks had been dug into a slope of
land and hidden to the smoky sky by camouflage
netting and more well placed rubble. It would be
difficult to find from the air.

The Waffen SS, he thought: the *Schutzstaffel* of
the death's-heads and double lightning flashes. The
bastards. Arno's blood type was newly and sorely
tattooed in his left armpit; only the SS ordered
that, their quick recovery more important than simple line troops.

Now he was forced to stand beside them, but

he would never be one of them—the fanatics, the murderers. They soldiered on the lines only when called in to plug some desperate tactical hole. Once they had been elite fighting troops; now they were reduced to butchers eager to bloody their knives with traitors, slave laborers and malingerers in the rear area. They were the mailed fist of the Gestapo, also in the rear to glut themselves upon foe and condemned friend alike.

Schutzstaffel Obergeldwebel Arno Hindemit: it did not sound proper.

Ducking, he stooped through the heavy beam doorway where sentries lolled at either side, boots propped up and Schmeissers lying casually at their sides. Arno now packed one of those, so new that flecks of packing grease still clung to it. But the fit and feel of it was different, not as comforting and familiar as the worn weapon he had depended on for the last five years.

It had been blown to hell in the same firefight that slowly killed Hauptmann Witzelei, schoolmaster. That old friend also had been comforting and familiar, and his death still made an empty place in Arno.

Inside, in the echo of barked *attention!*, the *leutnant* announced Arno's name and rank, pointed to a bare bunk, spun on his heel and stalked out.

"What have we here?" A scar-faced sergeant said. "Let me see— Ah yes! We have the hero of the Third Reich descending among us peasants."

Pushing by, Arno placed his gear on the bunk and sat beside it. The squad room was brightly lit, despite the brownout across the city, and men lounged in it, reading, smoking, arguing; two of the SS men shared a bottle of schnapps. The perfume of cheese and sausage wrinkled Arno's nose. The SS were the favored in all things.

Scarface would not let it drop. "Well, hero, please demonstrate for us how to be brave."

Schmeisser and cleaning rags pulled across his lap, Arno looked up without saying anything.

"Come now," Scarface said. "Do tell us how to kiss ass and be promoted and then admired by all the *frauleins.*"

Arno didn't move until Scarface climbed off the cot and leaned over him. Then he hooked the toe of his right boot behind the *schwein*'s heel and slammed his left foot against the knee. Scarface's ass jarred the floor, and his mouth gaped wide. Arno swung up and over into a crouch and stuck the muzzle of his Schmeisser into that mouth, careless of the teeth.

He said, "Do not fuck with me again."

The bunkhouse went quiet, men looking this way and that, nobody staring at the man on the floor. Arno sat down and wiped spittle from the muzzle of his Schmeisser, then went about field-stripping and oiling the weapon, one eye on Scarface as the man struggled up.

"A-all right, all right," Scarface said. "There will come a time, hero."

Clicking the magazine into place, Arno said quietly, "My rank is *oberfeldwebel;* use it when you speak to me, you miserable whelp of a diseased bitch. I have buried a dozen men better than you, and I will not mind helping any friend you may have to dig your last shit hole, now or in your imagined future."

Somebody chuckled and someone else said, "Welcome to the Führer's Guard Sergeant."

SHAEF HQ, London—Sept. 29, 1944: War News Summary—Enemy withdrawals were reported in the Arnhem area of Holland as U.S. paratroopers fought their way out of the bridge pocket there.

The U.S. Third Army delivered combined land and

air blows at the fortifications defending Metz, and there was little change in the Aachen area.

In the Pacific, Australian-based planes flew more than 3,000 miles to deliver the first blow of the war to Batavia in Java. Only one mountain and a small area of land remain in Japanese hands.

Eddie Donnely watched the neat rhythm of the nurse's hips moving within the thin shell of her starched white uniform. Her thighs whispered one against the other, softly spoken by the rubbing of nylon, the just-before-wartime invention that had fast taken the place of silk stockings. A good thing, too; Jap silkworms had a lock on the silk market, except for the Chinese worms, and they were kept busy trying to stay a wiggle ahead in that part of the war.

The stockings had cost Eddie a goodly bit of the money that had been piling up at Finance since he returned to the theater. It wasn't all that much, he admitted; the bulk of his pay went home in an allotment—not that Gloria needed it. But it was theirs, no dime owed to the family fortunes.

And no, not home—just to Gloria; they didn't have a home yet. The frowning fortress of Sandhurst Keep would never feel comfortable to Eddie, and he had seen too many ragged-assed, overpriced apartments sprout near army posts. He and Gloria would work something out, something better to fit them both. Before, he had never thought of a wife following him from post to post, but in Big Mike Donnely's time, there wasn't much roving around. You practically had to re-up to pick a new post, and then see if the CO there would accept you.

(*Barracks talk: You shipping out? When you get to Cash Street in Panama—and you will—watch out for all those great whores and cheap booze. The cross-bred kids say, "Gimme something, dogface, no mama, no papa, no Uncle Sam." You say, "Get the fuck out of here, you little bastard." And if you did a hitch there before, he might be yours.)*

Caught in the trail of Sister Tina's faint perfume, he drifted in its wake to Schofield Barracks and more Spartan posts. Wherever, there were always women to be found, and often without searching.

Gloria—as usual, the army had scared the hell out of her with its dire telegram, but her high-brass clout had gotten a call through to here. Though tiny and far away, her voice had held that special thready tone that always shook him a bit. "I'm okay," he had told her. "I'm doing fine; not crippled up. I'll be back on duty in a month or so. A furlough home? I don't think so, darling."

She could no doubt persuade old Crusty Carlisle to stretch regulations and bring him back, probably for the rest of the war. But that wasn't for Eddie; he wouldn't give the Carlisles any other reason to look down on him. Come down to it, in reality an infantry sergeant should outrank anything to the rear, no matter the brass. His was an immediate command over life and death.

He thought of Gloria—her scented skin like fine satin, the shape and dampness of her body—and his groin stirred. He needed her.

Sitting up in his cot, eyes following Sister Tina Avery's movement through the ward where the post-op patients rested and the walking wounded got back into shape through physiotherapy. Sweet, hesitant Sister Tina; that was what the Aussies called their military nurses: sister or sister of mercy?

Tina wore his gift, a much better thing for her than painting her legs tan and drawing black lines on them to simulate seams. He couldn't have reached an Australian woman with anything better.

When she accepted his gift, Eddie checked around to line up a meeting place for them; it was still officer and enlisted man.

But still man and woman.

Shifting his legs to the side of the bed, Eddie helped the heavy one with his hands. The right leg was weighted by a thick plaster cast, as was his right arm to the elbow. It was the new English-Australian wound treatment system: dig out bullet or fragment, stitch, bandage lightly and spoon on a cast. It was supposed to keep out bad bugs and, by holding the area still, to speed recovery. It might even work, but in the meantime, the awkward weight was always in his way. He would devise a system to overcome that, with the help of Sister Tina Avery.

And Gloria?

He pushed aside a dull edge of guilt; he would be faithful when he was with her. Being a world away and being wounded made a difference. Combat did something to the body that was stronger than the mind could handle. Maybe it was the powerful basic drive of a threatened species aroused to defend itself, to produce the young needed to replace too-quick losses, and they would be mostly boy babies. The species would live through to the next war.

CHAPTER 25

War News Summary—War Department, Washington, D.C., Sept. 30, 1944: In Italy, the 5th Army battled to regain heights below Bologna that were lost in counterattacks, while the 8th Army cleared the south bank of the Rubicon River.

In the Pacific, of 100 superfortresses, not a single one was lost in raids on enemy targets in Manchuria.

In Washington, leading government officials warned that the surface of Japan's ability to resist has barely been scratched. They reiterated that the enemy in the Pacific has sufficient resources to fight on for years.

In the Netherlands, a combined American-British airborne operation slowed and pulled back to strengthen its lines.

Preston Belvale propped his foot on a chair and rubbed his game leg. The Teletype had fallen silent for a change and no phones rang. The war room at Kill Devil Hill continued to operate, but it was quieter than usual.

A soft glow of desk lights played into the sorrel-blond hair of Adria and Joann as they bent over their files; their coloring was the same, this mother and daughter. Their loss was about the same, also. Husband and father, Major Dan Belvale had quickly fallen in the Pacific, too soon after son and brother Lieutenant Walt Belvale became the first family casualty of the war.

Stepping down, Belvale knuckled his mustache and moved over to where Adria sat. A half-smile lighted her face as she looked up. So badly hurt, Adria had slowly recovered to hold her place in the family. For a while there in the memorial grove, where services were held for her missing son, she had almost lost it, hating the army and blaming the family more. But like all the Carlisle-Belvale women, she had a special inner strength. The nonsense coming out of the War Department about Farley and about the misuse of family influence had not ruffled her.

It had devastated Minerva, but soon she raised her hackles and sharpened her claws. She visited or invited every old-money old family in Virginia and points south, calling in favors and gathering power for a counterattack.

He asked Adria, "Notice any difference in the reports lately?"

Adria continued to look at him. "Not quite as happy-happy?"

Joann stopped writing. "It feels funny—as if we're being warned of a coming disaster, but not openly."

Belvale said, "No major disaster yet, but bad enough. Cousin Ben Alexander says the War Department won't admit that the operation at Arnhem was a holy mess. Eight thousand men jumped on that bridge; only two thousand got out. We took about three thousand KIA and left twelve hundred wounded behind."

Adria's face tightened. "What happened?"

"A bridge too far, a lack of solid information, hurry-up efforts to win it all now. It was something they couldn't blame on the family. The enemy isn't finished; he's a damn sight more vicious with his back against the wall and fighting on his own land.''

"The children," Joann said. "The Germans are drafting kids ten and twelve years old."

"And grandfathers," Adria added.

"The sick and the lame," Belvale said. "The Gestapo took care of the lazy a long time back. The Germans are desperate, but Hitler is still in firm control. There won't be a mutiny by the military, especially since any officer remotely suspected in the Hitler assassination attempt was executed. That cost him many of his best tactical commanders.

"And only the blind fanatic doesn't realize that the Russians are close to knocking on the back door. When the Krauts fold, they will try to surrender to us. They know what awaits them if the Russians grab them. They brought it on themselves, following Hitler's orders to treat the Russians like lower animals. Kee-rist, at first the mistreated peasants were so sick of Moscow that they were eager to join the invaders, but not after word got out. Now they know they might as well die fighting.''

He moved back across the room and looked up at the ETO map. It had been rough, advancing through those miserable hedgerows in France. Every report pointed out the yard-by-pounding-yard battle that it took to grind through the thick stone and tree-rooted barriers. Even light tanks were at times held up by the ancient fences that separated the fields.

The GIs plodded on through mines, booby traps and dug-in Germans; they took brutal casualties and kept going. Painfully, stubbornly, they kept going, these incredibly tough Regular Army soldiers and the hardening draftees. Beautiful bastards, in the end better fighting men than the fiercely disciplined Nazi troops and their less willing allies.

Spread through every combat zone, the Carlisles and Belvales did their duty as fighting men, not desk commandos like Skelton and his cronies. In every war there were some rear echelon would-be soldiers not worth their salt. Ben Alexander was working on the present problem, ferreting out any detail, and Crusty Carlisle was bulling his way through Washington even now.

ASSOCIATED PRESS—The Philippine Islands, Oct. 20, 1944: Two years and six months after General Douglas MacArthur vowed, "I shall return," he announced that his troops, under strong air and ship-to-shore cover, had landed on the east coast of Leyte.

Monitored Japanese broadcasts listed at least three landings, all in the central sector, where American attackers could divide the island's estimated 150,000 defenders.

President Roosevelt's communication said in part: "You have the nation's gratitude for success as you and your men fight your way back to Bataan."

Lieutenant Nancy Carlisle sat with Penny Belvale and Kirstin Shelby in the always noisy PX coffee shop at Letterman General Hospital. The coffee-and-doughnut smell clotted the air, and the jukebox thumped "The Cow-Cow Boogie," with Ella Mae Morse rocking the lyrics.

Nancy said, "Crusty Carlisle is a hell of a man to have on our side. I never saw anyone so thoroughly cowed. Any prayers that chewed-out chaplain says will be for himself."

"In an Alaskan igloo," Penny said. "Where was it—Attu? Kiska?"

Kirstin stirred her coffee. "The most miserable place Crusty could think of, offhand. Wouldn't you know that he would be buddies with the Sixth

Army CG, so the orders could be cut immediately? The good chaplain had no time to squeal for his contacts. He might make it back to Washington before he turns blue, but by then he might know better."

"Crusty knows everybody," Penny added, "and now he knows who was behind all that crap about Farley. All of us figured General Skelton had a hand in Colonel Luther Farrand's plot, but nobody thought his backup was the Speaker of the House."

Nancy lit a cigarette. "Good old Boss Kawley from you-all land. That bastard never does anything for free, according to my earliest major mistake, Congressman Pailey—another son of a bitch. So our Crusty headed for Washington hot on the trail and with his teeth bared."

Leaning forward, Kirstin said, "It was a dirty thing for anybody to try, much less a man of the church. The psychiatrist says Farley's progress has been drastically slowed, if not stopped. Farrand needs stiffer punishment. And what about General Skelton?"

"Crusty won't let him off the hook," Penny said. "Not this time, and if it means meeting Boss Kawley head on, he'll do that, too."

Nancy drew in smoke and let it out gently. It was true that Farley might be a long time shaking off the effects of what Farrand had done. The slimy bastard had made certain that Farley sounded good and looked good before bringing in tame newspapermen to prod him, to know the reason he was sitting out the rest of the war in a hospital. . . .

Had he been severely wounded?

Those were Farrand's words, some of them. The rest were even more cutting, bewildering Farley and making the pack bay louder at him.

No, he had not been wounded. There was nothing wrong with him; he kept telling the doctors that.

Was he a member of the politically powerful, high-ranking Belvale-Carlisle family?

Had they pulled strings in Washington to bring him home and keep him safe?

Your chart says you suffer from battle fatigue. How is that different from shell-shock? How easy is it to fake?

Your aunt is your nurse. How much did she have to do with diagnosing your case? We know she escorted you home instead of staying at her duty post in Hawaii.

Farley flinched as the flashbulbs popped, and muttered that he was being kept away from his wife. . . .

"A full herd of sons of bitches," Nancy said. "The damage had been done before Crusty rode out there in the fastest army plane he could commandeer. General Belvale is being harassed by cheap journalists, and they're digging around for any dirt on the rest of the family. If they find nothing, they'll create some. Some of the general's newer friends suddenly can't be reached."

The family would stand strong, she knew. Technically she was no longer a member, but maybe it was like the saying "Once a marine, always a marine."

Once in the family, you could never shake its values. Even though she was being sniped at, too, Nancy would stand beside her own.

CHAPTER 26

UNITED PRESS—Off Leyte, the Philippine Islands, Oct. 26, 1944: The backbone of the Japanese fleet was smashed today as two strong Imperial forces converged upon Leyte Gulf. They were met by Vice Admiral Thomas Kinkaid's 7th Fleet.

One big Japanese carrier was sunk and two more disabled beyond use; one battleship of the Tomashiro class was sent to the bottom, four others were severely damaged, and several cruisers and destroyers went down. Many ships were hit by bombs and torpedoes. American loss was one aircraft carrier. General Douglas MacArthur said, "The Japanese navy has suffered its most crushing defeat of the war," and President Roosevelt has called a special news conference.

INTERNATIONAL NEWS SERVICE—European Theater of Operations, Nov. 4, 1944: The United States army fought its way back into the rubble-strewn streets of Vossmack today in some of the bitterest street fighting yet.

Three German counterattacks were repulsed. The sixth Army group made important advances in the Vosges Mountains, and in the Netherlands, Allied troops mopped up liberated areas.

Captain Owen Belvale hunkered down in the company command post, head pulled in against the vicious snap and whine of mortar fragments. The hole scraped in icy ground wasn't deep enough, but then, they never were when the shooting started. Newly made Sergeant Weintraub crouched beside him, shielding the precious radio. The company runner, a small man, managed to curl up on the graveled bottom. Owen couldn't remember the replacement's name right off.

There had been too many replacements, too many replacements' names passing swiftly by. Old-timers in his company drew closer together, avoiding intimacy with the new men until they proved trustworthy under fire. Even then, few replacements were drawn into the dwindling heart of the old outfit.

The old hands—and twenty-one-year-old platoon sergeants had the sunken eyes of the old and tired—were the veterans of the Arzew landing and the bloody defeat at Kasserine, of the almost overwhelmed Gela beachhead and the battering of Troina. And then there was Omaha Beach, H hour on D day—a thousand men of the 16th Infantry down in the first hour. It was a wonder any original member was alive, but by some quirk known only to the gods of battle, the replacements had been killed off much quicker.

Many went down at Aachen, the first city to be taken on German soil, and violently defended. It was also the first break in the heralded West Wall, Germany's concrete and steel defense line. The Big Red One solved the problem of the fanatic defenders of Aachen, ordered by Hitler to stand and die. They beat hell out of the town with artillery, tanks and even bombers, when they could call them in.

Then in typical infantry fashion, they had to fight their way in house by house. Owen heard later that two battalions of the troops they faced had been hastily pulled off the Russian front and freshly equipped to throw against them.

KA-WHAM!

"Shit," Weintraub said in the ear-ringing echo, "you'd think them bastards would take a break or run out of ammunition. They're too dumb to know they already lost the war, but even Krauts must need a rest sometime."

Owen tasted the sharpness of smoke as it swirled around them, and his nostrils flared at the all too familiar bite of it. Somewhere ahead, his weapon platoon backed up Second Battalion's rifle companies, and just ahead of the CP, in a narrow gully, the 81 mortars tried counter-battery fire. Their throaty chuff-chuff was reassuring.

Rubbing his hands in the damp, near useless woolen gloves, Owen peered over the top of the hole. Flakes of new snow warned of a bitter winter ahead, and suddenly Owen needed the skin warmth of Helene, that special woman-warmness that nothing else or no one else could match. He needed to bury his face in her hair and feel that tiny body squirm to him, lift to him, as he hid himself in the cave of her flesh.

KA-WHAM!

This time pebbled earth sprayed into the CP, and the concussion slapped Owen's helmet off. He spat out the bitter taste of black dirt and wiped at his face, eyes blurred and ears throbbing.

The company runner was obviously dead, chopped half a head smaller. And Weintraub— Oh, good Christ, Weintraub.

"Medic! Medic!"

Not a lot of blood showing, but Weintraub's narrow face was icy white. Knees propped against the radio, his shoulder angled into the side of the hole, bundled up as he was, he suddenly looked smaller.

He shrank as Owen knelt and ripped at the overcoat, at the field jacket beneath.

"Medic! God damn it! *Medic!*"

The wound whistled and pumped blood—a lung shot. Owen snatched his aid pack and crammed a bandage hard against the hole. The runner's puddling blood was wet and already cold on Owen's knees.

"Son of a bitch went slap through," Weintraub muttered. "Can't plug both holes, Cap'n."

Taking the man's weight across his knees, Owen pulled the thick bandage from Weintraub's packet and fumbled it into the exit hole. The whistling stopped, but the blood continued to soak warm over Owen's hand.

"Hang on, man. God damn it, don't let go."

He looked up at two smeared and bearded faces peering into the CP. One helmet bore a red cross in a dirty white circle. "Drag the other guy out," Owen said. "This man's hit hard."

Weintraub's eyes opened halfway when the medic propped him up and went to work.

"Near good as Mississippi bootleg," Weintraub sighed. "That morphine is mighty fine. Need to figure how to bottle it like white lightning and get rich." His voice was scratchy. "Cap'n, you know I ain't never been much for—for preachers or rabbis neither. Never put a yarmulke on my head . . ."

His eyes closed, and Owen pressed harder on the chest wound while the medic plugged and bound the hole in Weintraub's shoulder blade.

Weintraub wet his lips. When the medic took over the chest wound, Owen got off his knees to squat and put his canteen to Weintraub's mouth. "I wish to Christ it was whiskey," he said.

"Me, too. Cap'n . . . I know there ain't no—no time or way to do it. Ain't no rightful reason, neither, but I wish . . . oh, hell. Tell them I wanted somebody to sit shivah and say Kaddish for me."

His hand clamped around Owen's and then fell away limp.

"He's gone," the medic said. "What was he talking about?"

"Something he missed for most of his life."

Grunting, the medic climbed out of the hole with his kit. "Fucking shame he waited so long. I'll send a couple of stretcher-bearers for him."

A man reached out for something at the time of death, maybe a grip solid enough to hold him here, or for a thing of great importance he had passed by.

To sit shivah, Owen thought—the seven days of family mourning with all mirrors in the house covered? Something like that, and a number of men—he didn't know how many—would come to the house to say Kaddish, the prayer of mourning. He wished Weintraub had told him more about it during those long hours they had spent waiting for something to happen.

Snow came heavy, and Owen washed his bloody gloves in it. His knees were soaked and cold. The enemy mortar fire had stopped.

Cupping his freezing hands around his mouth, he yelled, "Anybody know anything about a radio? I need a man."

He needed Weintraub, the oddball redneck Jew from the deep South who had so much laughter to share, so much comfort to pass on to his buddies. Weintraub wouldn't be back. Maybe nobody would go home again.

INTERNATIONAL NEWS SERVICE: The Hurtgen Forest, Germany, Nov. 20, 1944: Here red and green backdrop dirty snow, but it doesn't look like Christmas. The

red is blood and the green is the cold, gloomy and
treacherous trap of the forest.

It is not primeval, but hand-planted in modern
times by order of the German general staff. Every natural advantage is screened; the thick balsams squat
to block movement through them. Artillery air bursts
hurl jagged splinters from the treetops to mix with
their steel fragments.

Seven infantry divisions and one armored combat
team tried to break the forest; only two seem to be
getting through—the 1st Infantry along the northern
edge and the 78th Infantry aiming for the Rur dams.

Statistics reveal that for every yard gained, the forest
is claiming more lives than any other objective the
Americans took in Europe.

Chad Belvale warmed himself at a small fire of K-
ration boxes and what dry branches could be
found. There was plenty of shattered green wood
around, but it would lift a telltale streamer of
smoke for Kraut guns and mortars to zero in on.
The regimental CP was a cold, damp hole covered
by a squad tent. Operators hunkered over radios,
and officers crowded each other at situation maps.

He stared at a letter that had finally come
through. Kirstin's strong, bold writing was not as
terse as he might have expected. She asked that
he keep her informed about Owen, who was no
letter writer, and told of Farley's problem, in case
Chad hadn't heard. She was righteously bitter
about the dirty tricks set up by Luther Farrand
and company. Chad marked that sneaky bastard
down in his payoff book, if there was anything left
of him after Crusty Carlisle and Preston Belvale
got through with him.

"Please," Kirstin wrote, "take care of yourself;
don't play the hero." She signed only her name,

no "with love." At least she hadn't used the cold and standard "sincerely." He had no reason to expect "with love." Kirstin was honest. She still had memories of their years together, a blood bond through their sons, and perhaps a little tenderness was left over. It was so with him, and maybe more than a little, if space remained beyond his need for Stephanie Bartlett.

Chad realized how lucky he was to have known both women, and luckier yet that they had loved him.

"Colonel?" Captain Finn was Chad's G-3, a small and intense man with a quick grin. "The Forty-seventh Infantry from the Ninth Division is attached to us and in place. You know division's plan for us to lead the way from Schevenhutte toward Munich. We're on line and ready."

"Okay. It's going to be a bitch struggling through that sloppy mud with tanks, much less the trucks. The Krauts have excellent OPs, as usual, and we'll catch hell from eighty-eights and mortars."

Finn flashed his grin. "So what's new?"

"Only the faces, Captain, only the new young faces."

CHAPTER 27

NORTH AMERICAN NEWSPAPER ALLIANCE—The Ardennes Forest, December 17, 1944: It was considered impossible, but the Germans never hear that. The entire Ardennes front is in chaos as enemy divisions strike viciously beneath snowy skies to smash back stunned American troops. Two veteran and two untried U.S. divisions are battling for their lives against this totally unexpected attack. Brutal winter weather and a low ceiling have halted direct air support, and German armor is rolling almost unobstructed.

Intelligence sources reported the enemy incapable of this kind of strong offense and too badly mauled to be thinking in such ambitious terms.

A special force of English-speaking Germans wearing American uniforms and driving captured vehicles, is leading the drive. They infiltrate behind Allied lines, change directional signs, blow up communication centers and ammo dumps and murder soldiers who welcome them.

Lieutenant Sloan Travis shoveled in beside his fifth squad gun, cold wet snow swirling around the position. Sixth squad was somewhere off the right flank, mixed with the beat-up survivors of Fox Company. The other guns and 81s were supporting

Easy and George companies, both unseen, since the Kraut tanks crashed through the forest with all guns blazing. From time to time sharp firefights broke out ahead and on the flanks, stopping as quickly as they began.

Corporal Ed Barker blew on his hands. "Colder than a witch's tit, sir. Any news on the radio?"

Sloan stuck the entrenching shovel into the front of his hole. "It's situation normal, all fucked up—only worse than ever. The Krauts have jammed some radio frequencies and crossed over into others, passing along phony orders. Some of the bastards were ODs and speak English. The best we can do is keep our heads down and wait."

"Sure," the gunner said—Sanford, Sutter?—"and wait for them goddamn tanks to run all over us."

On cue a motor rumbled down the frozen roadway to the left front where the pines grew thickest.

"Oh, shit," the gunner said, and swung the muzzle of the water-cooled .30 to cover the road. "I don't know if this mother is frozen."

"If it is," Ed Barker said, "just piss on the water jacket and thaw it out."

"Does that work?"

"What I hear."

"I may not have any piss left. Some of it's running down my leg."

Sloan squinted down the barrel of his carbine; snow swirled around the dark pines as a darker shape bulked into sight. Not a tank, but the familiar outline of a deuce-and-a-half, its canvas cover on.

"Hold your fire!" he called, and peered at the bumper markings—the 104th Infantry Division, one of the new outfits on line. This was a hell of a way to receive their baptism of fire.

Standing up, he lined his sights on the windshield and yelled: "Hold that truck!"

It braked immediately and the rider climbed down; the driver followed. The passenger wore a dirty field jacket, the dull gold bar of a second john showing, hands in his jacket pockets. The driver was a PFC, his neck pulled deep into his overcoat collar, his helmet dented and blackened by cook fires. Both men looked legitimate.

The lieutenant walked toward Sloan. "Hundred and fourth division. We're lost. Back at the crossroads, some stupid MP pointed us this way. Do you know where our CP is?"

Sloan lowered the carbine only a little. "Do you know Lana Turner?"

"I would like to, but I am no movie star. Lieutenant, what the hell—"

Four men climbed down from the back of the truck.

Sloan said, "Gunner, keep an eye on those guys," and to the officer, "Who holds the home run record, Joe DiMaggio or Ty Cobb?"

"Damn it, Lieutenant, I have no time for this horse shit—Joe DiMaggio, okay? Now will you point us right?"

"Keep your hands where I can see them! Both of you! Gunner, cover."

The lieutenant swept a .45 from his jacket. Sloan shot him twice and nailed the driver in mid-body, spinning him onto the city road. Grenades fell out of his overcoat. The four men at the tailgate of the truck scattered, firing M-1s.

Sloan yelled: "Fire, God damn it—fire!"

Late, the .30 caliber took off, skipping bullets off the Dodge, off the roadway. The gun stopped. On his knees in the foxhole, Sloan triggered the rest of his clip below the truck bed and ducked to heel in a fresh one.

Barker's scream tore from his throat. "You bastards! You got Sutter—you bastards!"

The gun hammered again as Barker pulled the

gunner's body away and rolled behind the tripod. Aimed low and deadly, the bullets raked below the truck and spanged holes through the body and tires. A snowy branch fell off a pine tree. Behind Sloan, the rest of the squad took up the fire, carbines banging.

That odd puddle of combat silence spread suddenly as all weapons fell quiet for a moment. Through it, a man shouted: "Okay, okay! Coming out—don't shoot!"

"Hold your fire!" Sloan yelled.

Grimy snow streaked the long OD overcoat and clung to the wool cap. The man held his hands high. "I give up; I surrender."

"Are you the only one left?"

"Yes. The others are dead. I wear my own uniform beneath this one. I am entitled to treatment as a prisoner of war."

The slamming of the machine gun made Sloan flinch, and he tasted the tart blue flavor of the gunsmoke. A hail of bullets chopped down the German, tearing at his body and rolling him in the snow.

"Bastard," Ed Barker said. "What the fuck made him think he could just walk away?"

Carefully Sloan stood up, eyes searching the stand of dark pines beyond the truck. "He would have been shot as a spy anyway. The outside uniform counts."

"I'm glad I nailed his ass first. Lieutenant?"

"Yeah."

"I ain't no baseball fan. Who does hold the home run record?"

"Guy named Ruth—Babe Ruth. Like the candy bar. That wasn't all, though. His English was too damned good, too precise."

"Suppose that Kraut wasn't no baseball fan, neither? Suppose he knew about Babe Ruth? Tough shit, right? We had to do it quick, on account of not wanting to fire on those GI uniforms got old Sutter killed.''

Lord, Sloan thought, the American soldier turned into a cold son of a bitch when he was pushed.

The company runner slid panting up to the gun, breath cloud steaming around his head. ''Lieutenant, shit's hitting the fan everywhere. Everybody shooting at everybody else, with those fucking Krauts in American uniforms. I goddamn near got my ass shot off getting up here, and had to hide out for a while. You got orders to report to battalion, but anybody with good sense ain't moving.''

''I agree,'' Sloan muttered, and wondered what the hell now. He hadn't wanted to be a soldier in the first place, but now that he had been dragged into the army, he ought to be allowed to do his job.

Friggin' battalion; this mess in the Ardennes was far from over, and his men were more important than whatever bullshit the battalion had cooked up.

CHAPTER 28

ASSOCIATED PRESS—The Philippine Islands, Jan. 1, 1945: To deceive the Japanese about the timing of the upcoming invasion of Luzon, American troops carried out mopping-up operations on Mindoro. Feints and nuisance raids are under way in the southern part of Luzon.

Eddie Donnely itched—in his crotch, under his arms and chin. If he could lie bare-assed in the sun for a while, the heat rash would dry up. But any die-hard Jap sniper would love to zero in on that. This island campaign was officially at an end, but the holdout Japs didn't care about that. Theirs was to do and die for their bucktoothed emperor in Tokyo, and so be guaranteed a place among the warm geishas and hot sake in warriors' heaven. To be sure of a good seat, he should take a *gaijun*—any round-eyed foreigner—with him.

(Barracks talk: If you're getting your ass kicked, go down swinging.)

There was nothing mystic about that, but it probably worked for Japs, too.

The goddamn jungle rot had come creeping back, attacking his toes and trying to get into his ears. So far he had fought that off, scrubbing into his ear channels with his fingers or twisted bits of brush, and if he got around the medics, alcohol swabs were a help.

"Happy New Year, Sergeant," Captain Destefano said. "I'd imagine that hospital in Aussie Land looks better all the time. It figures that you don't ride with both feet in the stirrups, or you'd be at stacked arms in Melbourne or, God forbid, even San Francisco."

He tweaked a little black and silver mustache, a man not long out of OCS at Fort Benning, but proven solid in combat. "I'm damned glad to have you in my outfit, but how many GIs go AWOL from the hospital and return to the jungle?"

Scratching, Eddie watched the tree line across a field plowed for a spring planting that might never happen. "Had a hell of a time finding the outfit, and then I didn't see familiar faces."

"We all go," the captain said, "quicker than one by one, the dead and the wounded. You're the only man to come back, so far."

(Barracks talk: The hole in his head matches the one in his ass.)

There was no use trying to explain why he went over the hill from the hospital and back into combat. Eddie wasn't that much of a hero. It was difficult for him to face the reasons. He wasn't familiar with the guilt that sawed at him after a lovely weekend with the sweet Aussie nurse. Sister Tina had a streak of innocence and shyness that delighted him.

She was soft and pliable, and when he kissed her polished white body from throat to belly, he knew she had never known that kind of love. Tina struggled a little, but he gently pinned her hands and continued, slow and probing and finally penetrating. Her faint screams were half sobs as she let herself go, surrending fully to him and admitting to a secret inner self.

Later in that first night Tina hesitantly took the initiative, at times turning her face away from him, even in the dark. Still later, after they drank some golden wine, she turned on the bed lamp and smiled like a mischievous girl. In their days together, Tina became a marvelous lover, a woman freed of ancient, throttling mores.

After the weekend passed, though, Eddie slowly went downhill. There had been moments when Tina's eyes became Gloria's, times when a sensuous move was Gloria's, when the flavor of Gloria overlaid Tina's silvered sweat.

Shortly after the casts were removed, Eddie equipped himself through an agreeable supply sergeant and took off. The newest latrine rumor had shipping orders being cut dated three days ahead, and Eddie wasn't ready to go home. For the first time, he wouldn't be sure of himself with his wife or possibly with any other woman.

And there was always this war to be fought, the war that had killed Big Mike Donnely.

"Movement," Captain Destefano said, lowering his binoculars. "Just into the tree line to the left front."

"Mortars," Eddie said. "Indirect fire from Dog Company's thirties?"

"Go! We'll cross after they fire for effect—and call up the flamethrower man. Jap bastards will have another cave or tunnel dug in. We'll fry some ass."

Or bury some holdouts alive; it made no difference, so long as they died quick and stayed dead. So long as they didn't play the corpse and rise to kill some unwary GI.

Hurrying with the extended line across the plowed field was tough; wet earth dragged at Eddie's boots and made him stumble. On his left flank a man stumbled and went down; he didn't get up.

(Barracks talk: Fuck 'em if they can't take a joke.)

"Goddamn sniper!" Eddie yelled. "Haul ass, haul ass!"

Then the brush closed around him and men crashed through it, firing at shadows, at anything. Eddie worked his way over to the poor bastard lugging the flamethrower. "Stay close; I'll nose out and see where we need you. Got your breath back?"

"J-Jesus—I think so-so. This is a heavy son of a bitch."

Eddie stared at the man's face, the boy's face. They were so damned young. "You ever fired this in combat?"

"Just in training. I'll do okay, Sarge."

It was a high-casualty-rate job; you had to get in close to a bunker or cave and cut loose the hosing of killing flame. The enemy had you at point-blank range where he could leave you dead while smoke leaked around you—smoke or gas erupting from a bullet-pierced cylinder to cook you to well done.

Easing through underbrush toward the sporadic fire of M-1s and carbines, Eddie found the camouflaged enemy bunker. It was a narrow-mouth cave slotted into a low hillside, with twisted vine trees above and below, hard to see. As he watched, a GI tried to reach it with a grenade. It fell short.

Wham!

The GI scuttled for cover as a hidden Nambu whacked-whacked at him.

A slant of ground rolled toward the cave from the right. It might furnish cover. Bellied down, Eddie called back and signaled the flamethrower up.

"Follow me and stay low. Drag that thing if you have to. When you get in range, yell and I'll bob up to cover you."

The ka-chung of the other rifles skipped bullets around and into the cave opening. Eddie figured the Japs were sandbagged and behind short logs. The machine gun would be placed at an angle where it was difficult to hit from head on, but Eddie waited in a slightly different position.

"S-Sarge!"

Up on one knee, Eddie sighted on the cave mouth and triggered eight fast shots. As the clip pinged out, he hit the ground and heard the furious roar of the flame when the kid snapped it on.

A tongue of fire licked below the bunker entrance, then lifted to spit a mighty gob directly into the target.

Sudden quiet came down with the shutoff of the flamethrower. A Jap squealed, the agonized cry of a stuck pig. Flailing his arms, he plunged outside in a spatter of flame. When he fell, his body made popping, frying sounds.

(Barracks talk: Medic, paint him with iodine and mark him Duty.)

"Jesus!" the kid gasped. "I got him."

"Sure as hell did," Eddie said. It was better not to think of how many caves lay ahead.

CHAPTER **29**

INTERNATIONAL NEWS SERVICE—New York, Jan. 16, 1945: Conservation Monday, which got off to a false start last week when many restaurants served steaks, roasts and chops, tried the other foot yesterday and stumbled even worse.

A dinner club across from Radio City filled a show window with red, juicy steaks and sold them quickly. Non-observance by eating places in all parts of Mayor La Guardia's city swerved away from rationing meat on Tuesday and Friday.

Specials at stool and counter shops were sirloin steaks with french fries for fifty cents.

Authorities blame the uncooperative attitude on good war news and anticipation of an early peace.

Crusty Carlisle downed a shot in Ben Alexander's Washington apartment and made a face. "Panther piss."

Alexander finished his drink. "Three Feathers, normally a fair whiskey. Like all the wartime distillers, it cut in far too much grain alcohol. It has this awful rotten-yeast taste, but it's the only game in town. And you're spoiled by Kill Devil Hill's wondrous bootleg."

"This new branch," Crusty said, "this Criminal

222

Investigation outfit. Do you have a connection? Big change in the army when we need secret cops. Hell, soldiers used to leave payday money on their bunks while they took a shower, and they didn't need to carry goddamn keys for wall lockers and foot lockers."

Nodding, Alexander said, "A caught thief would hope for two years in Fort Leavenworth before he got beaten half to death by his own platoon. I know a few people in CID, and one special hard-nose. No official power over civilians, you know, especially not congressmen. We might be better off to keep the investigation close to the family."

Crusty snorted and rolled a Bull Durham. "That's the problem. Nobody has any control over the duly elected, even though they're out-and-out crooks. If some son of a bitch gets caught with his paw in the public till, his buddies appoint themselves as a committee and finally get around to telling him he's a bad boy. He doesn't get locked up; he stays on the job. He just has to find another cash register."

Alexander said, "Boss Kawley is never far from a cash register."

"He's the power behind this fucking around with the family. How can that bastard Skelton pay him off? With what?"

"I may have a line on that. You know I finally got myself sent out of town on a bureaucratic inspection tour of some islands we've overrun."

Crusty scratched a kitchen match to his cigarette. "And?"

"There's an unbelievable amount of equipment being left behind the advance and more piling up in rear areas every day—tank engines, trucks, jeeps, refrigerators. Those are some of the civilian usables; then there are artillery pieces and shells. Any weapon difficult to ship—they'll be dumped."

"What the hell! You mean deep-sixed instead of

bringing them home or donating them to the natives? Millions of—''

''Billions, Crusty, billions. There'll be a great outcry from Mom and Dad to bring the boys home right away; every politician will faithfully echo it. And rear commanders will be led to understand that it's quicker and cheaper to roll the stuff into the ocean. They'd wait months, if not years, for enough ships to carry them back, and of course men would have to wait to load them.''

Taking a drag on his roll-your-own, Crusty said, ''And what would be easier than to run hired freighters to some of those islands before the dumping starts? It'd be a snap to offload the stuff on legitimate docks in the United States. Everybody's used to seeing that. Without much effort, it could all vanish. A million here, another few million there—oh, the bastards.''

''General Skelton has been flying the Pacific a bit, setting things up. I can't pinpoint the exact locations yet, or who'll make the payoffs this side of the ocean. I won't be surprised to find the operation already under way, now that the Jap subs have pulled back to protect the homeland.''

Crusty said, ''You've done a hell of a job, Ben. Now it's up to me to work out a way to nail these sons of bitches. But I will, down and dirty or however I have to play it, I'll run my hands down their throats, hook my thumbs in their assholes and jerk them inside out.''

Alexander smiled. ''I'm sure you will.''

NORTH AMERICAN NEWSPAPER ALLIANCE—Luzon, the Philippines, Feb. 1, 1945: General William Kreuger issued detailed orders for the next operation. Eleven Corps, which just landed, advanced on Manila along the base of the Bataan peninsula where it will link up with XIV Corps, also pointing for Manila.

Fighting has been heavy through the long months of this campaign, and at times gains were made only yard by yard, through matted jungle and over mountains. Fanatic to the last, the Japs battled for every tree and every piece of ground.

Filipino guerrillas have come out into the open—tough, ragged little men armed mostly with captured Japanese weapons, and all carrying razor-sharp bolo knives. They took to the hills after the Japanese invasion and carried on the fight.

Eddie Donnely held his M-1 at port and stared at the thing hung between thorn trees. Anytime you thought you had seen it all, something worse came up.

"Man, oh man," Corporal McElyea said, "I wonder how long it took him to die."

The old guerrilla's name was Golla; he squatted close to the earth, the smell of his sweat blending with the miasma of the jungle floor. He sucked at the butt of a cigarette, his gray-black hair bound by a strip of cloth that had once been red. He pointed and said, "Boy there. Japs shot down mother, father in street; he watched. We catch Jap officer seven, eight days back. Boy ask give to him, make present."

The kid hadn't shaved yet; his round brown face was almost cherubic, until you got a good look at his eyes.

Golla drew the final puff from the butt, and sparks fell over his fingers. "Boy take his time, skin Jap bastard little bit, little bit more."

Glancing back at the body, Eddie thought this particular Jap had earned a hitch in samurai paradise. From the lightly haired chin down, he had been skinned alive, each layer peeled back with great care, so he would not bleed to death too soon. He was left a twisty red lump that the flies buzzed over, rising in green-black clouds to crawl many-legged over exposed meat, and there was always an odor to death. The Jap stared wide-eyed into hell, his mouth gaped forever in a silent scream.

McElyea said, "There ain't no pretty way to die, but this is the ugliest I ever saw. How old is that little rattlesnake—sixteen, seventeen?"

"Maybe a thousand years. There'll be a lot of catching up by the natives; from the day the Japs landed, they were their usual murdering shits."

Handing the old guerrilla two cigarettes, McElyea said, "Man, oh man, I don't want these guys pissed off at me. Hey—the platoon's moving out. Look, this pair's coming with us."

"They're great scouts and know the land."

Manila, once the Pearl of the Orient, was a few miles ahead. What would the Japs leave of it? Rumor said that General MacArthur owned the city streetcar lines, and his staff was suggesting the artillery be a tad careful. The general had been stationed in the Philippines for so many years that he might own half the city.

Falling in with company headquarters, moving along an open dirt road as planes off the carriers roamed ahead. The regiment was in reserve for a change, and it was good to ease off for a few hours—if the Japs didn't pop out of nowhere with a suicide attack. You never let down completely; you couldn't. Nerves stretched only a little tight, and sleep balanced the knife edge of alertness.

Sweat oiled Eddie's cheeks and heat rash ate at his crotch. The goddamn jungle didn't smell any better than it had on all the bloody islands behind him. He should have gone back to the Zone of Interior when he had the chance; he knew that now.

Gloria waited for him, more woman than he had

ever known, so much so that he could no longer love other women freely and fully. He belonged with her, as much as he had ever belonged to the army.

Big Mike Donnely would understand; he had come so close to giving up the career he loved for the woman he thought he loved, but his great passion had turned out to be a great bitch. Gloria was Gloria.

Up ahead, American planes squalled down, and the rattle of their guns came back to the column.

Beyond Manila a string of fortified islands waited to become airstrips vital to the bombing of Japan itself. As stepping-stones, they would be a bitch for the marines and army to take.

For the first time, Eddie wondered how long his luck would hold out.

CHAPTER 30

AGENCE FRANCE PRESSE—European Theater, Feb. 3, 1945: Newly arrived German units got a shock today. English-speaking radio monitors could not understand transmissions within the American 442nd Regiment. And little wonder—the regiment is entirely Japanese-American—Nisei—barring a few Occidental officers.

They are all volunteers who fought their way up the length of the Italian boot, despite the fact most of their families are shut away in American concentration camps.

The Nisei soldiers tell captured Germans that Japan has surrendered and joined the Allies to fight against Hitler.

All Japanese on the West Coast, American citizens or not, were gathered up shortly after the sneak raid on Pearl Harbor and herded into desert camps for the duration of the war. Panicked officials in California feared sabotage.

So many young Nisei volunteered to prove themselves that the first carefully segregated unit, the 100th Infantry Battalion, soon grew to be the 442nd Regiment, the "Four-four-deuce." It has earned more awards for valor and more Purple Hearts than any other regiment in the American army.

The regiment's motto and war cry is "Go for Broke," which means shoot the works, or bet it all.

Keenan Carlisle had never been so cold. Wet, icy wind whipped off the high ground in bursts that saw-toothed to the bone. He thought he would never stop shivering, and locked his teeth to keep them from rattling.

After so many years in the tropics, and so many jungle bugs crawling in his thinned blood, he was inviting pneumonia. The transfer had come in red-stamped "Expedite and hand-carry." At first he thought the family was pulling him back to the ZI for some arcane reason, but when he only touched down in Hawaii to change planes, he began to realize his transfer—or shanghai, more likely—was actually something else.

Eyeing the snowy ridges before the battalion position, he thought about the between-planes time left to him on Oahu. He had screwed up his courage and called, and Susie had come, hurrying in the old Ford with the A Card sticker on its windshield. It was a wonder she had come; it was a wonder she would talk to him at all, after what he had done to her in her home, and before her parents.

"Keenan," she had said when she saw him, eyes soft, hands held out. She smelled of wonders, of sun and sand and flowers.

"I'm sorry. I've been such a damn fool, and I . . ." He felt foolish, without the words or the way to say what he so desperately wanted to say. She looked so good it made him hurt.

"Hush," she said. "I understand. I wasn't too bright about it, either, you know. I don't know what I was expecting."

"Susie, I've balled myself up into an awful thing, where hate has blotted out almost—"

She put a finger to his lips, then came into his arms, pressing tightly against him. She tasted of soft warmth, of quiet little flames. She didn't try to hold back the tears.

Yen Ling, Kennan had said silently to the memory, you will never leave me, but there is room for another. This must be as it was with your first love, the one you also lost. Part of Susie is like you, and part is very different. I know you will understand. . . .

"I love you, Susie Lokomaikai," he had said aloud. . . .

The harsh wind of a new continent raked at him again, and Keenan huddled closer beneath the GI blankets and ponchos that partially shielded the command post group against the savage winter. There had been time only for that much talk with Susie, almost no time for holding each other. But he had smiled as he waved at her from the plane that winged him east.

In New York he had called Kill Devil Hill to find out what was going on.

"What?" General Preston Bevale had asked. "You're in transit where?"

"The ETO, sir. Specifically, a battalion command in the Four-four-two Infantry, no delay en route."

"Hang on a moment," Belvale said. "Let me take a reading."

It wasn't much of a wait before the general told Keenan that he was targeted for trouble by General Skelton, that the 442nd was almost entirely Nisei. Skelton and his cronies obviously figured that Keenan's deep hatred of anything Japanese would cause him to blow up, lose control, somehow discredit the family.

"I don't think that will happen, General. I've learned some things, and that last trip through the jungle closed an old and ugly wound."

"I'll put a stop to this crap, anyway. Stay where you are until—"

"It's okay, sir, I can hack it. Maybe that's what Skelton wants, interference with official orders so he can turn up the heat. Let's back off and wait. Now that we know where the enemy is, we're up one.''

As he thought back on the conversation, Keenan realized it was easy to apply jungle tactics to almost everything, but what, he asked himself, had he learned lately? Was there ever an end to win or lose, hate or die? Pinned so close in that hole with a dying Jap, Keenan hadn't been so intent on revenge. The guy had turned human, and at the end had made Kennan a present of his own life, given him a gift when there could be none in return. The man could have fired right away; he might have alerted the Jap patrol. Instead, he chose to die quietly and to let Keenan live. The man had even known how to laugh.

Christ, it was impossible to hate so much that you were willing to choke on your own life's blood. And that left Susie, with Japanese blood, Hawaiian blood, all mixed to the beat of his crippled heart. When he let go of the hate, he suddenly had room for love. She was Susie, uniquely Susie, and he loved her.

There were also the volunteers of this special Nisei regiment; they were as tough as the Japs in the South Pacific, though in his eyes they were a hell of a lot smarter. They all had that don't-screw-with-me look, and they were more than good soldiers—they were dedicated. Keenan still had problems with the set of their features and the sound of the language; that much of the *yonsei* stayed with him. And some of the looks the soldiers had given him made him wonder if latrine rumors had preceded him, rumors about the wild jungle spirit that ate heads.

"Krauts moving across the front of Able Company, sir." Lieutenant Yamoto held a sound power phone and looked at him.

"Heading where?"

"Looks like they mean to hit Charlie Company on the flank; Charlie sticks out on a salient."

The crackle of small arms fire echoed over the CP, followed by the crump of mortars. Able Company wasn't waiting for orders.

"I haven't been here long enough to know everybody. Who has Able?"

"Captain Ohara, sir. A real sharp *ka-tunk*."

"*Ka-tunk?*"

Yamoto grinned. "What we call Hawaiian Nisei—it's the sound a coconut makes when it's thumped. They call those of us Stateside Buddha Heads."

Digging for a cigarette, Keenan said, "Your suggestion, Lieutenant?"

Yamoto showed his surprise. "Ah, Able Company to advance and take the Krauts on their flank?"

"Sounds good to me."

Yamoto thumbed the phone switch, rattled off a quick string of Japanese, and then added: "Go for broke, brudder—go for broke."

CHAPTER 31

ASSOCIATED PRESS—London, Mar. 16, 1945: Buzz bombs—the German V1 and V2 rockets—still wing out of the sky to explode in and around London, still causing many civilian casualties and further battering to this often-bombed city.

The newer V2 rocket weighs eight tons and carries 2,000 pounds of explosives. While RAF and American bombers search for the launching sites, plucky Londoners go about business as usual.

Said one publican of the Chelsea district: "If this is old Adolf's mighty secret weapon, he had better look for another while he can."

But there have been rumors of yet another secret weapon developed by Hitler's scientists, a so-called jet plane that flies at incredible speeds without visible propellers.

Penny Belvale sipped a glass of half-and-half, more or less used to beer being warm and flat. God, did the British believe that everything had to be at room temperature? Whether one ate it or drank it, it was all served the same. She had just brought in another light bomber, and she was tired. But Stephanie had promised to meet her here at the Blacksmith's Arms, and she would wait all night if she had to. She hadn't seen Stephanie in months, and after the closeness they shared in the Jap POW camp, it was as if a part of her body had left her.

The camp. Lord, how it stayed with her, intruding upon thoughts little connected with the war. The stink and sweat crowded in on her at night, choking off her breathing, dragging her gasping from sleep.

And always Major Watanabe's smooth yellow face taunted her. The things he had done, the life-and-death control he had over her, continued to gnaw at her belly. Somehow, some way, she had to see the bastard dead. She was going to use family strings to catch a slot ferrying planes on the other side, because if God was good she would get a chance to kill Major Wobbly herself.

"Penny!"

She looked up. Stephanie Bartlett now wore the three pips of WAAF captain, but her face hadn't quite regained its pixie gleam. Penny wondered if her own eyes still held that slightly out-of-focus stare.

Standing up, she hugged the woman close. "Stevie—oh, God, it's good to see you." Stephanie smelled of soap and woolen uniform. Was there an odor to a deep and abiding sadness? After the stink of the camp, what was the perfume left to wrap around a soul?

Stephanie smiled across the table. "Lass, you look a bit worn at the edges. Haven't the Yanks got enough bombers here?"

Penny reached for her hand and held it gently. "I'm tired, but we're still losing planes, I guess. If not, I wouldn't be in the ETO at all. How are you? How do you feel? Talk to me."

Stephanine was quiet for a while, squeezing Penny's fingers. "My husband was alive at last word.

They tell me our land forces are getting close to that bloody prison camp. The question is, will the Japs worry over their own bums and begin to treat our people well, or will they murder every prisoner—man, woman and child—before escaping into the jungle. Puir Dacey. With no legs he wouldn't even have a chance to run."

"How close are the Brits to actually liberating that camp?"

Stephanie stared for a long moment. Pub talk and tobacco smoke swirled around them; a woman laughed, a sound close to the barking of a seal.

"Within ten miles," Stephanine replied.

"Close enough," Penny said, smiling.

"Close enough for what? . . . No, you're not thinking . . . Not even you would be crazy enough—"

"The hell I'm not. I can swing a plane, a C-Forty-seven probably. There's military muscle to be used, and I'm more than willing. And if you want to go with me—"

"I know; that big Belvale stick can do almost anything. But, Penny, it's so far, and the plan is more than a wee bit insane."

Penny swallowed beer; it didn't taste good. "There are new jungle airstrips in Malaysia. It's a long way from over on that side, and the Brits can always use supplies."

Stephanie hesitated. "If the timing is right, I might get to see Dacey."

"You have a better chance of meeting Chad if you stay right here in England."

"I suppose so. Oh, damn."

Sipping the last of her beer, Penny said, "Have you heard from Chad?"

"One wee V-mail note. His unit is rolling forward at speed. He didn't mention any chance for

London. I don't think he will come until this
bloody war is completely done."

"I'm not asking you to choose."

"Not that it matters. I'm an officer, assigned.
I'm not one of those who can go running all over
the bloody world."

"Easy, easy. It's all right, Stevie. I can find
whatever crew I need."

Stephanie toyed with her glass. "And your own
husband?"

"Seems I added to his troubles," Penny said. "I
had the effect of a one-woman mortar round, and
if that wasn't bad enough, he had a setback because of some stupid thing with the press. Several
barking reporters chased him into a hole and he
hasn't come out yet." Penny looked into the beer
glass, then pushed it away. "I wonder if I could
be as steady as you—if another man loved me as
Chad does you, and if Farley remains condemned
to the prison of his mind. I don't know, Stephanie,
I just don't know."

Cigarette smoke thickened around her, and there
was the closed-in smell of people, filtered by the
bitter odor of beer. At the battered piano, men and
women in uniform sang about the white cliffs of
Dover. Penny thought of the times when she would
have loved to lay hands on a bluebird—and have
it for lunch.

"I'm only sure of one thing," she said. "I must
find Watanabe. Suppose he escapes. Dear Christ,
I want to see him dead."

Her hands pressed low on her belly; the phantom pain was always with her, from the thing she
had carried there—Watanabe's child; her child too.

Possibly her only child.

UNITED PRESS—Warm Springs, Ga., Apr. 12, 1945:
Franklin Delano Roosevelt, wartime president of the

United States and the only chief executive chosen for more than two terms in office, died unexpected at 4:25 P.M. today.

Less than two hours after the official announcement, vice president Harry S. Truman took the oath as the 32nd president. His first official statement was that President Roosevelt's cabinet members would remain in place.

Burial will be at the Roosevelt's Hyde Park home.

Korporal Schmitt poured Calvados for everyone. "The Führer toasts the health of the new American president with champagne. We must make do with the leftovers liberated during the glorious days in France. We still have at least a rail car filled with spirits."

Never smooth, this particular stuff was green and brought tears to Arno's eyes with its coppery flavor of rotten apples. He took another swallow. The weather was miserable, and so was he; so were the men around him in what was left of Berlin. Skies were heavy this day, bellied low with fog as gray as their hopes. Such a ceiling might hold back bombers.

The Allied bombers had come calling again and again. Buildings looked like rows of broken teeth. Pipes were ripped out so that no water came in and no sewage went out. Power was undependable and the people around him less so.

Always in the background, artillery rumbled so that at times Arno felt it through the soles of his boots. Not all that much was defensive 88 fire anymore, the sounds replaced by the heavier Russian guns. On the other front, the Tommi and Ami tanks slowly ate the few miles to Berlin. He hoped they would reach the city before the Russians did. *Gott*, according to the stories from the Eastern

Front—what used to be the Eastern Front—anyone would be better than the Russians.

He said, "Dead or alive, one American president is like another. It will make no difference to the outcome of this *verdammt* war."

A wolfish sergeant licked his glass and held it out for a refill. "You are so familiar with the Ami way of politics, *Oberfeldwebel?* The Führer considers the Jew Rosenvelt's death to be a sign of Providence."

Arno shrugged. "The Führer has second sight. All I have is experience fighting, first the British and then the Americans. Shoot a captain, a lieutenant takes his place; shoot the lieutenant, and a sergeant commands. No different from us, but I think this is also the way with American presidents. Who will succeed Hitler if he dies suddenly? Which of our strutting generals is capable of holding Germany's fate in his hands?"

The sergeant lifted an eyebrow. "You are a true Nazi, then?"

Arno's face showed nothing. "I am a soldier."

A rangy *oberleutnant* stuck his head through the blanketed doorway, bringing a sliver of cold with him. "*Oberfeldwebel,* fall in with your relief guard. Closely check any vehicles passing into the compound."

"Sir!"

The officer was gone, and the wolfish sergeant said, "Another strategy meeting. Perhaps you will discover another briefcase bomb, Hindemit, another act of Providence to save the Führer's life."

Arno wasn't sure which way the man leaned, but it would make little difference. This was the *waffen* SS, and each had sworn to die with his Führer.

CHAPTER 32

NORTH AMERICAN NEWSPAPER ALLIANCE—New Orleans, Apr. 17, 1945: Uncle Sam's scrap metal drive is still under way, although with much less impetus than in the beginning of the war. Housewives in this glamorous city donate everything from hair curlers made of aluminum to the elaborate iron fencing brought from Europe in sailing ships.

In Detroit, the former automakers are turning out military trucks, jeeps and tanks in ever-growing numbers, using the metal collected by such patriotic drives.

Fifteen miles of docks stretched along this side of the Mississippi, and rusted freighters from across dangerous seas bumped softly against the pilings. Plimsoll marks rode high on the empty ones, though the seasonal markings to warn of an overloaded ship had been ignored since the beginning of the war. Mixed gangs of longshoremen and servicemen loaded and offloaded cargo.

Crusty Carlisle, back in the shadows of baled peat moss stacked high on the pier, watched a big crane suck up its steel cables and hoist the first deuce-and-a-half over the side of the *Titania Princess*. The moss had a peculiar green and brown odor that vied with the smell of engine exhaust and the river's mud.

New Orleans always made Crusty uneasy; it was too smooth, too full of wrought-iron curlicues and overdone politeness. It was a city of dandies and old European ways, with an emphasis on pleasure. He suspected men raised here would wear perfume and take a liking to silk. It also had the weirdest damn graveyards he had ever seen. Because of the groundwater level everyone was buried in crypts, of so many sizes and shapes that a cemetery looked like a miniature city constructed by a ghoulish child. This was not a town that made him happy, and now he had even less reason to like it.

Beside him, Major Irving, over the metallic whine and grind of the crane, said, "The first one off, and check those bumper markings. The One Hundred Forty-first Field Artillery, a National Guard unit. Used to be based here at Jackson Barracks. Nobody would look twice at these vehicles. Your thief is smart."

Crusty said, "He isn't mine, or won't be until I get my hands on the bastard. And he isn't all that smart, just slick, slick as a rat. Jesus, I saw a wharf rat just at daylight; damned thing was big as a tomcat, wouldn't run. Tried to stare me down. Spooky red eyes."

"Word is you won't find cats along the wharf, General. The rats ambush and eat them. They develop strong jaws by cracking river clams."

"Still," Crusty said, "a rat is just a rat, and it can be trapped or stomped, the same as this thief. Are you sure he's still on that rusty old bucket?"

Just looking at the ship made Crusty's bones ache and his mouth go dry with the need for a drink of water. Getting knocked off a ship and slapping around in a skin-scraping life raft was not an experience that was going to go away. Ships,

boats, rafts and rubber duckies—they could all
stay with the devil. A good horse and solid land
were all he wanted for the rest of his life, and here
he was again, playing pattycake among things that
were too by-God wet.

"We've kept a close tail on him all the way,"
Irving said. "He boarded the ship at the mouth of
the river from a pilot boat, and no way he could
have come off without us knowing."

It wouldn't be like Skelton to stay out of the
picture, the way Boss Kawley did. It wasn't so
much that Skelton was a hands-on, on-top-of-the-
action kind of person—his series of desk commands was proof of that. No, it was that, like all
power-grabbing, self-serving bastards, he didn't
trust anyone. Kawley, with that innate instinct of
soulless politicians, kept enough distance to avoid
responsibility. Skelton, eager to keep on top of his
leverage in Washington, and to be sure of his
profit, wasn't about to take any chances, even if
he had to count every truck himself.

It was a typically military approach, and Crusty
bit his lip with the thought of the double-dyed son
of a bitch bringing discredit on the entire army.

"There," the major said. "Is that Skelton coming down the gangplank?"

"In civilian clothes, by God—a real peanut."

Irving stood away from the moss bales. "My
people are in place. Let's nail him."

"Wait," Crusty said. "Could you give me a minute? This is something I've been looking forward
to." Crusty had been waiting years to take a chunk
out of Skelton—a man so stupid that he hadn't just
exposed his ass; now his jugular was about to be
opened—and Crusty wanted to taste the blood.

"Your call, General. Show a signal and I'll blow
the whistle."

"Thanks. It won't take long."

He caught up with Skelton as the man hurried

along the wharf beyond the warehouse, heels thumping the scarred wood, chest thrown out despite the civilian dress.

Crusty touched his arm, and Skelton's face went pale, his stride breaking into a stumble. "General!"

"Do you have a god, asshole? If you do, boy, you better pray hard, 'cause me and the Criminal Investigation Department got you by the short hairs."

"Carlisle . . . damn it, you don't . . . you don't know what you're getting into." Skelton's eyes darted away, then back, then slid off again.

"Looking for a way out? Looking for help? Looking for Kawley, maybe? You oughta know better, boy. He's gonna say he never saw you before. He covers *his* ass, not yours." Crusty moved a bit closer.

"Wait, wait, damn it! Think of what you're doing. Think of what the press will do to the army . . . the army, when the war's not even over."

Crusty stared at him, watching a rat twist and turn.

"It's a setup!" Skelton's voice lifted to a squeak. "I'll claim this whole thing is a setup; everybody knows about the bad blood between me and your goddamn family."

Planting his feet solidly, Crusty said, "You thieving son of a bitch, I'm gonna give you a choice: resign and retire immediately or get hung out to dry."

Eyes round and glaring, jaw twitching, Skelton bulled his way over the edge. "I have press contacts, connections, people who remember Lieutenant Belvale faking his way out of combat and being covered up by your goddamn family. And you can't prove that this equipment isn't legal, that I wasn't saving the taxpayers' money."

"You should know me better. I can prove every

bit of it." Crusty lifted his right arm; a whistle shrilled, men shouted and motors began to stop. "And that's twice so far you've bad-mouthed the family. I don't think I'm going to wait for a third." Crusty looped the same right hand in an arc and popped Skelton solidly on the left eye.

Skelton staggered off balance, tried to run, slipped and hit the guard plank. Arms flailing, he pitched into the swift, muddy river.

Major Irving ran up, his expression caught between disbelief and amusement. "Is he . . . are you . . . I'll get a boat in the river. Can he swim?"

Uncurling his fingers, Crusty shrugged. "My guess is that he swims as well as any river rat."

ASSOCIATED PRESS—Southern Philippines, Apr. 20, 1945: Assault units of the U.S. 24th Infantry Division, supported by aircraft, cruisers and destroyers landed on Mindanao Island today. The landing force made rapid progress with no opposition from the Japanese 35th Army.

On Cebu, the American Divisions occupied positions abandoned by the Japanese on the hills around Cebu City.

Eddie Donnely watched close and listened hard and barely managed to pick up Filipino guerrillas before they eeled into the company CP in bright sunshine. They were good; they had to be, to take on the Japanese occupation forces and survive. They could blend with the twilight jungle or remain unheard in the night. Daytime they vanished and let the Jap patrols probe the brush for them while they moved to a different sector.

Golla was the old one, his lived-in face a tight overlapping of wrinkles. Eddie glanced at the kid

and tried not to remember that he had peeled a
Jap officer inch by inch.

Squatting, Golla showed his broken teeth and
accepted C ration cigarettes. "Jap patrol not far.
You come, Sergeant?"

Eddie looked at Captain Destefano, who said,
"Take two men. Nobody plays hero and you're
back before dark. Password is lalapalooza."

"Yes, sir. McElyea and Bailey."

Once out of the CP and into the leafy brush,
McElyea touched Eddie's shoulder. "Thanks a
bunch for volunteering me, especially to follow
that little rattlesnake."

Bailey, a squirrel-hunting mountain boy out of
Tennessee, walked the jungle almost as quietly as
the Filipinos, M-1 at the ready with bayonet fixed.

A faint path appeared, winding past some high
ground, and Golla squatted beside it. Eddie waved
those behind him down and eased up to the man.
Golla pointed, and when Eddie didn't see it right
away, the Filipino aimed his crooked brown finger
again. Eddie picked out the well-hidden giant flyswat, its handle green bamboo drawn far back and
attached to the swatter, which was laced with sliv-
ers of sharp fire-hardened bamboo. A trip vine was
snuggled somewhere across the path.

They waited. When Eddie began to think his leg
muscles would cramp from lack of blood, Golla
stiffened.

The Jap scout came warily around the slope, Arisaka and overlong bayonet thrust ahead. One sliding step, two; a jungle bird wheeped overhead, and
the Jap halted to peer at the green canopy. He was
still looking up when he tripped the vine and the
flyswat whipped around to impale him on half a
dozen points. Dropping his rifle he tried to scream,
but his punctured lungs leaked air and he could
only hang and gurgle, toes scraping at the grass.

When a pair of his stubby companions eased

around the slope, Eddie could hear their indrawn hiss of surprise. Tugging at Eddie's arm, Golla pulled him down. The Japs fired upslope and down, working rifle bolts and firing blind into the jungle. Green leaves drifted down with bits of brown bark, and gun smoke eddied into the brush.

Golla didn't wait to see the man's comrades pull him off the trap, although it would have been a good time to catch several Japs in the open. Instead, the old Filipino and the kid snaked off through a stand of sharp-edged grass, leading the way to another booby trap. Eddie panted in the heat, sweat plastering his fatigues to his body.

McElyea whispered, "What the hell? What are we doing?"

"Demonstration," Eddie murmured. "I think they're leaving us soon, and Golla wants to show us, or maybe warn us, how the guerrillas operate."

This time the Flips hid themselves on either side of a straight stretch, a slice through the jungle that was mostly open to the sky. Here the Jap patrols could see a good distance without brush closing dark and tight along the trail, and they could move faster.

Until the guerrillas opened fire.

"Oh, Jesus," McElyea said. "That's a combat patrol. Must be thirty of the little bastards. Man, oh man, now it hits the fan."

Bailey went to earth beside Eddie, went into the prone firing position as if he'd been doing it all his life. He cranked off eight rounds, and McElyea joined in. Eddie was about to rise to one knee to pick targets when the return fire whipped over them, the snap and pop of rounds mixed with the sound of twisted twigs and ripped grass.

Fire came from both sides—random, blind, no one daring to rise up high enough to do more. But the Japanese had them clearly outmanned. The firing stopped briefly, then began again. Eddie squeezed into the soft ground, wishing he could melt away. Smoke and dust rode the air currents, slowly sifting down the miniature valley into the splayed and tattered thickets of bamboo and grass.

In a lull Golla suddenly popped up, firing. Eddie's body uncoiled, lifting him off the ground. Through the smoke and dust the Japs stumbled up the trail, and they began screaming as they came.

The firing became frantic as the soldiers blundered through the brush, ignoring the bullets that ripped and snapped around them. Eddie watched puffs of dust erupt from the tan uniform of a Jap, and as he twisted down into the grass he was replaced by another, seeming dazed and firing without looking.

Eddie unhooked a grenade and snatched out the pin. He lobbed it high, and the wait was too long, the explosion muffled. He worked loose a second one and let the spoon ping off—one thousand one, one thousand two. It cooked in his hand, and he steeled himself to wait—one thousand three, you can't trust these goddamned things—four, one thousand—he chucked it up and out. The explosion was sharp and crisp, and he knew he got the airburst he wanted. The jungle absorbed the burst when a grenade hit the ground, but this one worked, and he was rewarded with the sound of screams.

He saw guerrillas snaking backward, working their way uphill. He thumb-signed McElyea and Bailey to start falling back. "This is going to get worse," Bailey said.

"No shit" was the only reply McElyea could think of.

The guerrillas quickly disappeared, sucked into the jungle with little more than a quiver of grass and vines. The Japs were still screaming and shooting, though the intensity of the shrieks rose and fell in choppy waves. Eddie turned and elbowed his way upward, wriggling through brush that snagged and caught and tried to hold him.

At one point he passed a guerrilla lying on his back, mouth open, empty eyes staring at the sky. He held a fairly new M-1, bolt cocked back. He wouldn't be using it.

The drone of a fat blue fly made Eddie realize the jungle was quiet, far too quiet. He listened to the silence and felt a wave of dread. This was not going well; sweet Jesus, dear Gloria, this was not going well. The color of leaves around him changed, became more vivid as the adrenaline pumped. He could smell the dank earth and the sour stench of his own sweat. He felt nauseated.

Suddenly there was an explosion of rifle fire, mixed with excited voices as the Japs found someone, or maybe more than one. "Holy shit." Eddie quit trying to be quiet. He lunged forward and up-hill, moving in a low crouch, yanking himself free of the jungle fingers that kept clutching at him.

The top of the slope flattened into a clearing, and he burst into it before he could stop. Kneeling on the far side were Golla and the skin-specialist kid, and Eddie felt a wave of relief. He just reached them when Bailey rolled out of the brush, gasping and wiping blood from a thorn-ripped cheek.

"We've got to set up a perimeter," Eddie said.

Golla looked at him and shook his head.

"I think McElyea got hit," Bailey said, eyes focused on the bloody tips of his fingers. "Jesus, everything went crazy as shit."

"Too many," Golla said. "We go quick."

Eddie wanted to argue with him, to get organized, to find McElyea, but Golla was already gone, and the kid was moving behind him. Eddie had only time to suck in a breath before Bailey said, "They're coming. I can hear them coming."

Eddie eased into the brush and motioned to Bai-

ley to follow him. Two steps and he turned to see
Bailey still at the edge of the clearing, clutching
his weapon and looking wildly around. Eddie
opened his mouth to call out, but saw the results
of the bullet before he heard the shots. Bits of
fatigue jacket blew into the air as the slug sliced
through Bailey's shoulder and then, oddly, came
out the side of his neck, leaving a stream of red.

Bailey pitched to one side and hit the ground
facedown, unmoving.

A chunk of tree above Eddie's head turned into
dust, and a clump of bamboo to one side started to
fall, cut in half by something invisible. Eddie ran.

McElyea was missing—dead or captured, what
was left of him fallen somewhere behind the advancing Japanese line. Bailey had died standing
up; what hit the ground was only so much leftover
meat. Eddie could hear the jungle behind him
being shredded by rifle fire, and in front he could
barely pick out the fleeting forms of the guerrillas,
moving faster than cats.

He pushed ahead, out of options, out of breath,
struggling to keep up. In the descending twilight,
throat raw and legs aching, he found himself repeating something from childhood, the words
matched to the ragged rhythm of his legs, said
again and again, "Now I lay me down to sleep, I
pray the Lord my soul to keep, and if I die before
I wake . . . and if I die . . . and if I die . . ."

It was so goddamn dark Eddie couldn't see his
hand in front of his face. He was cold, he was
hungry, and he had no idea where they were. They
had gone to ground at nightfall—Golla, the kid,
and two more Flips who had appeared from nowhere, materializing out of the green background
as if God had made them then and there. And
Eddie, hot-shot Pacific jungle fighter, felt like a
slow-witted elephant following them.

They couldn't build a fire, of course, and he felt

lucky for the ball of cold rice someone handed him. Under a bush, out of the path of even an accidental trail, they had snugged in, scooping small depressions in the humus. Eddie watched Golla take a palm-sized rock and tuck it under his shoulder blade.

"No sleep too deep," he said when he saw Eddie staring.

After feeling around for his own rock, Eddie lay staring into the black, awake, exhausted, choking on bile that kept rising in his throat. Bailey was dead, probably McElyea too. Christ knew how many Flips got away and how many died in that ravine or scattered on the hillside. The Japs got cut up, went berserk, then everything came apart. That patrol was too big, and there might even be more running around.

Gloria, I'm sorry. I never realized how much of this I thought of as a game. Now time is running out, the rules are running out, I have this feeling someone is about to turn the lights out. Lights out. Taps. End of the time. Big Mike raised me a certain way, but I walked through it, playing a part, feeling as if I was being judged by outsiders: Big Mike, officers, your grandfather. Judged by all the women, but like all actors, judged by the performance, not the person.

It's not a game, and this isn't a stage. People all around me are dead, and tonight I know I can die, too. As quickly and as soundlessly as Bailey. Even being wounded didn't sink that home. Lord, how dumb can one man be? Gloria, I love you. Not as part of some game, or as part of a play other people are watching—I love you man to woman, me to you. I won't take that lightly or treat it childishly, ever again.

I promise you, Gloria, if I ever get my ass out of here.

ASSOCIATED PRESS—South Pacific, Apr. 24, 1945: The island-hopping tactics of the Pacific Command appear to have paid off in huge gains as the Allies sweep toward Japan. Leaving behind fortified Japanese strongholds, Allied forces concentrate only on those islands they will need to use as stepping-stones in the march on Tokyo.

Penny stood on the tarmac wondering how long backward evolution would take. Amphibians were obviously the next step on the Darwinian ladder, at least for anyone who lived on these godforsaken islands. The air was so humid she had to take shallow breaths, and every inch of her skin was layered with moisture.

The heat beat up from the runway, and light bounced off the metal Quonset huts, some reflections so intense they hurt her eyes. But back inside the plane would be even more miserable; being stuffed into the metal and glass cockpit while the plane sat on this airstrip was the same as being baked alive.

Island after island, she was part of a fleet winging west, increasing waves of bombers moving up to knock on Tojo's door. This particular island wasn't much more than a fuel dump, a launch point for both fighters and bombers sweeping one area, a restaging stop for equipment still moving on.

The overnight stop promised a meal, a shower and a cot, which together added up to more luxury than she'd had in a week. She made a last check of the plane before heading for the huts pointed out by the on-deck sergeant.

The water was tepid, the soap wouldn't raise a lather, and the water pressure was so low she got a crick in her neck long before her hair was clean—but it was still heaven, and she loved every moment of it. She even managed not to mind that the sweat put a sheen on her skin as soon as she toweled off.

"You with the wing that came in this afternoon?" Penny, leaning forward to run her fingers through upside-down hair, looked down the bench and read the insignias on the fatigues: U.S. Army, nurse, lieutenant.

"Yes. First time I've washed the dirt off in days," she said. "Is the mess hall here worth a damn?"

"Not bad, believe it or not. I suspect they clip part of everything that comes through, but nobody's going to ask, just in case it's true. Not much else to do here lately except eat, sleep when it gets cool enough, and spend the rest of your time fending off men."

Penny managed a chuckle. "Tough, huh?" The woman wasn't all that young or thin, but who was she to judge? She hadn't even thought of a man since the prison camp. Well, not quite true—she thought of one man, and her thoughts usually concerned ways to kill him. Of course she sometimes thought of Farley, but fleetingly, with a quick twist of guilt. Farley, to be honest, was less a thought than a mixed memory of childlike romance and adult regret. He certainly didn't fall into the realm of male aggression the nurse was talking about, of men who were hard and hungry for women.

"Seriously," the nurse said, "the enlisted men are no problem, of course; the brig is just one holler away. But the officers . . . particularly the damn flyboys. Those guys think they own everything, including your ass."

Penny gave her hair a last shake and gave up on it. "Something to the breed, I guess. Right now

I'm only interested in something decent to eat and a chance to grab forty winks.''

The mess tent had the canvas flaps pinned up in the hope of letting in any possible breeze. The air was still, however, and the few people scattered at the tables were almost as motionless, as if trapped in the thickness and afraid of friction.

Penny had just set the tray in front of her and was reluctantly eyeing the compartments of ham and beans, whipped potatoes and what purported to be peas, when a man's voice said, "It's not so bad. The potatoes may not be real, but the meat usually is.''

He was standing behind her, so she just nodded and picked up her fork. She kept her eyes on the tray when he came around and took a seat opposite her, and because of that there was no easing into it. When she looked up, his face was a complete shock; she had no chance to hide her reaction.

Penny was instantly embarrassed by her measurable flinch, the instinctive movement away. Half of his face was a scar, shiny and purple. He turned that side away from her, eyes downcast. "I've frightened you, haven't I?'' he said, soft and hurt.

Her skin flushing red with guilt, she automatically lied. "No, no. It's just the surprise, that's all. My thoughts were somewhere else.''

He made as if to get up. "I'll just spoil your meal. I'm sorry, I'll sit somewhere else.''

"Please, stay. It'll make me feel terrible if you leave.'' She smiled at him, forcing her lips into place. "Give me time to get collected. I've just come off a very long flight.''

"If you're sure,'' he said, turning his head slightly so that only part of the scar showed. He heaved a small sigh and looked up at her. Penny felt some part of her click on—there was something wrong with his eyes; they didn't fit his mannerisms. His gestures were boyish and uncertain, but the eyes were hard and cold. And they stirred a memory.

"Are you with a crew?" he asked. Half his smile was frozen.

"I'm a pilot," Penny said. "Transporting a bomber one more hop before hitching a ride into Singapore."

"I am too," he said, turning full on so that she saw all of his face. "That's how I got this. Shot down in the ETO, but that didn't keep me from becoming an ace—on both sides of the world."

Her amusement at the strut in his voice disappeared in the jumble of quickly connected facts that popped into her mind. "The ETO? Did you go down in the Channel?"

"Why, yes," he said, unable to control the jut of chin. "I guess you've heard of me; I've Gavin Scott." He held out his hand, fingers curved and ready to caress.

She kept her hands where they were. "I should say so. Seems we're family. My name is Penny Belvale."

"Belvale! Christ, you're married to one of my cousins—one of Uncle Chad's boys!"

"Farley. My husband is Farley Belvale. You and I met years ago at Kill Devil Hill."

"Pretty Penny—goddamn, you're right. But you weren't a Belvale then." He put on a smile and leaned forward. "We may be family, but we're not blood related. We're even past kissing cousins."

She put her fork down carefully and looked him in the eyes. There were many different kinds of family—by blood, by marriage and by experience. The last category was created when you were bonded to someone by time and shared pain and by the nurturing of hope within each other—the hope of seeing just one more sunrise.

"I heard you don't kiss," she said.

"What?" The bafflement may have been the first real emotion he let show.

"I heard you just grab the crotch and just stick it in. A real world-class lover, the story goes."

"What the hell are you talking about!"

Penny saw a couple of heads turn their way, so she raised her voice a notch, making sure she was heard. "I spent time in a POW camp with Stephanie Bartlett, you pathetic son of a bitch. I know all about your sad little rape. Is that always your routine? Cry first, slap them around a little, then grab a thirty-second screw? You really are laughable."

The cords stood out in his neck, and he was drawn so taut she thought he might snap into pieces, parts flying off like shrapnel. His voice came out in a keening, rage-flicked shriek. "You whoring bitch! She had it coming. She deserved it. She—"

Penny stood up, and her words cracked through the tent like the tail end of a bullwhip. She had been used, humiliated, starved and hung out in the sun like a piece of meat. She had eaten rats, choked back tears and stabbed a man until his blood ran to her elbows. She was not about to back away from this psycho—never again would she back away. "Stephanie laughed! She laughed, you twisted piece of shit. You're a joke! A whining, slobbering pud-puller who couldn't keep it up if your life depended on it."

She turned to the round, white faces floating in the tent heat. "Gavin Scott, air ace and rapist. This bastard is as ugly on the inside as he is on the outside." She bent across the table and hissed a cold whisper: "And the family knows, you slimy little fuck. The family knows. I made sure of that."

CHAPTER 33

INTERNATIONAL NEWS SERVICE—The Eastern Front, Apr. 25, 1945: The great battle for Berlin has begun. The biggest breakthroughs are made by the 1st Ukraine Front over the Neisse, where three Russian armies advance toward the river Spree.

ASSOCIATED PRESS—The Italian Front, Apr. 26, 1945: The advance of Allied troops goes on without pause. In the western sector, the U.S. Fifth Army makes for Sarzana, while the Polish II Corps pushes on west of Medicina.

Preston Belvale placed a handful of file folders on Gloria's desk. "The first listings of war criminals," he said. "As yet technically not proven. The proof is piling up, though, and more names will be added. Hitler won't avoid paying the price, as the Kaiser did."

Behind him the Teletype machines clattered, and Adria was putting down yet another box of blank paper rolls that constantly fed the noisy metal monsters. She now had to hurry to keep up with the swiftly changing picture on the big situation map.

Gloria said, "These are all from the ETO. How about the Japanese?"

Preston could tell when letters from Eddie Donnely were overdue. Her face would grow thinner, her eyes deeper set and vaguely accusing, as if she thought he might be withholding information from her. The news would of course be something she must know but could not stand to hear: Eddie killed? Missing? Badly crippled? He sighed, knowing that nothing would change those fears until Eddie was home, or until one of the nightmares came true.

"We have a line on some of the early criminals; the butchers of Bataan, for instance. A few have already been sent to their samurai gods, and we have every intention of rounding up the others."

She straightened the edges of the files, then lined them up. "It's such a long war, Uncle. It looks like the fighting in Europe may be over soon, but what about the Pacific? God, it might go on forever if our soldiers have to land in Japan. Can't we just cut them off the way we've cut off other islands? Just let them starve? Can't we just bomb the hell out of them and . . ."

Touching her hair lightly, Belvale said, "Such tactics almost never work. From Troy to Rhodes, history shows a siege too often to be ineffective. The process is long, ugly."

"Who cares?" Her face was tense, dark half-circles of fatigue under her eyes. "Those goddamn fanatics—"

"I know," he said. "And I know what you're worried about. There are no promises in combat; you know that, my dear. And we're both aware that a man like Sergeant Donnely is hard to kill."

"Why didn't Eddie come home after he was wounded again? What made him think he was so different? I had a right to see him, to hold him, to be with him again. Damn! You could have ordered him—"

"No, I couldn't. That is not the way." And why wasn't it? Preston Belvale could order around more people than he could count. He could move equipment, quail government agencies and ask for the head of anyone who moved too slow or jumped too low. Why in hell was he obligated to let members of his own family keep getting killed? Must honor always be steeped in blood?

Turning her face away from him, Gloria went back to work. He watched for only a moment, feeling how it was for her, how it was for most of the family women. Because of who they were, what they were, in uniform or out, the women soldiered as much as the men. At times they suffered even more and tried to show it even less. Locked up here in the war room Preston understood their side of it now, how the endless waiting was more frustrating, more emotionally painful than combat. At least there you could do something, or act like you were doing something—move, fight back, bitch, sweat, feel involved and maybe lose yourself in that rush of adrenaline.

What the women were going through was like holding on to the earth, pinned under the merciless hammering of mortar fire or an artillery barrage, nowhere to run, no way to fight. It was a time for eyes squeezed tight, for catching up on prayers. God, nothing was worse than helplessness.

He sighed again, something he found himself doing a lot of lately. Although it seemed the German armies would soon collapse, Japan remained. The "divine wind" attacks were hurting the Pacific Fleet far more than the public knew, with higher casualties than the navy wanted to admit. It was easier to make fun of the little bastards, to toss off their suicide runs as desperate, ineffective stupidity. Washington didn't want the American people—or even the Japs, for that matter—to get a fix on the kind of success those assholes were having. From oil tenders and LSTs to destroyers, battle wagons and the precious aircraft carriers, everyone was taking hits. Besides the hell-bent kamikaze planes, the Jap Special Attack Force hurled the *oka,* a piloted bomb; the *kaiten,* a piloted torpedo; *fukuryus,* navy frogmen used as human mines; and a host of other suicide weapons that didn't even have names.

G-2 Washington recently flashed a quote from a Jap admiral to his Special Attack men: "Die, die—all of you!"

It couldn't get any crazier than that, and now, with penetration still hundreds of miles from the home islands, so many Japanese were eager to die if there was any chance of taking an enemy with them that the invasion was going to be house by house, Jap by Jap. What bloodbath waited for Allied troops on Kyushu, Hokkaido and Honshu?

The War Department had put together a secret estimate of what the casualties would be when they finally had to overrun the islands of Japan: one million men.

INTERNATIONAL NEWS SERVICE—European Front, Apr. 28, 1945: Count Bernadotte arrived in Berlin with the Western Allies' reply to Himmler's offer. The Allies demanded unconditional surrender on all fronts.

From the Alpine fortress in the south of Germany Hitler ordered the war to continue. He appointed Grand Admiral Doenitz his successor as head of state.

Friendly fire—a contradiction in terms not so funny now. Chad Belvale stared at the sheet-covered hump at the end of his hospital bed. Under there was a metal cradle designed to keep any weight from the end of his leg. It was the end of his leg, not his foot. He stared, trying to get used to the fact that under that hump in the sheet was nothing, because he had no left foot. Friendly artillery fire and a short round; simple as that, he had lost part of his body, a random piece just blown off.

Propped up on one elbow, Chad drew deeply on his Lucky Strike. His colonel roommate, officially classified as an ambulatory patient, was off to the PX coffee shop. The room was too bright and clean and polished, too different from the place he had come from. It was more than a world away from the combat zone and his son; Europe and Stephanie were a mere world away, and he had been sent from a even that.

He twitched; phantom pain was another contradiction. There was nothing ghostly about the pain that racked the missing ankle and foot. The nerve ends were still there, lying to him, sending signals from the heel and sole of a foot long gone, left on a muddy knoll in Czechoslovakia.

Ask, complain and plead all he wanted, he had been held over in London just long enough for a Harley Street specialist to fix his leg and pump him full of the new pencillin drug; the family had decided it wanted him home.

But there had been time enough for Captain Stephanie Bartlett to come to his bedside, to hold his hand. Though her face was thinner and older, there was still pixie in her eyes and that special tenderness hovering behind her sadness.

He knew he was about to get wounded all over again—more friendly fire.

"Dacey is alive," she had said. "On the mend and to be flown back with the other badly hurt men. British troops reached the camp not long ago and sent a list immediately. My husband will soon return to Scotland, and I must meet him there."

Okay, so another piece gets blown away. The body goes numb anyway—self-defense. Don't make it worse.

"Scotland," Chad had said. "I'll never forget

breathing the morning sea and heather, and watching you sleep."

He watched her try to hold them back, but tears slowly brimmed over. He didn't want her to cry; enough pieces were enough. Her fingers closed hard on his hand. "Wheest, I shall not forget a single moment of us. You understand, don't you, love?"

His voice was shaky, and his eyes gave him trouble. "I understand. And I can accept it. But I'll be damned if I have to like it. Duty, honor, fidelity—Christ, my entire life has been chained to tradition and duty. Stevie, I know how you feel, maybe more than is good for me. If I were someone else I might scream and rave and beg . . ."

He sucked up a big breath and let it out slowly. Pieces flying off, random bits. "Look, there's always time. . . . Maybe later, however long it might take—"

"No. That would be bad, like desertion. Och, God, Chad, this bloody, bloody war."

"It brought us together. That was something."

She rose and bent and brushed soft lips across his. He drew in the flower scent of her hair and skin.

"Aye," she murmured. "There was that. I thank you for at least that, Chad Belvale."

"Stevie—"

Small, breathy noises trailed behind her. Stephanie Bartlett was gone. He shut his eyes. Phantom pain. That part of his heart was already torn out, so it had to be phantom pain.

REUTERS—Burma, Apr. 29, 1945: The 17th Indian Division took the town of Pegu, and British forces of the XV Corps sailed from Rangoon.

Penny Belvale clamped a sweaty hand on the door of the British Land Rover. The old fears and hatred came welling up the moment the vehicle passed through the gates of the POW camp. Her eyes locked on the spot where Stephanie had killed the Jap sergeant.

She had pulled every string, spent family favors and deliberately broken rules to be here at this moment. Frontline troops had already swept through and moved on; paratroop commandos had smashed into both camps, this one and the men's down the road, to save prisoners the Japs might murder. But she rode with the next wave of Allied forces, a wave breaking on Japanese holdings with both speed and confusion.

As she swung her stiff legs out of the Rover, the driver said, "Caught the bloody Nips cold. There was some fighting, but not for long. A few committed hara-kiri, or whatever they call it. Saved us the trouble. None made it to the jungle."

Penny stared at the women gathered in protective groups, dazed and uncertain, not yet believing in freedom. She ran to them and began hugging and shaking hands, crying with those who had tears left.

"You came back," one said. "You came back for us."

A thin, hunched woman hugged her hard, refusing to let go. "Only after you were gone did we find out what you did for us. My God, I'm so sorry for thinking of you as Watanabe's whore. We didn't know, and then it was too late."

"Were you punished for our escape? Did the camp suffer?"

"It didn't happen." Her laugh was more choking cough. "The loss of face would have been too great, so it just didn't happen. They claimed you were sent away to join the Korean whores who serve the Japanese soldiers—that was the story and no questions were allowed. You and that lassie were just gone. But the guards knew, and in time we did, too."

"Watanabe," Penny said. "Did he get to commit suicide?"

Two tall, gaunt women looked at each other and then at Penny. Sisters, she remembered, the Kirk sisters, Margaret and Sheila. She didn't recall which was which, but they were tempered and tough and as unbending as an English sword. Penny started to speak, but stopped as too many things crowded in—the dripping heat, the memories of reflex bowing to the guards, being slapped and spat upon. Watanabe.

"I'm Margaret, luv, and I'm ashamed that it took so long to discover what you did for the children." She hugged herself and held her head up. "Major Wobbly had suicide in mind, and that great ruddy blade in hand when we got to him. He was all dressed up in a silk kimono. Can you believe that?"

Sheila joined in, her voice flat and cold. "There was a crowd of us, all beating on him with sticks and fists and whatever we could grab. The little bastard had no chance to get off his knees, much less save his sodding honor."

Penny breathed deeply. Was she relieved, disappointed, angry? She tasted memories—the jungle, her sweat, his soaped body. "You killed him, then?"

"Not right off, luv. Most of his people had run off, and any left were dead or about to be. The paratroopers shot any Jap who flinched. But they stood back for us."

"I don't—"

"You remember how proud Wobbly was of his appearance, how he played the strutting peacock? Well, we dragged him around to the prisoners' *benjo*—that stinking cesspool of our crapper. It was just full enough to cover the top of his head every time we poked him under with bamboo poles. He was determined to be quiet at first, but after a while he began to scream—although it was really more of a choking noise."

Blinking, Penny thought it was the heat more than the image that made her sway. The filth there, the bloody flux and puddles from sick, loose bowels. She closed her eyes and tried to shut her nostrils.

Margaret said, "Major Wobbly was properly drowned. We've left his body there, out back. Would you care to see it?"

She didn't. All the traveled miles and sobbing dreams, the fantasies and pent-up hate—all came to this moment, and she didn't want to look at his corpse. It was done, and what she wanted was to let go. "I came back to kill him," she said, "but you've done a better job."

"Oh, yes," one of them said. "That we did. Poetic like, you might say."

NORTH AMERICAN NEWSPAPER ALLIANCE—Somewhere in the South Pacific (delayed): The Japanese have thrown a wild card into the sea battles here. It is called "kamikaze," the divine wind, after a howling gale that sank a Mongol fleet on its way to invade the home islands centuries ago.

Any type of plane still capable of staying in the air is flown by pilots intent on suicide as they deliberately try to crash their bomb-laden craft into American warships. These suicide attacks have gone on for some time, but are becoming more frequent as the line of battle draws nearer to Japan. Although they keep trying, most encounter a concentrated hail of antiaircraft fire that throws up a solid wall over American ships.

Admiral William Halsey said the psychology is too alien for Americans to understand. "We fight to live; they fight to die," he said.

Major Gavin Scott wore his new oak leaves as if they were medals, which in a way they were. If he had jumped senior captains here, too bad. They all had a chance to build themselves a reputation, and if they couldn't measure up to him, it was simply because none of them were that hot.

Or that lucky. He had to admit to an element of that. How many pilots had been downed three times and come out of it? This time he had walked away, just inches from being splashed in the drink again. Damned few land-based pilots could have brought a shot-up aircraft down on a carrier deck. And it was his fortune that it happened to be the *Franklin*, an Essex-class carrier with a vice admiral aboard.

"You're the most charmed flyboy I ever saw," the lieutenant commander said. "That P-Thirty-eight skidded crosswise all the way to the lip and hung up just long enough for you to clear the cockpit. Like it waited before flipping itself into the sea. And that was on top of the fact we'd just airlifted forty-five planes and hadn't brought up the next thirty-one. You had a clear deck and more luck than God."

"You don't know," Gavin said. "Splashed in the English Channel, downed in Tunisia, and they still can't get me. This time I didn't even see the goddamn Zero that jumped me. I was after a Betty bomber, so I had to slow my dive; that's when the Jap burned me." He sat down at the wardroom table, liking the feel of the first-time story, knowing it would polish well in the retellings to come. "The P-Thirty-eight climbs like a homesick angel, but it won't make a tight bank like the Zero, so we have to dive hard and keep going. In a dogfight they can cut us up."

The lieutenant commander poured coffee into two cups. He was a big, shambling man with deep-set eyes. "But damned if you didn't drop one of them anyhow. We got a radio report."

"I dropped the wrong one. The right one nailed me. But I have confirmation on one more kill."

The navy man sugared his coffee and stirred. "I heard you're not far behind Pappy Boyington's score."

Gavin tried not to smirk. Boyington, the drunken marine and darling of the press. His clock was ticking; no way he had the luck, the gift. "When I get another plane—"

The ship's alarms kicked in, knifing to the bone. *Whee-oo! Whee-oo!* Sounding general quarters.

"Shit!" The navy officer bumped his knee jumping up. "It's probably those damned suicide planes!" He leaped for the wardroom door.

Seconds behind him, clumsy in the too-big borrowed work clothes, Gavin scrambled after, awkwardly ducking through hatchways until they reached the deck. The salted wind licked his face as the antiaircraft guns in their tubs on the flight deck slammed away. Tart powder taste rode the wind and puffs of black smoke splotted against the sky. Gavin looked up and watched two Jap planes kick over, pivoting on a wing tip, and begin a screaming descent on the carrier. His mouth opened. They weren't really—

Three—no, four—coming down from different heights. The guns slammed in a continuous sound, and the sky blackened. One plane took a burst of gunfire and cartwheeled away, blowing with a water-muted roar when it hit the sea. A second exploded close above and the blast tore a chunk off the ship. Its tail actually slapped down across the deck, and men in one of the gun crews began to scream in the wreckage.

Gavin stood rooted. This was all wrong. Planes weren't supposed to do this, and he wasn't supposed to be here, not like this.

The third plane pulled out only feet off the water and came all the way in. It plowed into the port side of the ship, and the giant carrier rocked. Flame and smoke poured up. Seamen ran back and forth, yelling. There was another explosion below-decks; then suddenly the carrier listed sharply to port.

The concussion knocked Gavin to his knees. Stunned and feeling oddly disoriented, he struggled erect. He looked up to see Navy Corsairs jumping on a scattered group of kamikazes. Turning at a sound he saw another Jap plane belly in to lay two bombs on the flight deck.

KA-WHAM! KA-WHAM!

Gavin was knocked down, and he stayed flat when the .50 caliber ammunition on the burning Corsairs blew up. As the gallery mounts caught fire, 20 and 40mm shells also exploded; then it was the Tiny Tim rockets from the planes parked aft. The flight deck turned into a section of hell with deadly fireworks pinwheeling and spitting and clanging off a sinking island.

A roaring tongue of flame seared Gavin's face and he screamed. He threw his crossed arms in front of his eyes and backed away from the inferno, but there was no place to go.

No! This was wrong! He was meant for more than this; he had too many scores to settle. A plane, God damn it! He needed something to lift him out of this and into the sky. He should be the one screaming down from above, bringing vengeance and fear.

Hot metal touched his back. He choked down a whimper and staggered forward. The wall of fire swirled before him. Head down and holding his breath, he plunged into it, tripping over things, bodies, sliding downhill.

Gavin went over the side, arms flailing and clothing ablaze. He hit water as hard as concrete.

CHAPTER **34**

SHAEF Press Pool—May 1, 1945: Hamburg Radio announced today that Adolf Hitler died yesterday in his Berlin bunker. Admiral Karl Doenitz has been appointed his successor.

Arno Hindemit stood just inside the Führerbunker entry on the first stairwell landing. The bunker itself was drilled deep, with Hitler's compartment at the far end, best protected, the war room close at hand. Arno had seen the Führer after the last assassination attempt, after more than four thousand German officers had paid with their lives for that failure.

Hitler looked terrible, his left arm and side paralyzed by the bomb blast, drooling from time to time, unsteady on his feet. Even the well-known power of his voice was gone. His eyes still glared, and Arno thought the man at least understood that Germany was beaten, that he would try to save what he could.

But no; he moved imaginary armies around on the map table, voice shrill as he blamed backstabbing traitors for losing the war he never wanted and international Jewry for starting it.

The ground shuddered from the impact of Russian artillery, reaching ever closer. Dark with smoke, the sky rumbled with crisscrossing fighter planes—Russian, Ami and Tommi, all watching for small escape planes that darted low over the ruined city. There were such planes; Arno had seen them. They carried a few desperate general staff survivors, anxious to surrender to the Allies before the Russians caught them. He heard no German tanks, saw not a single *verfkuchten panzer*.

Two SS junior officers pushed past Arno, each carrying one end of a blanketed body; Arno saw black trousers and shoes. A third man followed with another bundle, then came more SS with sloshing fuel cans; the smell of gasoline was overwhelming.

"The thousand-year Reich," the old Wehrmacht colonel sighed. "The Führer is dead, *Oberfeldwebel*. He shot himself, and Braun—Mrs. Hitler—took poison. And Reichminister Goebbels—my God!—all poisoned, the wife and six dead children; six!"

A Russian shell exploded, and Arno felt the ground shock through his boots. The stench of Berlin's funeral pyre choked him, and he spat. "The Führer—"

"Burning, and to be covered over." The colonel's thin hand shook as he ran it through his hair. He talked half to himself. "How did we ever allow this to happen? How?"

"Soldiers do not question, sir." The reply was automatic.

The old man lifted his head and blinked. "We should have."

Then he left the bunker and walked slowly, his back straight, toward the bursting shells of the Russians.

"A little late," Arno muttered. He looked around, then slung the Schmeisser muzzle down and walked away from his post. He might find a way through the ruins and encircling Russians. Around him the survivors of the bunker, Luftwaffe officers, Wehrmacht generals, outlaw SS chiefs already shedding their black uniforms, scurried for alleys of safety. All, it seemed, had decided to surrender to the Allies.

Reaching the first gate at the outer perimeter of the bunker defenses, Arno saw a thin and shaking *Oberleutnant* clutching a Luger in his fist, pointing it at a sergeant and very young corporal. The officer was wild-eyed, on the edge of hysteria. "Get back to your posts, you stinking cowards."

The sergeant looked at the kid and shrugged, then turned away. Then in a blink he twisted back, swinging a large fist in a roundhouse at the officer. It was far too slow.

Arno watched as the Luger coughed once, then again. In slow motion the sergeant folded and fell to the ground, bits of blood and bone from his head still hovering in the air. The corporal threw both hands up in front of his face and shuffled backward. A low moan escaped him.

Arno swung the Schmeisser from his shoulder in a fluid motion that came with a thousand repetitions. He barked, "Asshole!"

The officer turned, and in that split second Arno resigned from the army. He squeezed off a short burst, and the officer was slammed up and backward, body twisting, pistol thrown away. He hit the ground lifeless, eyes and mouth open wide.

The corporal stared at him, tears brimming, and Arno realized he was facing a child, twelve, thirteen years old. The boy started to stammer something, but Arno threw up his hand, fending off the words. His anger held back the numbing sorrow: "Go! Run, you stupid bastard. Find your mother!"

The boy spun and stumbled away, and Arno sat on a pile of rubble not far from the body of the SS officer. "What do you think, Father?" He talked to the past and to the man who had taught him how to be honorable, dependable, a good soldier. He cradled the rifle across his lap. "I've killed a German officer. One of my officers. A stinking, shitty, cowardly, murdering member of the SS, but still one of mine. You taught me to be decent and obedient, so . . . do you approve or not?"

Arno began to laugh, the sound thick and choking. "And if you don't approve, what are you going to do? Throw me out of the army?"

The ground shook and then shook harder, artillery rounds coming closer. Black smoke drifted toward him in waves, and the smell of powder hung in the air. Arno drew in a ragged breath. He was a soldier, this was a war, and the basic rule was to survive.

"Ho, schoolmaster," he said to his last friend, his only friend, a man long dead on a different battlefield. "You should have seen this—rats in uniform hunting their holes, and each other. You might have enjoyed this, and you could lecture me on what history will have to say about all of it."

Another artillery barrage rolled closer and heavier, rounds slamming into buildings he could see, spewing fire and smoke and ripping metal fragments. The old Wehrmacht colonel had marched directly into that.

Arno stood and slung his weapon and turned the other way. He smoothly moved around wreckage and didn't flinch at the whine of steel. He moved west, and the smoke closed around him.

AGENCE FRANCE PRESSE—The Western Front, May 1, 1945: The city of Berlin surrendered today to occupying Soviet forces. There are rumors of a breakout attempt by German armies trapped to the north of the city.

Captain Owen Belvale shifted his weight carefully and looked down the draw. Boulders cluttered the slopes, and the fragmented trunks of trees poked upward at odd angles. Twice he had had mortars walked through there, and yet when a patrol went in, it got cut up pretty badly, with some men still missing.

Owen tried to hold down the anger that kept rising, blotting out his ability to think. Goddamned krauts were whipped and wouldn't admit it. They started this thing, grabbing land and entire countries, one after another. The greedy bastards had tried to take half the world, and now the world was paying them back. Still, little pockets of the "master race" were inflicting damage, lashing out and drawing blood.

Brutal bastards. They had stomped all over Europe, smashed most of it flat with tank tracks and rocket fire and bombs. They'd bombed the hell out of England, too, but somehow missed the one building that should have been knocked flat. Owen shook his head, trying to clear it. Concentrate, stay with the here and now. . . .

They had missed the house. They started the war, and because of that he had met her and his entire life turned inside out. They kept up the goddamned war and took him away from her, took away his chance to make it work. She stayed behind and did what she did, and the sons of bitches couldn't even hit the building.

Owen had wrangled a quick trip to SHAEF headquarters, then applied some emotional blackmail for time to visit his wounded father. He hadn't seen his father, of course. Instead he'd made a swift trip to Southampton to see Helene. His need to be with her had become a pain, an ache that tormented mind and body.

He had caught a taxi out of London, hurrying the driver through twilight and crowds of people who had begun to throng the sidewalks in the evenings. The end of the war was near—people could sense it—and hints of celebration seemed to filter through the air. The driver was elated at the fat fare, and talky: he chatted through the long trip, and Owen answered mostly in grunts.

He had written letters and received no replies. So many things could have happened since he had gone—she might have gone into the service and been shipped away; her building could have been bombed; dear God, she might have been killed, all that wondrous beauty and passion forever lost.

The driver had to ask around to find the area, and finally turned into the street Owen recognized. Owen had to hold his breath until he saw the building, solid as ever. He gave silent thanks, handed the driver a wad of bills with instructions to wait, and bounded up the steps.

Light showed beneath her door. Belly drawn tight, he knocked, heard a stirring beyond the panel and knocked again. And suddenly there she was—the light rainbowing a halo around her, wrapping her in an incredible loveliness. For a moment he could not breathe beyond the light musk of her perfume. The whisper of her silken robe made him shake.

"Owen!" She stared at him.

"Helene . . . oh, God, how I've missed you."

She didn't move. He started to reach for her, then stopped. She glanced over her shoulder, then turned back to him, those eyes able to slide so deep inside him and touch things he had not known lived within.

"Owen . . ." That sultry voice that had haunted his dreams across Europe, that some nights whispered to him, calmed him when even the ground shook.

Suddenly afraid, he grabbed her hand, that soft, experienced hand with its butterfly fingers.

"I love you, Helene. Marry me, come with me, please."

She moved back, opening the door so he could see beyond her. The tiny apartment had always fit her—the slashes of bright color, the beckoning of soft, shadowy places.

A naked man was stretched out on the bed Owen remembered so well.

"I made you no promises," she said.

Throat so dry it was difficult for him to talk, he closed his eyes. "Why? You didn't have to—"

"I don't love you, Owen. It's as simple as that."

"You could have had everything."

One corner of her mouth twisted. "What, even lovers?"

He swayed. "You bitch."

"Well, I guess so," she said.

And closed the door. . . .

"Captain Belvale, sir?" Owen turned to see a boyish PFC, a company runner.

"What is it?" Owen had to unclench his fists, bring his mind back. Focus, concentrate, pay attention to the immediate problems.

The kid spread a soiled and wrinkled map across his knees. "The CO wants to know where you're going to put your platoons."

"I'm not putting anything anywhere until I unjam this bottleneck." He pointed down the draw. "The CO can get his ass up here and help."

"Sir?" The kid blinked, confused. He held out the map.

"What's your name, Private?"

"Farrell, sir. John Farrell."

"Do you know what it's like to try to gain ground, Private? To move forward, then get pushed back? To think it's yours, then lose it? What does the goddamned CO know about it?"

"Sir?" The kid looked away from Owen's red-rimmed eyes, turning to look behind him as if he had taken the wrong path.

Owen looked down the draw, trying to focus. What were the lessons in school for a situation like this? He couldn't remember. Nobody ever lectured about tiny canyons and big boulders, that was for sure. He shook his head.

The private folded the map, stuffed it in a jacket pocket, not saying anything.

Owen ran his fingers through his hair, then over his face, rubbing hard. Christ, it was hard to keep a straight thought. That ugly scene with his father, all the anger and embarrassment, the pain that came with each memory of Helene, and the pictures—God, the pictures in his head of her with other men.

"Sir, do you think you ought to be standing out in the open like that?" The kid's voice was thin, uncertain.

"What?" Owen looked down at him, a young boy squatting on the heels of his boots, tightly tucked behind the rock. "What are you talking about?"

The bullet ricocheted off the granite with an oddly metallic sound, like the banging of a pipe. Owen turned slowly. A puff of dust kicked up on his chest, and he blinked hard. Another slug spun him, and he dropped to one knee. The sounds of the shots echoed down the defile and faded away.

"Sir? Captain Belvale?"

Owen let out a breath, then fell over.

CHAPTER 35

ASSOCIATED PRESS—Manila, Philippines—May 13, 1945:
With the fall of Manila, the chief task of the Americans on Luzon is the elimination of elements of
the Japanese Fourteenth Army. Today part of the
American 25th Division, reinforced by a regiment
from the 37th, succeeded in scaling the cliffs of the
Balete Pass.

The clearing of Japanese from caves and pillboxes
in the pass area continues while main forces push down
the northern slopes toward the village of Santa Fe.

They'd moved all morning in spurts, suddenly stopping and holding motionless for reasons Eddie
couldn't figure out. Now they were frozen halfway
up a slope, the Flips training their weapons uphill.
Fat beads of sweat broke out on Eddie's face as
he hunched in the dry dirt, surrounded by tall,
sharp-edged grass and brush. The grass had
opened minute cuts on his face and the salt-sweat
made them burn.

He waited. The only noise was the touching of
leaves in the light breeze. The little hairs on the
back of Eddie's neck moved. He did not like this.

Golla began silently moving upward, pushing
vines and bamboo sticks out of his way. The rest

followed, easing forward, the only sound that of flys buzzing around their heads. Sweat seeped down Eddie's back, little beads ran sticky down his legs and the loose fatigues bunched uncomfortably around his crotch. He could feel the grime in his skin and bits of grass pricked his neck. It was too damn quiet. His brain was flashing danger signals, sputtering like a short circuit.

Golla halted and they clustered around, tense and skittish.

The sound of the shot froze Eddie's brain in adrenaline. The first feeling that broke through was relief that the creeping around was over. But the Flips reacted like startled cats, heads snapping around as they went up on their toes, backs arched. Their faces were drained of color, eyes black smears on bloodless skin.

Eddie knew instinctively it was a signal shot, and its echoes were just fading when he heard the Japs coming through the brush, moving in a line.

Golla motioned everyone together and pointed uphill. There was only one way out of this.

UNITED PRESS—May 13, 1945: The last organized resistance by German troops in Czechoslovakia has been crushed by the three Russian armies closing in the region northeast of Prague.

Six days after General Alfred Jodl of the German High Command signed the brief document that committed Germany to unconditional surrender, the final remnants of the Third Reich army have been extinguished.

Keenan Carisle walked into the CP trying not to slouch and display even more disdain than his face probably showed. It was all winding down, and now the rearward brass was moving up and putting on a spit-and-polish show. With his scuffed boots, ratty fatigues and two-day beard he figured he looked like one-half of a Willy and Joe cartoon, and the stares he got from the nearest officers left little doubt.

He couldn't bring himself to give a damn. His family, his training since childhood, was about as ramrod-stiff and khaki-creased as anyone could get, but in the several lifetimes he'd spent since this war started he learned there was more to soldiering than snappy salutes and a tin of shoe polish. Some of the best warriors he had ever seen had baggy pants and rice bowls, or sun-blistered British skin coupled with a mad stare.

His go-for-broke boys had been more interested in kicking butt than in looking smart, and the statistics proved it. So much paperwork got put through for medals that some in the chain of command began to doubt if it was all true. But those who checked found out the paperwork wasn't the half of it. The 442nd was one tough, balls-out outfit, but any Mauldin cartoon depicting Nisei would have been just too weird.

"Can I help you, sir?" It was a captain, squeaky-clean cheeks and upright brush cut, trying hard to acknowledge a doubtful superior.

"Where's the CO, son?" Keenan was certain the guy was at least his own age, probably older. He was equally certain he hadn't just made a friend, but anyone that neat he didn't want on his side anyway. Where the hell did all of these people suddenly come from? Two weeks ago his unit was short on radios, C rations and transport. Now there were men running all over who goddamn shaved every morning.

"Staff meeting, sir. Perhaps I can help?"

Keenan stuck a cigarette in his mouth and thumbed out his battered lighter. "I understand my guys are going north, but I'm not going with them.

I'd like to get clued in as to what the hell is going on."

The captain's eyes widened just a bit, and the cut in his voice disappeared. "Major Carlisle? Are you Keenan Carlisle?" He didn't click his heels, but he did find an ashtray and moved it to where it was convenient for Keenan to use. "The old man shouldn't be much longer, and I'm sure he wants to meet you, to tell you himself."

Keenan wondered which set of stories had reached this far—headhunter? Chinese guerrilla? Burma mystic? After the 442nd Regiment, he was supposed to be the Asian warlord or something, able to deal with the inscrutable races. He did nothing to stop the tales; an edge was an edge, and he'd long ago learned to take any one he could get.

"I appreciate that, Captain, but I'm in something of a hurry. I'll wait for the CO, of course, but maybe you could fill me in. . . ."

He had to smile at the speed with which the commanding officer's personal information got handed over. Good news was easier to pass around, of course, and since when wasn't going home good news?

Washington, D.C., this time, though Keenan had a feeling the orders could just as easily have read Sandhurst Keep or Kill Devil Hill. He wasn't going to complain at all, or insist on hightailing it off in another direction. Heading west was fine, because it would take him at least a third of the way to Hawaii.

The idea of palm trees, Honolulu sand and Susie struck him as just fine. The thought of warm winds, iced drinks and the soft taste of Susie's skin could make him dizzy if he let it. And, he had to admit, he also liked the idea of a mixture of people around him—Nisei, Hawaiian, *ka-tunk*, even a round-eye or two. It was never going to be the way it was before; he wasn't what he was before.

"The orders are all cut," the captain said. "Looks like the next stop is home."

"In this case, home is just a stop," Keenan said.

REUTERS—Manila, Philippines—June 10, 1945: The 9th Australian Division struck at Borneo today with a landing in the Brunei bay area. A foothold was also secured on Labuan Island, and from there operations will be directed at important oil fields.

INTERNATIONAL NEWS SERVICE—Vicinity of Luchow, China, June 15, 1945: The Chinese have taken the city of Ishan after all but a handful of Japanese defenders withdrew. Free China forces are moving on to Kweilin.

Stars & Stripes—June 16, 1945: The War Department today reminded Americans on the home front that sacrifices were far from over. Buying bonds, conserving gas and tending victory gardens should still be part of every citizen's life, a spokesman said.

Sloan Travis bit his lip and tried not to make too loud a sound when he sighed. The flash of brass and campaign ribbons was everywhere, separated by dark suits and ties and the loud voices of politicians. This was a fund-raiser of some kind, with drinking and hard laughter and much slapping of backs.

"The chicken-and-peas circuit, boy," some senator had said. "Smile at 'em, don't sign anything and grab as many women as you can get. You're a hero, the real thing, so men want to be your buddy and women want to be a conquest. You earned it, son, and you ought to take it."

Travis tried to stretch his neck and ease up the

collar chafe; the damn tie was too tight, and half the time he felt as if he was choking. What was it that some poet said about too late the hero? The real heroes weren't late; they were dead. The ones walking around showing off medals all had to have some doubt. It was a mistake; they had been given the awards by accident.

Since when did going out of your mind with fear and anger make you a hero? You were crazy, you were berserk, you were too goddamned lucky to know better. You took the medal because you were afraid to tell the truth—that most of your mind hadn't been there when it happened, and as long as you were whole and sane you'd never do anything like that again.

Medal of Honor—Christ, they gave out more than two dozen of them to guys on Iwo Jima, most of them dead. Question was, how could you be alive and have really earned it?

"What do you think of dividing Germany into four occupational zones?" the man asked, taking a short pull on his drink.

Travis didn't dislike him; he was sincere enough and polite, but he belonged to that sect of the State Department that Crusty called "pen-stripped cookie pushers." And besides, what was a split-personality field-commission lieutenant supposed to know about postwar political policy?

"I'm not sure, sir. Anything that keeps the Germans from coming back in twenty years has to have its advantages."

"Seems to me it's pretty much dividing the rubble into four parts. Everything's so flattened there isn't enough left to argue over."

"All of Europe's like that, I guess." Travis looked around, trying to figure a way out. It was easier to work your way over a mountain than out of a cocktail party. He had thought that maybe he was finally going to be able to get with the program, go military all the way, make the family proud. But being shown off like this just made him feel cheap and dishonest.

"Except Paris," the man said. "Amazing that the Germans were civilized enough to leave it stand. If anything deserved to be kept whole, the city of painters and poets—"

"The city of light." Travis nodded. "It is special."

"I wouldn't mind getting myself a piece of it. Can you imagine, with the economy in ruin, what the dollar is worth over there? Like after the First War, when Hemingway and Fitzgerald and that goofy woman—what's her name—all lived there?"

Travis quit looking around. "Yes, sir. They went so they could stand aside for a while, so they could get a fresh look at the society and lives they had come from. Seems to have worked."

"Not to mention wine, women and the ability to pay the rent." The man laughed and took another sip of his drink.

INTERNATIONAL NEWS SERVICE—Pacific Theater, July 10, 1945: In the wake of the predawn fire raid by super-fortresses on four Japanese cities, aircraft carriers launched their planes against a complex of airfields in the Tokyo area.

Stars & Stripes—Home front, July 15, 1945: The U.S. Navy has begun staff reductions of the more than 77,000 WAVES (Women Accepted for Voluntary Emergency Service), almost all of whom are in the ZI.

Kill Devil Hill looked so good she wished she could wrap her arms around it and hold on for dear life. Penny Belvale had thought herself wrung empty of most emotions, left limp to dry and stiffen. But the sight of that great home, rising so white above the green of long-grass pastures, pulled at some unexpected, hidden place. She had to wait a moment and adjust; it was not easy to let herself feel so much.

She took her time once she passed through the great front door, even though she was told the generals were available and she could go right up. First she made a stop in the ground-floor library, smelling deep of the old books and thick, faded carpets. Then she swung through the dining room, collecting there the scent of lemon polish laid over dark mahogany crisscrossed with kitchen odors and tile wax.

The smells were the memories. They triggered most vividly the flood of scenes, words, feelings. Home is where the heart is, but it was all attached to the nose, too. Roses, fresh sheets, the mint leaf crushed and dropped into iced tea. She collected the aromas in a mental basket until the weight of them began to convince her that she was really home, and it was right.

"Good God, girl, it took you long enough." Crusty Carlisle had a tough time blustering, the eagerness showing through. "We put the whole damn war on hold, waiting for you to come up, and it took you so long that for all we know the Japs could be back in Rangoon."

"Sorry," she said, and gave him a kiss. She crossed to Preston Belvale and he unbent enough to hug her back. The two old generals looked pretty decent, she thought. The war hadn't worn them down as much as some. Of course that was something like trying to wear down a file with a piece of meat—bloody and useless. "There's nothing I can tell you two that you don't already know, so I didn't hurry."

"It's your opinions we want, not just numbers,"

Crusty grumbled. "Otherwise we'd have a room full of Washington clerks."

Penny took a seat and peeked a smile at him. "You may have to settle for that. It looks as if my commission might get pulled any time. Deactivation is in the wind."

"Not until Japan goes to her knees," Preston said. "Everyone is starting to pretend the war is over, and the worst may be yet to come. Do you know the Japs are preparing for house-to-house fighting, that they're training women and kids to use bamboo sticks as weapons?"

"We can bomb them from one end to the other and back again," Crusty said, "but the infantry will still have to go in and dig them out. If Iwo Jima was tough, then by God, think how they'll be in downtown Yokohama."

"Pilots are a different story," Penny said. "With the ETO shutting down you've got male pilots coming out your ears. Guess what's going to happen to those of us who wear our hair too long."

"So?" Crusty wasn't just pretending to be offended. "It's not like you don't have enough to do." The unspoken thoughts of Farley hung in the air; who dared assert rights—wives or leaders of the clan?

Penny had once again stopped off in San Francisco, once again made the journey to see Farley. He had seemed happy to see her, an honest joy in his eyes when he looked at her. But again she'd had that disconnected feeling, that constant sense of his mind being elsewhere. The more she tried to bring him out, the more responsiveness she sought, the further away his mind moved. How far could his need reach? How far did her duty extend?

"No, there's a lot to do," Penny said, and her voice was calm and unbending. "Aviation is turning a technological corner, and I want to ride with it. Not only is everything going higher, faster and farther, but there are even planes without propellers. I do not intend to sit around and knit or tend the home fire.'' Or pour sake or bow exactly forty-five degrees or wait for any man's permission.

"That's understood,'' Preston said, rubbing at his leg as usual. "You pick your own direction, go at your own speed. We're with you, Penny, whatever you choose.''

"What if I'm no longer family?'' There, it was out. What if Farley cracked like a hollow eggshell, sucked empty inside and waiting for the slightest pressure? What if he held together and their marriage didn't? What if she wanted to do something besides wipe brows and serve tea?

"You are family!'' Crusty half-roared, half-spit. "Come hell, high water, or Huns!''

Preston was a bit more diplomatic, and for the first time in a long while Penny noticed the smooth southern burnish on his words. "You're a Belvale,'' he said. "Like it or not, now or next week, here or away. This is your home, girl, whatever future you choose.''

ASSOCIATED PRESS—Potsdam, Germany, July 17, 1945: U.S. President Harry Truman, British Prime Minister Winston Churchill and Soviet leader Joseph Stalin, in a show of harmony, announced an intention to continue in peacetime the Grand Alliance.

ASSOCIATED PRESS—Potsdam, Germany, July 28, 1945: U.S. President Harry Truman, British Prime Minister Clement Attlee and Soviet leader Joseph Stalin, in yet another decision by the Grand Alliance, today agreed to divide the Korean peninsula along the 38th parallel.

"That Stalin is an ugly bastard,'' Crusty said, "and I trust him about as far as I can throw him. Jesus, the two best ones are gone.''

"I think we ought to ask Winston to help us plan the invasion," Preston said, and it took a moment for Crusty to realize he was completely serious. "That man has one of the best tactical minds of the century, and Brits be damned, it shouldn't go to waste."

"I can't argue with you," Crusty said. "But you'll have to go through your people over there. Seems I screamed at one Redcoat too many, particularly after Monty screwed up that drive from the coast."

"More like they just found out what you call that piece of rock you claim to be home. What if someone had a castle called West Point Shame? Not much of a chance you'd offer them a drink."

"Speaking of which . . ." Crusty held out his glass, holding one finger up. When he'd had a sip he set the glass down and folded his hands across his stomach. Softly he said, "Preston, what do you think of the rumors about the desert—New Mexico or wherever the hell it is?"

The Teletypes were quiet in the war room, however briefly, since for the moment the western half of the world was dark. Preston shook his head. "I don't understand it. Something about the sun and the brain boys tapping into it. Frankly, it's a bit beyond me."

"Probably doesn't mean a damn." Crusty reached for his glass again. "Won't make any changes in the foot soldier's life."

CHAPTER 36

AFP, July 30, 1945: A group of American Office of Strategic Services (OSS) agents parachuted this month into northern Vietnam to help coordinate guerrilla action against the Japanese.

The guerrilla chieftain, a slight, middle-aged Vietnamese with thinning hair and a wispy goatee, is called by his followers Ho Chi Minh—"He who enlightens."

The Keep was as imposing as ever, and Keenan Carlisle had an unexpected appreciation of the towering bulk and all it represented. He guessed he enjoyed it because he knew his time would be limited. It was an old rule that the temporal was difficult to take for granted. School friends knew of looming graduation dates; adulterous lovers suspected a limited number of tomorrows, and all of it was made more sweet by the ticking of the clock. In short, it was easier to acknowledge what Sandhurst Keep represented when it wasn't seen to be a permanent burden.

His conversation with the generals, the two warhorses now confined by age and ailments to the rear echelon, hadn't been as difficult as he'd anticipated. He had been prepared for arguments about obligation and duty, family responsibility and social caste. Instead, he got a lot of questions.

"Hawaii," Crusty told him right off, "may not be the best place for a Carlisle, seeing as I left a lot of hide stuck to that particular wall. Then again, the career carnage might have left enough of an impression to help."

"It's a good location," Preston Belvale said, "and not a bad jumping-off point for different parts of the Far East. You say this lady is mixed—does she think of herself as an Oriental?"

"She thinks of herself as American," Keenan said, voice tight. "And she's not the kind you want to underestimate."

"That's not what I meant, and you should know me well enough not to make that mistake. Continual inbreeding weakens the stock; if you paid any attention to horses you'd be aware of that. What I was trying to ask was, if she travels through Asian countries, will she be at ease or awkward?"

"I haven't the faintest idea," Keenan said. "And what does it matter? The question is highly personal."

"Whoa, both of you." Crusty bit the end off of a cigar, looked around, then had to spit the nub into his hand. "If those damn women don't stop taking the ashtrays out to wash, I'm gonna start using the floor, by God." He turned to Keenan and locked his eyes. "How good is your Chinese?"

"Fair enough for someone who hung out with foot soldiers. But I should think Japanese is the language someone should know."

"I don't think so," Crusty said. "We're gonna whip them; then we're gonna occupy every Jap island for some time to come. But armies of occupation tend to be made up of clerks—administrators and lawmakers. The real soldiers have moved on. No, as far as the family is concerned, some different tongues will be handier."

"And cultures," Preston added. "There seem to be as many countries in Asia as we have states, most about the same size, but all a lot different."

"It's the Chinese who have the numbers and the potential," Crusty continued. "They're a serious factor, but that whole area is going to boil over as soon as the Japs are gone. The Europeans will want their colonies back, Malay and Indochina, but I don't think that's going to happen. Damn Russians are trying to spread halfway down the Korean peninsula, and they have to reach over China to do it. Mark my words, that whole area will be trouble."

Keenan looked at the ceiling, attempting to hide his smile. "And?" He could see his position at yet another family outpost had already been plotted on one of the war room maps.

"And nothing. Go to Hawaii. Get married. Take naps on the beach. You've earned enough R-and-R to last a lifetime."

"But we want to meet her," Preston said. "If she's to be family, she has to know she belongs here, too."

"Kill Devil Hill, the Keep and a little grass shack," Keenan said. "Quite a circuit. So what happens if I get tired of lying on the beach?"

"Well, we'll see when the time comes." Crusty leaned forward. "Like the man said, Hawaii isn't such a bad jumping-off point. It's the closest you can get to the Far East and still get decent ice cream. So you go get your lady, and bring her back when you're ready to let her find out about this part of your life."

Keenan made one more trip around the grounds of the Keep, the summer stillness hanging in the dry trees, wilting the courtyard flowers. There were no trade winds, no mix of salt in the air; it was different from the islands, different from the layered scents that blossomed with the Pacific rains. What would Susie think of it here, of the dark colors and crisp edges of the Keep? Would she be glad that she was only visiting? Would she like it only because it was temporary?

Running his eyes once more over the high, bare walls that symbolized the strength of Sandhurst Keep, Keenan Carlisle realized there was a lot he didn't know about the woman he loved, but now he had the time to find out. He would share places with her, including this one, and Susie could simply tell him what she thought—and this time around, he intended to listen.

Eddie Donnely lifted his right arm and put it around Gloria's shoulders as they walked the wooded path from the stables toward the house. "What with uncles, grandfathers, assorted cousins and the busybody staff, I don't get much of a chance to hold you outside of our room."

She snuggled closer and tightened an arm around his waist. "Sometimes there's more etiquette at home than when walking down Main Street. But that's all right; it makes the little moments more special."

Eddie took a breath and savored everything. Cicadas counted off the afternoon minutes, and the taste of dry grass and dusty oak flavored the air. He could taste the scent of Gloria, too—soap and warm skin and the after-bite of shampoo. He reveled in the sound her dress made as it brushed against her legs, the touch of her hair under his jaw, the feel of her muscles beneath his hand. He was alive and able to lose himself in the wonder of it all.

"I can't believe how you're getting along with the family," Gloria said. "I mean, I believe it, but I didn't quite expect it. You're . . . I don't know. . . ."

"Not so hostile? Not on edge all the time?"

"I didn't imply—"

"Hon, it's okay. It was true. I was so busy being defensive with everyone I didn't have time to even smile. Surrounded by all that brass, you know, officers and in-laws. Not a combination that put me at ease."

"That gave me doubts about my own commission, Eddie. It was just one of those wartime sops that are handed out in the family like gas masks, but I almost said no."

He stopped and nuzzled the top of her head. "If you come across any more childish traits of mine like that, kick me in the butt. There's a limit to how self-centered a man should be allowed to get, and that should be just a shade past not at all."

"You were never self-centered—just a little insistent on having your own way, that's all. And dead set on proving yourself."

"A lot closer to just plain dead." He put both arms around her and squeezed, holding on for several counts, then slowly let go. He took her hand as they continued up the path. "If none of it matters when you're dead, then how much of it can be really important when you're alive? If you've got a family and a home, someone to hang on to in the middle of the night, then how much can be taken away? I'm telling you, Gloria, if you stick with the basics, there's no need to give a damn about what others think."

"I read a speech by Mrs. Roosevelt where she said no one can make you feel inferior without your permission."

"That's a fancy way to put it, but that's it. I don't mean opinions aren't important, or there aren't things to be done, things to accomplish. It's just that from here on out I choose—we choose—according to what's important to us. We decide, no one else, and the devil take the rest."

She raised his hand to her lips and kissed the back of it. "And what is your decision, my love?"

He laughed. "I've decided I like your family. They're good people—smart and hard and dependable. It's a good group to be a part of." He grinned at her. "I've also decided it's great to be alive and in love."

She kissed his hand again. "Well then, Eddie Donnely, it's my decision that you should take me to our room and prove it."

The rubber tip of the cane slipped on the waxed floor, and he swore under his breath. To say anything aloud would have been to make a show, to complain. Chad Belvale sucked in the pain created by the slap of pressure between his stump and the lump of wood that was supposed to replace his foot. He eased up on his good leg and brought the cane back until he could balance his weight. Damn the servants and their floor polish. And damn if he was going to say a word about it.

He moved across the library until he reached the couch set in front of the fireplace. He took his mind off the hurt by considering the books. The collected volumes of Kill Devil Hill braced the walls from floor to ceiling. Art, history, political science—many tastes for a hungry mind; but the longest shelves, the thickest volumes, were concerned with a single subject: war. Whether it was treated as the art of war, the science of war, or the history of war, the gory topic spread itself behind leather bindings and gold-leaf lettering and wound its way around the room.

He hooked the cane over the back of the couch and turned so he could lift the bum leg and rest it on the cushions. Then he saw her standing in the shadows.

"Kirstin?"

She moved away from the curtains and into the

half-light of the fire. "Hello, Chad. Sorry if I startled you, but I didn't know how to announce my presence."

"I didn't know—no one told me you were here."

"I'm delivering a colt. Seems General Belvale has decided a Morgan or two wouldn't hurt Kill Devil Hill. They told me you might be here when I arrived."

"You came anyway?"

"Of course. You're the real reason, actually. We're not enemies, Chad."

"You can't tell me you don't hold me responsible for Owen's death. Not only did I let him be raised as soldier, he was under my own command when—"

"You were in the hospital when he got killed, and there was nothing you could have done about it. Yes, he was a soldier, but this whole family is soldiers; the whole damn world has become soldiers."

Chad eased his leg off the couch, giving her the option to sit if she wanted. She was thin, her face more angular than he remembered. Her hair was drawn back, held with a faded ribbon.

"I am sorry, Kirstin. You've had so much pain—"

"He was your son, too; I don't think you hurt any less."

"Between Owen and Jim Shelby—"

"Yeah, war is hell on horses and women, as Preston is fond of saying." She sat on the couch. "Look, my main concern now is Farley. I can keep my ranch together, and I dearly hope that no one else in this extended family dies too soon, but I have one son who came through, and I'd like to make sure he comes back all the way."

"I'll do whatever you ask." Chad shifted his weight and grimaced.

"Army-issue prosthesis," she said. "Throw it away and get a good one. With the money you've got, you can have one made that will do everything but teach you how to dance. I'll give you some names."

"How do you know about things like that?"

"You'd be surprised at how much I know, Chad. About surgical scars and cut-up egos." She turned to face the fireplace, back held straight. "I've become something of a specialist in working with the maimed, it seems."

"Then teach me what to do with our son." He reached out and patted her arm. "And if you've got the time, maybe you can tell me a thing or two about myself."

Nancy Carlisle put down the coffee cup and turned to the window to look out at the runways. Everything was moving west in one final push against the Japanese. Planes, equipment, personnel—all were backing up at the piers and airports, then flowing toward the far edge of the Pacific in a river that swelled daily.

The coffee shop was jammed with servicemen, duffel bags jammed under tables and stacked up along the walls. Out in the terminal she knew they were being used as seats or beds or makeshift card tables.

Not much longer and she would be able to move from the endless wait for the airplane to the interminable ride on the airplane. It was always hurry up and wait in the army, so the tired joke went. Run for the chow line, then stand forever. Move at double-time, then don't move at all. But this time catching a ride out to the islands seemed to take forever, and she was bone-tired of the delays.

Fitz DiGama; it was a strange name for a guy who smelled of orchids and tobacco smoke, after-shave and surf. God, she wanted to see him, and the wait was about to drive her over the edge. Each thought of him made her happy and impatient, anxious and content. It was a jumble, and only Fitz could solve it. Everything with him was simple, uncomplicated. It didn't involve all the pressures, all the bends and twists and pushes of the Carlisle family. It was direct and clean and filled with sunshine, and she intended to hang on to it with both hands.

"Lieutenant?" The counter girl looked as if she should still be in high school, learning student leadership and home economics. "Isn't that your flight they're calling?"

Nancy listened. "Yes, thank God."

"Jeepers," the kid said, pleased with herself. "I guess you've been waiting long enough."

The wind lifted through the pines, and the branches shook softly. Penny and Farley Belvale walked over the needles that carpeted the ground, as quiet as the sunlight filtering down. The Presidio of San Francisco had to be one of the most beautiful places Penny had ever seen; one side overlooked the Bay and its islands; the other side opened onto the Pacific Ocean where it narrowed down to pour through the narrow opening called the Golden Gate. The bridge, less then ten years old, arched over the opening, looking as if it could have been spun from sugar. The post itself was neat, orderly, spread thick with trees.

Penny had been in San Francisco for nearly a week, staying in one of the downtown hotels, since any extra billets were taken by troops in transit. She could easily have afforded the Mark Hopkins, had she wished, but she still had a hard time with soft beds and being waited on. She preferred clean and spartan places now, with the emphasis on clean.

"Farley, they're not putting any pressure on

you, none at all. Your mom and dad just want to visit, to see you for a while. You can stay here as long as you want.''

He looked at her, eyes large and soft, his long lashes keeping his face young. He stuffed his hands in the pockets of his hospital coat. "I know. I know. I'm just not ready to go." Ten words.

"No one wants to rush you. You can set your own speed. It could be a nice time, though—almost like old times."

"Old times were nice, but they're gone now . . . mostly so." Ten words.

Penny pulled her sweater tighter against the breeze. Farley could be frustrating. He listened, but part of him seemed always to be somewhere else. The conversations were strained, slightly off kilter. Sometimes she felt the two of them were normal, beginning to understand each other; then she was equally certain there was a gulf between them, a clear gap separating two distinct realities. She didn't know which feeling was right; worse, she didn't know which one she wanted to be true.

"Farley, there's a company here in California, down south, that's putting together some air routes—commercial freight, they say—and I've been asked to talk to them. The general wants me to take a look. So I'll be leaving for a while, but not for long. Is that okay?"

"It's no problem, Penny. Don't you worry about me. Sure." Ten again!

She sighed. He could go along just fine, looking at her, face alive to the conversation, acting as if he had just come back on spring break from VMI, and then everything would go stilted and stiff. Well, sooner or later she was going to have to make a decision, but she had to give it time; she had to try so there would never be a doubt. She was strong enough for that, and there was no such thing as being too strong.

"It's getting chilly. Let's go back now," she said.

"I'm ready whenever you are. We can turn around now." Ten again! No, wait. Was "whenever" two words? Then it would count eleven. It must be one word, but it's no good if you cheat! Oh, God.

"Farley, what's wrong? Why are you crying? Farley?"

CHAPTER 37

AFP The Marianas, July 30, 1945: Nearly 1,000 men were reported killed yesterday after the heavy cruiser *Indianapolis* was torpedoed and sunk by a Japanese submarine.

The ship had just left these islands after dropping off a heavily guarded cargo identified only as "Little Boy." The Indianapolis was en route to the Philippines.

AGENCE FRANCE PRESSE—Aug. 1, 1945: Many Frenchmen began their traditional annual holidays today, free to travel as they wish for the first time in years. Despite shortages and continued rationing, a festive spirit has begun.

Sloan Travis looked through the window of the shop at the typewriter. It was used, but had obviously been lovingly restored. The metal gleamed black and the name Royal was lettered in gold above the keys. It stood high, was undoubtedly heavy, and certainly was solid. He loved it.

An old-fashioned bell tinkled when he entered the shop, rung by the opening door. Sloan smelled leather and oil, saw the muted shine of brass and new paint. It was a secondhand store mainly, a repair shop of sorts, a nondescript opening in a block of nondescript businesses. But it also struck Sloan as the hiding place of a craftsman. With clocks and cash registers, hand pumps and big-handled adding machines, the room held a collection of metal moving parts, carefully fitted and intricately meshed, brought back to prewar condition.

"Can I help you?" The shopkeeper was close to what Sloan expected: gray, slightly bent, pale hands with long fingers.

"The typewriter in the window, how much is it?"

He looked at Sloan with watery blue eyes, face expressionless. "That one's a bit expensive, son. It's a quality piece of work, built to last a long time."

"Will it take some licks? Can it hold up to travel?"

"I suppose so, as long as you don't really abuse it. But it wasn't meant to go to the North Pole."

"Just Europe." Sloan moved to the window, reached out and ran a finger over the big silver return bar. "I don't expect I'll move around much once I'm there."

"You in a business?"

"No. I want to be a writer."

The old man stood straighter, and the pale eyes focused. "I'll be damned. Great idea, young man, and that's just the kind of machine you should have. It was built for something like that, writing books and such. As soon as this war is over, people might even have time to read again." He waved a hand at the counter. "Bring it over here and take a good look."

Sloan grunted at the weight, then grinned as he reminded himself it was a hell of a lot lighter than a mortar plate. He set it between them. "This thing will last longer than I will."

The old man smiled for the first time. "It's quality, like I said. But if you're a writer, maybe we can talk about the price. You intend to write quality stuff?''

Sloan brushed the keys, black and silver with white letters. ''I intend to stay honest and do the best I can.''

''You can't be expected to do more than that. What are you going to write about?''

In the pause before he formed the words, Sloan heard the sound of artillery walking through hills, of men moaning in their sleep, saw stubbled faces grinning and a hand holding out a heated C-ration can.

''Love and hate,'' he said. ''It's the only thing there is to tell.''

AFP Guam, Aug. 2, 1945: The chief of staff of the U.S. Army's new Strategic Air Forces, Major General Curtis LeMay, arrived today to meet with the 509th Composite Group, a bomber squadron.

Eddie Donnely took a chair opposite General Crusty Carlisle and declined the offer of a drink. Half the maps in the war room were gone, those remaining having only to do with the Eastern part of the world. The Teletype machines still clicked, and a large chalkboard was covered with notations, but the room was somehow calmer, as if pressure had been let out.

''It's over, but it's not,'' Crusty said. ''No doubt we're going to win, but it's going to be very bloody. We've flattened just about every factory the Japs have, but that's not going to keep them from fighting with pitchforks if they have to. Assuming they have pitchforks—which you don't need for growing rice, do you?''

''I get the point, sir,'' Eddie said.

"Right. Well, what I'm saying is that there's a distance to go, even after the war." He took out a cigar, looked around and stuck it back in his pocket. "I'm not much for beating around the bush, so let me say it right out. There's enough time left to arrange a commission for you. Most of the battlefield promotions awarded will be rescinded, but I've got the strings to make it stick once it's all over. Now I know you get all stiff when—"

"Do it," Eddie said quietly.

Crusty's eyebrows went up and he forgot to close his mouth. "Goddamn," he finally said. "No argument?"

"I used to mouth off about RHIP—rank hath its privileges—but I never said much about RHIR—rank hath its responsibility. I'm ready to be responsible, in a lot of ways. I think I can shoulder the weight, so there's nothing to argue about."

Crusty nodded, reached for his cigar again, stopped. "You've thought about this."

Eddie stood, walked to a table and returned with an ashtray. "I've thought about the family and the future. My future, and the next generation's future. Gloria belongs here, and we belong together. I can be a part of this family—add to it, help it. Pinning on a set of bars is a simple way to start."

"Next generation? By God, is Gloria . . . ?"

"Not yet, General, but we intend to try, and the sooner the better."

Crusty leaned forward, hands on both knees. "That's good, I like that. Would you consider . . . I mean, Sandhurst Keep, it's big and—"

"And it's home, I know. Again, the answer is yes. I'll bring some of my own traditions, if that's what you can call the advice handed down to me by Big Mike. But I don't suspect that's much different from how you think, anyway."

Crusty finally struck a match, bit the end off

the cigar, and puffed it to life. "We can use the strength," he said. "Welcome, son."

INTERNATIONAL NEWS SERVICE—Washington, D.C., Aug. 7, 1945: The White House announced that an "atomic" bomb was dropped yesterday on the Japanese city of Hiroshima. The result was said to be the devastation of nearly the entire city.

Colonel Jerzy Prasniewski rubbed the side of the gelding's neck; then his hand traveled up to scratch it in the crease of the jaw. "Magnificent animal," he said. "Well shaped."

"Yes, good conformation," agreed Preston Belvale. "Handles almost as nice as he looks."

Jerzy brushed his hands together and gestured out over the field. "The grass is so thick and dark. I don't think I've seen such colors."

"That's bluegrass," Preston said, "actually native to Eurasia." They walked along the fence and the horse followed for a couple of steps, then lost interest. "It's good land for growing. And it's family land, which is why I'm grateful you've brought Walton Belvale home."

"It had to be done before it was too late. My country is a nation of corpses; it's littered with bodies from end to end. His grave might have been kept, but perhaps not."

"He belongs here."

"It was an honor. He was my friend—saved my life, you know, in that rather intense American way. It's hard to believe that was six years ago. Seems like a lifetime, and it seems like yesterday."

One of the stable hands came running toward them, waving an arm. "General Carlisle wants to see you," he yelled. "He says come quick. Somebody just declared war again."

Crusty was reading a telex, several more in a pile at his feet, when Preston and Jerzy entered the war room. "The Russians," he said. "The big, brave Russians have just declared war against Japan. A million and a half of their troops have invaded Manchuria."

"Land grab," Preston said. "They're gobbling up as much as they can while Japan is on the ropes. I guess that's their answer to the Jap request that they act as go-betweens in negotiating a settlement with us."

"The Soviets," Jerzy corrected. "Why does everyone insist on calling them Russians? Russia is only one of the republics in the Soviet Union. What if people referred to all of you as Texans, no matter what state you lived in?"

"They call us Yanks, even though not everyone qualifies," Crusty said.

"Which is why his point is well taken." Preston took a seat and waved at the other two to do the same. "I've been offended at that more than once." He stretched out his bad leg and unthinkingly began to knead the muscles. "Stalin is a coward and a bully, which are the main reasons he's a ruthless son of a bitch. Now's the time for him to take all he can get, and you better believe he's going to."

"He controls everything between Moscow and the Elbe," Crusty said. "Including your country, Colonel."

Jerzy lifted a disdainful hand. "He can't keep it for long. Poland belongs to the Poles, not to the Soviets. He may push to the east as much as he wants, but Europeans will not stand cossack boots any more than they did German."

"Who is in a position to say no?" Preston asked. "You just told me Poland is mostly a graveyard. Who else could stand up to the Soviets—Latvians? Serbs?"

"We, of course, can handle our own problems," Jerzy said, "but one might expect the other countries to turn to the Americans."

"Right now we've got our own damn problems." Crusty pointed at the pile of paper on the floor. "The Reds may have declared war on Japan, but we're the ones who actually have to finish it up."

"There has been no response since that bomb was dropped?"

"This is the second day and not a word. Truman says he's going to keep dropping more until they quit, and even though he's a politician, that man tends to mean exactly what he says."

"I hope you're right," Preston said. "Invasion of the islands is going to be a costly and bloody campaign." He turned to Jerzy. "In fewer than ninety days some thirteen divisions are scheduled to land on Kyushu. And it won't be until next year that we go after Tokyo. Personally, I don't mind if we spend all winter bombing the hell out of those islands."

"This bomb—it's supposed to be very big, isn't it?"

"Not so much big as powerful," Crusty said. "One carries as much explosive power of all the loads of an entire fleet of bombers. I don't understand how it works and don't expect I ever will. All I know is that it packs one hell of a wallop."

"Will you use it again?"

"If it were up to me," Crusty said, "I'd drop another one tomorrow."

INTERNATIONAL NEWS SERVICE—With the Pacific Forces, Aug. 15, 1945: Emperor Hirohito in a radio announcement to the Japanese people today urged acceptance of the Potsdam Declaration, in effect asking that the nation surrender.

"Close the damn door!" a man yelled when the freezing wind skidded across the room. Then, seeing who had come inside, he said, "Oops, sorry, Chaplain."

"That's colonel to you," said Luther Farrand, slipping off his greatcoat and scowling at the handful of men scattered around the communication room. "And straighten up, all of you. Just because you're assigned to this godforsaken place doesn't mean you've quit being soldiers."

With sighs and nearly inaudible mutters most turned back to what they were doing, except for the sergeant sitting behind the ops desk. He folded his hands in front of him and looked directly at Luther.

"Well?" Luther said. "I mean it. This place is run like some logging camp, with everyone sloppy about appearance and procedure."

"We're on the Bering Sea," the sergeant said. "We're closer to Russia than the United States. The weather is measured in minus degrees, and if you take a piss it's frozen before it hits the ground. This is worse than a logging camp, because there isn't a tree for hundreds of goddamn miles. So we're not doing so bad, considering."

Luther sucked in a breath, going stiff with surprise. He was stationed out on the edge of nowhere, pushed far from the centers of power. He had written to every connection, contact and passing acquaintance he'd ever made, begging some and threatening others, and he didn't intend to be here much longer. But more importantly and immediately, he was a colonel, and no subordinate dared talk to him like that.

He walked to the desk. The sergeant, not moving, continued to stare at him, face impassive. Luther noted the man's hair was graying at the temples and that he had a jagged white scar on the back of one hand. Although no faces were turned toward him, the room had gone completely quiet.

"Are you bucking for brig time or a section eight?" Luther hissed. "You cross swords with me, Sergeant, and I'll make you a project. Now, you stand at attention and you address me as sir."

Reaching up past his chest pocket flap, the sergeant deliberately rubbed the CIB pinned there. Then he leaned back in the chair and crossed his arms. "I don't know that you're going to have much time for all that. You're going to have to catch a flight out of here pretty soon, I think. You do all that messing around, it could be too late. When night falls around here, sport, it takes a long time to get up."

"Flight out?" Luther's mind fixed on the phrase. Sweet Lord in heaven, someone had finally processed the papers to get him out. "Did my orders come through? Where are they, man? Now!"

The sergeant smiled, slow and easy. He reached into a pile of papers and pulled out a sheet. "There's a bit more to it than a transfer, sky pilot."

Luther grabbed the paper. "I'm telling you for the last time, you will address me by rank." And when I get back, Luther silently promised, I will most certainly make it a point to stretch your non-com hide, combat soldier or not.

"To be polite, I guess I should." The sergeant stood up and looked down his nose at Luther. "Seeing as how you're going to be a colonel for such a short time. That list you're holding is names of people being decommissioned. You're being mustered out, sport. Oh, sorry—Colonel, sir."

Luther tried to look at the paper, but his eyes wouldn't focus. The family had finally found the time to start cleaning house.

CHAPTER 38

INTERNATIONAL NEWS SERVICE—Tokyo, Sept. 2, 1945: Japan surrendered to the Allies today in formal ceremonies on board the battleship Missouri in Tokyo Bay. The most destructive war in the history of mankind is officially over.

The sole source of light in the library at Kill Devil Hill was the glowing logs in the fireplace. All the lamps had been left off when twilight turned to night and darkness expanded through the room until held off only by the fire. Preston, Crusty and Jerzy sat in high-backed chairs, feet extended toward the embers, faces lost in the shadows. The clink of ice in their drink glasses sounded clear in the silence, as an arm occasionally moved up, then down.

Only part of the book-lined walls now showed, disappearing as the shelves receded up into the black, swallowed by the deepening shadows that wrapped themselves around the room. The small semicircle of light thrown from the fire held, but wavered back and forth when flames grew or shrank. The curve of darkness could just as easily have hidden cave walls, and the fire might have guarded an entrance to hold the outside world at bay. Fire meant warmth and food, but it began as protection. The bodies caught in the glow could have traced an arc through time, belonging to other places, other wars.

They had dressed in uniform, automatically and unthinkingly. It was the instinct of victors, unconscious and deep-rooted. Their boots were polished, gleaming in the licks of light, and brass flickered from chest and shoulders.

One man finally stirred, and Crusty Carlisle spoke: "This is the first time in half a dozen years that I haven't felt I could wake in the morning to news of disaster."

"It has been a long time," Jerzy said. "It was 1939 when I first met a member of your family. I feel I've known your people all my life."

"It's been a lifetime," Preston said. "Yet another war and yet another lifetime. And here we still are, more scarred, increasingly bent, but still hanging on."

"You have to hold on, at least until it's over. The problem is, it's never really over." Crusty lifted his glass, his hand disappearing into the darkness. "Eastern Europe, the Far East. Trouble over there is as certain as sweat on an overworked horse. Thank God we're separated from each of those by an ocean."

"You're quite lucky that way," Jerzy said. "You haven't people running over your borders every time they've nothing better to do."

"No, but that doesn't mean we can stay clear of it." Preston gently shifted his bad leg. "We won't be left alone any more than the Romans were. They were the most powerful empire in the world, and that didn't keep the barbarians from grabbing whatever they could. Every time you relax a little, some bastard is going to try to sack a village."

"That's why I'm glad you talked to Ike," Crusty

said. "He's as smart as he is popular, and he shouldn't just retire, by God. You stay on him, Preston."

"It wouldn't hurt to have the family politically as well as militarily protected. That last lesson with the chaplain and his politician shouldn't be lost on us."

"I agree. There'll be battles at home as well as abroad, and neither will ever get completely won. We have to stay prepared, because some animosities never die."

Preston gave a short laugh. "I saw a picture in the paper of Mao Tse-tung and Chiang Kai-shek, smiling and toasting each other. It's the first time they've met in nearly twenty years, and I bet each would have paid a fortune for the chance to cut the other's throat."

"Mao will be the victor," Jerzy said. He slid a palm back and forth on the leather arm of his chair. "Mao has control of the land. The cities will never be enough."

He leaned back and thought once more of the fields of Poland and how they had been ripped open by German tanks, the ground torn and soaked with the blood of defenders. There he had lost the best horse he ever owned in that ridiculous charge against panzer armor, and there he had met Walton Belvale.

Their ragged retreat had taken them to Warsaw, a damned city, cut off and slowly choking. They had fought for the city section by section, house by house. They drank from broken water mains and ate from the carcasses of animals not yet bloated. They saved ammunition more carefully than food, and the ruins became a blur of sniper positions and exit routes.

Warsaw Radio would play music to show the world the city was still in Polish hands, and in the rubble a Chopin polonaise could often be heard.

Colonel Jerzy Prasniewski had grown to admire the young American for his dogged refusal to quit, even though his country wasn't yet at war.

The music had stopped when the last wave of Stukas came over the city and dropped their noses into a howling dive. He and Walt had been searching for a sewer opening, one last possible exit, when a bomb split the world open. Jerzy had crawled away wearing Belvale blood.

He lifted his drink to the firelight and gave a silent toast.

"We'll at least be able to keep some eyes and ears around Mao," Preston said. "Keenan was accepted to some degree by the inner circle, and had their respect."

"As he damn well should have, given what he went through," Crusty said. "Not that it was too much for a Carlisle."

"It seems to have made him half Oriental." Preston shifted again. "He walked over most of China with that communist nurse, and when she sank with that boat he went nuts."

"Became a Jap ghost," Crusty said with a trace of cheer. "Ate heads and left a trail of fear all over Indochina. Spent more time in the jungle than Tarzan."

There was a pause while they mulled over the image, flavored with the spice of survival. Insanity and pain were acceptable, if one managed to come away upright and breathing.

"Then we should let him walk with tigers. He's comfortable in that part of the world, and we have to let him prowl it as he sees fit."

"He'll see what needs to be seen." Crusty coughed to hide his pride. "His first reports on the fitness of the Japanese army were a lot more accurate than those pinheads in Washington were willing to admit. If they had listened and learned more, we might not have been caught with our pants down."

"You've had family throughout the Pacific war," Jerzy said. "It must have gained you a fair amount of knowledge."

"Not really," Preston said. "They've been fighting more than learning."

"Depends," Crusty said. "Eddie learned a lot about himself. Went off to fight a war so he could measure himself against his father, and came back with an internal yardstick that allows him to judge himself. He seems to like what he finds."

"I wonder what happened to him in the Philippines." Preston rose and collected glasses.

"Found out he could actually get killed, from what I understand. Confronting your own mortality tends to either break you or make you."

"That which does not kill me, makes me stronger," Jerzy said. "War is the best example."

"Again, it depends," Crusty said. "Sloan Travis won a Medal of Honor, found a hero's courage and used it to go in another direction. That boy intends to have his own head and wants to move as far away from the army as he can. Christ, a writer—the family has had a lot of odd ducks, but nobody I know of who spent his whole day sitting down."

"Anything that you can't paint, salute or ride makes you nervous," Preston said, adding ice to the glasses. "Sloan has the blood, and whether he likes it or not, he's good at soldiering. If the bugle blows again, who knows if he can keep from answering the call?"

Crusty grunted agreement. "But it takes more than the ability to hold off fear. Gavin Scott, for all his bravery, was curdled and spoiled. There was more than a streak of evil in that boy."

"Honor must accompany courage," Preston

said, handing out fresh drinks, "just as duty should be bound to love."

"Fancy words," Crusty said, "and probably not much of a salve to a family as sliced up as yours has become. You've got dead, crippled and broken. It's going to take a while, Preston."

The aging general, lord of Kill Devil Hill, acknowledged the truth by hanging his head for a moment, gray hair falling into the light. "It's Chad who had the greatest wounds to heal. He's lost a son, maybe two, and a foot into the bargain. Owen was killed by what may have been the last known fighting German soldiers. And Farley appears to have left his mind behind on some Pacific island. Christ, maybe they were all trained too hard, pushed to do too much."

"Unlike the women." Jerzy sipped his drink, and his voice was soft. "They have no training and get pushed as hard and must endure just as much." A coal popped in the fireplace, stressing the silence that followed.

"I don't know what Kirstin is going to do," Preston finally said. "She has a son and an ex-husband to try to put back together. If she handles them as well as she handles her horses, it should come out all right."

"Ex-wives are supposed to be emissaries from the devil, but in this family they seem to be a source of strength and understanding. I hope we get that woman back."

"If she is as good with horses as they say," Jerzy interjected, "I may wish to talk with her myself."

"Sorry, Colonel, but this one would be too much even for you." Crusty shook his head, leaned forward to show a sad smile. "Nancy Carlisle is gone for good, and that's another loss. She wasn't built for this family, wasn't built to be the stay-at-home, quietly suffering military wife. She hurt too easily, stayed bruised too long."

"But she's found happiness," Preston said, "and bless her for it. She has a man and a future, and after what she did to help Farley, I'm going to make sure both work out."

"Don't try to take all the responsibility," Crusty said. "It was my family she was married into." He flexed his shoulder, then worked his fingers gently over the muscles. It had bothered him since the day he pulled a shark into a life raft and beat it to death. It was, he figured, a small price to pay.

"I'll tell you who's built for it," he continued. "Gloria. That girl is family all the way, blood and tissue, bone and marrow. God, she just as easily could have been a man."

Preston waved a chiding finger. "You better be glad she's not. She's going to bear your next generation, and right there in the Keep. That woman is much of the family's future."

"True enough for the Carlisle side. I only hope the same can be said for Penny Belvale. If I were thirty years younger, by God, I could probably kill for that woman."

"That woman could do it for herself. Now, there's the example—talk about steel hardened in the fire. It's as if she were a blade held over the flames of hell, beaten and pounded by the blows of Vulcan." Preston took a long pull from his glass. "And look what's been produced—strong, sharp-edged and damn capable of drawing blood."

"Mars is the god of war; Vulcan only has control of Hades, a much smaller territory." The fire was dying down, the semicircle of light decreasing, and Crusty spoke from deeper in the shadows. "There's what your philosopher was talking about, Jerzy. They couldn't kill her, and in her is the blood of warriors." He drew a breath, long and shallow, the sound of a careful effort to fill tired lungs. But his announcement was firm and final.

"Penny Belvale is to be respected and treasured, and if she doesn't want Farley, we have to keep her even if it means adoption. That woman is too much of an asset to let slip away for any reason."

They grew quiet again, thinking of the future. There were bloodlines and breeding, history and traditions to consider, so much that was carried down the unending years, locked in to the cadence of the military heart. It was the arterial flow of a caste, a clan, that moved to the rhythm of marching drums, the steady pounding of war chants. They were a type, certain of position and place, sure of strength and pride. And they paid, always, the asking price, and carried the scars.

In the room, layered under the shadows, if an eye searched for such things and if the men were given to such thoughts, the soldiers might have traced images in the dark behind them—faint traces of men bearing clubs and swords, of outlined lances that flickered into long-barreled rifles, which in turn shifted from flintlock to snubbed machined blue steel. There could have been other shapes folded into the dark—horses with tossed head and high-stepping gait, the round wheel of a caisson, the flat bulk of armor.

And if the men listened, and listened hard, there behind the pop of burning wood and the soft crump of log falling into ash, they could have sorted out the sounds of men grunting, breathing hard, moving in groups, spaced into columns and rows, rank and file. There, in counterpoint, they might hear the sporadic clang of blades in battle, the strike of hoof, the whisper of bowstring. And rising, wrapping itself around the human cry of surprise and pain, would be the growing clank of tank tread, cough of mortar, rumble of artillery.

While sitting still, frozen in that moment, the

men might have been able to follow the sounds shifting behind them, curving through the blackness, becoming audible as they brushed the edge of the light. There, to the far side, the soft pop of musket rounds repeating, slowly blending into the extended staccato of machine gun fire. There, behind and slightly off center, the fizz of powdered fuse changing, evolving, erupting into the sharp splay of claymore. And there, too, far in one corner, with growing precision, the whomp-whomp of helicopter blades.

Mixed through it all, the human sounds would never change. Growls and laughter, a roar of rage, followed by quiet, choking sobs. They were, as always, the sounds of pain and fear, fatigue and joy, love and hate. And the shadows, as always, would remain.